The Glass House

"In Captain Gabriel Lacey, Gardner has created an intriguing protagonist . . . a quickly paced read with engaging characters and a multilayered plot sure to satisfy her fans . . . an intricate puzzle that subverts the classic love triangle in a novel way." —*The Mystery Reader*

"A perfect choice for mystery readers who like an intelligent historical as well." —*The Romance Reader's Connection*

"Compelling . . . Newcomers and fans alike will quickly become enamored of Captain Lacey." —*Romantic Times*

A Regimental Murder

"An exciting, read-it-in-one-sitting novel, thoroughly enjoyable with genuine edge-of-your-seat suspense . . . Eminently satisfying." —*Roundtable Reviews*

"Ashley Gardner is a name worth following as this author shows deep talent for vividly re-creating the era and people of the Regency period inside a powerful mystery." —*BookBrowser*

"Gardner has inhabited this world with recurring secondary characters rich in personalities, who continue to evolve. The icing on the cake is the intriguing, masterfully told mystery." —*The Best Reviews*

The Hanover Square Affair

"With her vivid description of the era, Gardner brings her novel to life." —*Romantic Times* (4½ stars, Top Pick)

A BODY IN
Berkeley
Square

ASHLEY GARDNER

BERKLEY PRIME CRIME, NEW YORK

THE BERKLEY PUBLISHING GROUP
Published by the Penguin Group
Penguin Group (USA) Inc.
375 Hudson Street, New York, New York 10014, USA
Penguin Group (Canada), 90 Eglinton Avenue East, Suite 700, Toronto, Ontario M4P 2Y3, Canada
(a division of Pearson Penguin Canada Inc.)
Penguin Books Ltd., 80 Strand, London WC2R 0RL, England
Penguin Group Ireland, 25 St. Stephen's Green, Dublin 2, Ireland (a division of Penguin Books Ltd.)
Penguin Group (Australia), 250 Camberwell Road, Camberwell, Victoria 3124, Australia
(a division of Pearson Australia Group Pty. Ltd.)
Penguin Books India Pvt. Ltd., 11 Community Centre, Panchsheel Park, New Delhi—110 017, India
Penguin Group (NZ), Cnr. Airborne and Rosedale Roads, Albany, Auckland 1310, New Zealand
(a division of Pearson New Zealand Ltd.)
Penguin Books (South Africa) (Pty.) Ltd., 24 Sturdee Avenue, Rosebank, Johannesburg 2196,
South Africa

Penguin Books Ltd., Registered Offices: 80 Strand, London WC2R 0RL, England

This is a work of fiction. Names, characters, places, and incidents either are the product of the author's imagination or are used fictitiously, and any resemblance to actual persons, living or dead, business establishments, events, or locales is entirely coincidental. The publisher does not have any control over and does not assume any responsibility for author or third-party websites or their content.

A BODY IN BERKELEY SQUARE

A Berkley Prime Crime Book / published by arrangement with the author

PRINTING HISTORY
Berkley Prime Crime mass-market edition / December 2005

Copyright © 2005 by Jennifer Ashley.
Cover design by Marc Cohen.
Interior text design by Kristin del Rosario.

ISBN: 0-425-20728-5

BERKLEY® PRIME CRIME
Berkley Prime Crime Books are published by The Berkley Publishing Group,
a division of Penguin Group (USA) Inc.,
375 Hudson Street, New York, New York 10014.
The name BERKLEY PRIME CRIME and the BERKLEY PRIME CRIME design are trademarks belonging to Penguin Group (USA) Inc.

PRINTED IN THE UNITED STATES OF AMERICA

10 9 8 7 6 5 4 3 2 1

CHAPTER 1

AT two o'clock in the morning on the fifth of April, 1817, I stood in an elegant bedchamber in Berkeley Square and looked down at the dead body of Mr. Henry Turner.

Mr. Turner was in his twenties. He had curls of brown hair arranged in the drooping, poetic style and wore a suit of black with an ivory and silver waistcoat, elegant pantaloons, and dancing slippers on his feet. An emerald stickpin glittered in his cravat, and his collar points were exceedingly high.

Only a slight red gash marred the waistcoat where a knife had gone in to stop his life. Except for the waxen paleness of his face, Mr. Turner might be asleep.

"And he died where?" I asked.

"In a little anteroom off the ballroom downstairs," said Milton Pomeroy, my former sergeant, now a Bow Street Runner, who had summoned me here. "Right in the middle of a fancy ball with the crème de la crème. Lord Gillis had him brought here, so his guests would not be disturbed by a dead body, so he said."

Lord Gillis was an earl who lived in this opulent mansion on Berkeley Square. Apparently, tonight he had hosted a ball which the top of society had attended, including Lucius Grenville, Lady Breckenridge, Lady Jersey, and the Duke of Wellington.

Colonel Brandon and Louisa Brandon had been invited also because Lord Gillis had been an officer before he'd inherited his title, and he loved to gossip with military men—at least those ranked colonel and above.

At about midnight, after supper had finished and dancing had recommenced, Mr. Turner had been found dead in a small anteroom, alone.

"What about the weapon?" I asked.

For answer, Pomeroy held up a knife. It was slim and utilitarian, with a plain handle, unmarked. I'd had one much like it in the army and regretted its loss when I wagered it away in a game of cards.

Pomeroy laid it carefully on Mr. Turner's chest.

"Belongs to one Colonel Aloysius Brandon," he said.

I stared at it in sudden shock, then back at Pomeroy.

"I am afraid so, sir," he said. "He admitted the knife was his, but has no idea how it came to be a-sticking out of the chest of Mr. Turner."

I at last understood why Pomeroy had so urgently sent for me. Colonel Brandon had been my commanding officer during the recent Peninsular War. He'd also at one time been my mentor, and my friend.

Currently, Brandon was my enemy. His actions had ended my career as a cavalry officer and brought me back to London tired and defeated.

"And where is Colonel Brandon now?" I asked tersely.

"At Bow Street. I sent him off with my patroller. He'll face the magistrate tomorrow."

Like a common criminal, I thought. The magistrate would examine him and decide whether there was enough evidence to hold him for trial.

I studied the knife. Nothing remarkable about it except that it had belonged to Colonel Brandon.

"Did Brandon offer *any* explanation as to how the knife got there?" I asked.

Pomeroy rocked on his heels. "None whatsoever. Our colonel looked blank, said he didn't do it, and that I should take him at his word." He cocked his head. "Now what kind of Runner would I be if I believed every criminal what told me that?"

I could imagine Brandon, his back straight, his blue eyes chill, telling Pomeroy that his word should be enough to clear him of a charge of murder. He had likely marched off with the patroller, head high, indignation pouring from every inch of him.

"That the knife belongs to Brandon does not mean that he stabbed Turner," I pointed out. "Colonel Brandon could have used the knife at any time this evening—to pare an apple or some other thing. He might have laid down the knife, and anyone might have picked it up."

Pomeroy tapped the side of his nose. "Ah, but the good colonel told me that was nonsense. He never remembered taking the knife out of his pocket. Or so he said."

I hid a sigh. It was typical of Brandon to make everything worse with heated protests. He would expect Pomeroy simply to obey him, as though we still stood on the battlefields where he told us where to ride and who to shoot.

But it was three years since we'd left Spain, Napoleon had been defeated, and Brandon and Pomeroy and I were now civilians. Brandon, with a large private income, lived in a rather opulent house on Brook Street, and I, with no private income, lived in rooms over a bake shop near Covent Garden.

Even so, Pomeroy's instant acceptance that Brandon had stabbed this young man through his so elegant suit irritated me. Pomeroy liked solutions to be simple.

"I do not ever remember Brandon mentioning having acquaintance with Mr. Turner," I said. "He does not look like the sort of young man Brandon would even consider speaking to."

"True, the colonel did not know Mr. Turner, he says. I believe him, for the reasons you give. But he didn't have to know him, did he? Turner was annoying the colonel's paramour, and the colonel killed him in a fit of jealousy."

I stared at Pomeroy in abject astonishment. "Paramour?"

The Colonel Brandon I knew would never have anything so common as a paramour.

Pomeroy nodded. "A woman named Mrs. Harper, Christian name, Imogene. According to guests at the ball, Colonel Brandon became angry at Mr. Turner's pursuit of Mrs. Harper and threatened to kill him."

I continued to stare. Brandon in a temper might call out a man who behaved badly to a lady, but what Pomeroy said was unbelievable.

"Sergeant," I said. "You are speaking of Colonel Aloysius Brandon. He does not have a paramour. He never did. He is the most moral and faithful husband a wife could have. He is tiresome about it. The idea that he murdered a rival lover in a fit of jealousy is beyond absurd."

Pomeroy held up his forefinger. "And yet, not a few witnesses put him walking off alone with her several times during the evening, never mind escorting her in to supper, and these same witnesses say they overheard quarrels between himself and Mr. Turner about Mrs. Harper. Besides"—Pomeroy played his trump card—"Colonel Brandon admitted to me that Imogene Harper was his mistress."

My mind whirled. "Pomeroy, this is astonishment on top of astonishment. I cannot credit it."

"It has much credit, sir, and 'twill be the colonel's debit, so to speak." He chuckled at his joke.

I stood still a moment, trying to take it all in. "Mrs. Brandon was at the ball with him, you say?"

"Aye. That she was."

"Did he admit this in front of her?"

Pomeroy nodded, losing his smile. "Aye, that he did. Mrs. Brandon refused to leave his side while I questioned him."

That was typical of Louisa. I imagined the blow of Brandon's admission striking her, imagined her face whitening, her gray eyes growing moist with pain. I would wring Brandon's neck when I saw him.

"Where is Mrs. Brandon?" I asked sharply.

"Gone home."

"Alone?"

"No, sir. Her maid toddled off with her, and the Viscountess Breckenridge and Lady Aline Carrington."

Lady Aline Carrington was Louisa's closest woman friend, and I was happy that the lady had taken care of her. The addition of Lady Breckenridge surprised me. She was a young widow, friend to Lady Aline, but she'd not been acquainted with Louisa. Also, Lady Breckenridge was a woman about whose motives I was not always clear.

Pomeroy went on, "Mrs. Brandon told me to fetch you here."

"Mrs. Brandon is a wise woman."

"Aye, sir. I always obey when Mrs. Brandon gives orders."

"Good man."

I lifted the knife and held it between my palms, the point touching one hand and the handle touching the other. The knife told me little. The blade was slim and stained with blood. Neither blade nor hilt contained any markings or engravings. In itself, the knife indicated nothing.

I sighed, laid it back on Turner's chest. "Please show me where he was found."

Pomeroy raised thick yellow brows. "Don't know what good that is. It's just a room."

"All the same."

I gestured him to the door. Pomeroy gave me the look he'd always reserved for my more questionable orders, but he lumbered away.

I looked down at Turner before I went. A young man, his life abruptly ended. Did he have a father and mother, brothers, a wife, an affianced? His face told me nothing. He'd been a dandy and a well-to-do young man—his clothes and the emerald stickpin attested to that.

Lucius Grenville would know all about him. Grenville would know who the young man's crowd was, who his intimates were, who were his family. Grenville would also be able to tell me where Mr. Turner went to school, what wagers he liked to place at White's, and what kind of horses he drove. The Polite World knew everything about everyone, and this was definitely a crime of the Polite World.

I followed Pomeroy down the staircase. This house was opulent, with no expense spared to impress the invited guest. The staircase lifted three stories from a wide hall paved with marble, and paintings of Gillis ancestors covered the walls to the domed ceiling at the top. The stair railing was wrought iron, shaped in fantastic curlicues.

The footsteps of Pomeroy and myself echoed as we descended, footsteps that this elegant house disdained. Pomeroy's boots clumped swiftly. He was ever a quick walker. I followed more slowly, my footsteps punctuated with the sharp tap of my walking stick. At forty-one, I already walked like an old man, courtesy of a painful wound in my left leg—a wound for which Colonel Brandon was directly responsible.

The house did not want us there. The cream-colored walls and marble floor were cold. Ancestors by Reynolds and Holbein and other painters marching back through time frowned at us. Pomeroy in his black frock coat and dun-colored trousers and square-toed boots did not belong, nor did I in my worn breeches and top boots. Even my frock coat, a fine black thing tailored by a man recommended by Lucius Grenville, could not please the rather high standards of this house.

Lord Gillis had remodeled his house with all modern conveniences—large windows, airy rooms, and hidden halls and staircases through which servants could pass without being seen by the inhabitants or their guests.

It was a house that spoke of wealth and of the latest in fashion and taste. It did its best to shut out all that was not beautiful and glittering, and so was disdainful of a former sergeant and a captain of limited means tramping through its halls.

We left the staircase and trudged through an equally grand corridor that ran the length of one wing of the house. We had to climb another marble staircase, which made us enter the ballroom at the top of a graceful flight of stairs. Ladies and gentlemen would sweep down these stairs, announced by the majordomo at the top.

The ballroom had a lush floor of polished wood. The soaring ceiling was punctuated with ponderous chandeliers, each holding about fifty candles. Most candles had been extinguished, save a few, rendering the room gloomy and austere. I imagined that hours ago the room had blossomed with light and music, gentlemen in evening dress and ladies in green and gold velvets and sumptuous jewels moving about it.

Lucius Grenville waited with Lord Gillis in one corner. Lord Gillis drank brandy, and from his pink complexion, he'd consumed quite a few glasses.

Grenville came forward, brandy glass in hand, his cool sangfroid in place. "Lacey," he greeted me with a nod. "May I present Lord Gillis. Lord Gillis, Captain Lacey."

We might have been at a soiree. I bowed and shook his lordship's hand. Lord Gillis was fifty and gray, but he had the physique of a man who enjoyed hearty walking and riding. He looked up at my six-foot height with strong eyes.

According to Pomeroy, Lord Gillis had been serving as a major on the Peninsula in 1811, when he'd received word that his cousin, the previous earl, had died. He'd quit the army and returned home, but he still retained his military bearing and his interest in military men and events.

"I wish the circumstances of the meeting were happier, Captain," Lord Gillis said. "Our little ball will be a nine days' wonder."

"Will you show me where it happened?" I asked.

Lord Gillis pointed. "In the room just at the foot of the

stairs. Forgive me, but somehow I never want to see it again."

"I am sorry," I said. "Did you know Mr. Turner well?"

Lord Gillis looked surprised. "Not at all. Henry Turner was the friend of a friend of my wife's. But murder is a grim business, Captain. It was a gruesome sight."

Death in battle was far more gruesome. I recalled piles of bodies before the walls at Badajoz, young men torn in half by blasts, some ripped open but still alive, screaming in pain and fear. Henry Turner had looked peaceful, hardly touched.

Grenville volunteered to show me the room. His face, which was rather pointed, revealed no emotion, and his dark eyes did not glitter with as much curiosity as I'd thought they would.

Tonight, Grenville wore the finest clothes I'd ever seen him in. His coat was black superfine, cut in a style likely invented this morning and which would be all the rage by tomorrow. Next week, Grenville would return to his tailor and invent yet another fashion, and this week's coat would be discarded by one and all.

Black pantaloons hugged muscular legs that ladies liked to admire. I'd seen caricatures and cartoons in newspapers about his legs. The diamond stickpin in his cravat was large and elegant, though not so large as to be vulgar.

"It was not pleasant, I must tell you," he murmured as we crossed the polished inlaid floor toward the stairs. We walked alone; Lord Gillis stayed behind to speak to Pomeroy, or rather to answer his abrasive questions. "Mrs. Harper found him a little past midnight. She began screaming in a horrible way, half mad with it. She had blood on her hand and it seemed to make her crazed."

"Blood?" I asked. Turner's wound had been small and nearly clean.

"Yes, I saw it on her glove. The poor woman was horrified by it. The ladies near her seemed more inclined to recoil from her than to help her. I was able to take her off to pour brandy into her."

"Where is she now?"

"Home. Her servants rallied round and got her away."

I was becoming more and more intrigued by this Imogene Harper. Why had she gone into the room where she'd found Turner? How had she gotten the blood on her glove without putting her hand on the knife or the wound itself? And why the devil did Brandon agree to Pomeroy's accusation that Mrs. Harper was his mistress?

"I must meet this woman," I said.

Grenville gave me an odd look. "I'd never seen her before tonight. You did not know her?"

"No."

He said, "Hmm," but did not elaborate.

He opened a door whose panels were picked out in gold. The room behind the door was small, a retiring room for the convenience of the guests.

Scarlet damask covered the upper walls, framed by gold-painted panels. The wainscoting was pale gray, also framed in gold. The ceiling, much lower than that of the ballroom, had been painted with a gaudy scene of Apollo and his chariot chasing nymphs across an arch of sky.

The only furniture the room held was a slim-legged Sheraton writing table and a small Sheraton chair with two carved slats on its back. The tastefully austere table and chair contrasted sharply with the ornamentation of the room.

"Where was he found?" I asked.

"Here." Grenville pointed to the chair. "He was slumped forward, as though he'd fallen asleep or was foxed. Lord Gillis himself lifted him, and then we saw the knife in his chest. His eyes were open, but he was quite dead."

I studied the chair and writing table. Both pieces of furniture were innocuous, betraying nothing of Turner's sudden and violent death. Nothing lay on the desk. It presented a smooth, golden satinwood surface with an inlaid design on its edges.

The chair faced the desk, away from the door. I walked around it once, then stopped.

"Grenville, would you mind?" I gestured at the chair.

"Show you how he looked, you mean?" Grenville gave his usual cool shrug, but his face was white. He strolled to the chair and sat down. "Slumped over the desk, as I said." He arranged himself in an untidy hunch, resting his head and one arm on the desk and letting the other arm hang to the floor. "Like this, I think." His voice was muffled.

I moved to the door and stood, looking in. "Interesting."

Grenville sat up. "I found it rather appalling, myself. Are you finished?"

I started to tell him to stay there a moment longer, but I realized he found sitting in the dead man's chair distasteful. "Of course."

Grenville stood. He removed a handkerchief from his pocket and dabbed it to his lips. "I know you must have seen worse sights on the battlefield than a man dead in a chair, but the entire business gave me a turn. It was so quick—"

He broke off and patted his lips again.

I thought I understood his distress. The month before, Grenville had received a deep knife wound in his torso, one that had barely missed killing him. The sight of the knife and the fact that it had killed Turner instantly must have given him pause.

Grenville tucked his handkerchief back into his pocket and assumed his usual air of calm. If I hadn't come to know him as well as I had, I would think he'd found the whole thing a dead bore. But he betrayed himself with small signs like the twitching of his fingers and the tight lines about his mouth.

I swept my gaze through the room again. "If Imogene Harper entered and saw Turner sitting here, she might have thought him drunk or asleep. But as soon as she touched him . . ." I moved to the chair and laid my hand on an imaginary Turner's shoulder. "She would have noticed he was dead. How, then, did she get the blood on her glove?"

I saw Grenville's interest perk. "Yes, I see what you mean. He bled very little. If she merely shook his shoulder, where would she have picked up the blood? She would have had to reach down to grasp the knife or press her fingers to the wound."

"And why should she?"

Grenville looked grim. "Unless she did the deed herself."

"Then why scream and draw attention to herself and the blood on her glove? Why not quietly walk away and dispose of the glove somewhere?"

"Perhaps she never meant to kill him. Perhaps there was a quarrel, she shoved the knife in, then realized what she'd done in her anger. Horrified, she began screaming."

I wandered around the desk again. "He was sitting down when he was killed, or the killer took the time to arrange his body so. He was a healthy young man, would he not be able to deflect a blow from a woman? Even one crazed with anger?"

"Not if he were taken by surprise."

"As you were," I finished for him. "This is different. It was pitch dark when you were stabbed. You did not have a chance to defend yourself."

He winced. "No, I didn't."

I remembered fighting to save Grenville's life, remembered him lying in the dark on cold stone cobbles, his breath so very shallow. I had watched him, fearing every breath he drew would be his last. But Grenville's constitution was strong, and he'd recovered.

The incident had happened over a month ago, but the wound still pained him, I knew. It had made him a bit more nervous than usual, though he strove to hide it.

"The circumstances here are entirely different," I said in a businesslike tone. "A brightly lit room, a hundred guests outside, a strong man facing his attacker. In addition, if Imogene Harper indeed killed him, how did she obtain Brandon's knife for the purpose? I refuse to believe Brandon handed it to her and told her to kill Turner with it."

"She might have stolen it," Grenville suggested. "Or he

might have left it lying somewhere. Or it might be her knife, and Brandon lied to protect her."

I tried to picture each circumstance. "I do believe the knife belonged to Brandon. Such knives were common in the army—they are utilitarian and handy to have."

For a time we both looked at the desk and its intricate inlay in a herringbone pattern. I imagined Turner lying there, his curled brown hair, nearly the color of the satin-wood, splayed over the desk.

"Lacey," Grenville said in a quiet voice, "we can speculate all night, but the fact is, it looks pretty damning for your colonel. Brandon tried to place himself next to Imogene Harper from the moment he arrived. He was seen speaking sharply with Turner by more than one person—myself included. He even followed Turner into this room, although, admittedly, they emerged together not a few minutes latter. An overheard quarrel, the knife, and Brandon seen chasing Turner from Mrs. Harper, all point to one conclusion."

"I know that." I closed my fists. "And yet, it is the wrong conclusion. It feels wrong."

"Your Sergeant Pomeroy does not much care about how a thing feels."

"He is a practical man, Pomeroy. It makes him a good sergeant, but I do not believe it makes him a good investigator."

"No?" Pomeroy boomed behind me.

I turned. Pomeroy filled the doorway, the tall bulk of him crowned with pomaded yellow hair. His face was red and his right cheekbone was creased with a thin scar that he'd recently received from a thief reluctant to be caught. He grinned at me, his stalwart good humor ever in place.

"No," I answered. "You see much and see nothing at the same time."

Pomeroy guffawed. "Now that, Captain, is why you are the captain and I am the sergeant. You do the plotting and the planning and the inspiring, and I do the drilling and the fighting. We get it done in the end." He beamed at

Grenville. "You should have seen him on the Peninsula, Mr. Grenville. His men would have followed him to the mouth of hell itself. A fine sight."

"You flatter me," I said dryly.

My men had followed me because they knew I'd make damn sure they'd come back. I'd seen no reason for us all to die in a heroic charge to satisfy a general's lust for glory. The generals had often disagreed with me, and I'd told them exactly what I'd thought. Shouting back at those above me, many of them aristocrats, had earned me the reputation as a hothead and made certain I never progressed to the rank of major.

Wellesley, however, had liked efficient use of his resources, so I'd not been drummed out. But Colonel Brandon had, many times, had to intervene between myself and a superior I'd insulted, thus, if only temporarily, saving my future.

"He did not do it, Sergeant," I said.

Pomeroy shrugged. "That's as may be. But it's my duty to take in a man to face the magistrate. If you believe you can get him off, then I leave you to it. I won't hinder you."

He would not. Pomeroy liked getting convictions, because he would receive reward money, but if a man was proved innocent, well then, the gent had had a bit of luck, and who was Pomeroy to rob him of it?

"I will certainly try," I said.

"Best to you," Pomeroy said cheerfully. "I'll be off then. Done all I can do here."

"What about Turner?" I asked. "If the coroner's been and gone, what is to become of his body? You cannot leave it in Lord Gillis's spare bedroom."

Pomeroy looked surprised. "Already taken care of, sir. Lord Gillis sent for Turner's man, who will trundle it back to Turner's ma and pa." He tugged his forelock. "Night, sir. Mr. Grenville."

CHAPTER 2

GRENVILLE murmured his good-night. He'd leaned against the writing table and crossed his legs at the ankles. Pomeroy trudged out, whistling a tune.

"Tell me about Henry Turner," I asked him.

Grenville shrugged. "A young man about town. Cousin to the Earl of Deptford. Father is a retired MP, lives in Epsom."

As I had suspected, Grenville had everyone's pedigree in his pocket. "I would like to speak to them."

"I will fix an appointment," Grenville replied.

I had been thinking out loud, but Grenville was correct. I would not be able to visit a retired MP, cousin to an earl, even to express my regrets at his son's death, without an appointment.

"What will you do tonight?" he asked me. "Speak to this Mrs. Harper?"

"No," I said. I did need to visit her—she was key to this matter, I was certain, but I had an even greater need to see someone else. "I must go to Louisa."

Grenville shot me a look. "She is with Lady Aline."

"I know. But I want to reassure her—"

I broke off, not certain of how I could reassure her. But I wanted her to know that I would pursue this inquiry and find out what had truly happened tonight. Louisa loved her husband, and I owed it to her to help. Brandon might well be guilty. If so, I had to make that shock easier for her. If he was not guilty, I would work to get him free. I had to.

"Do you want me along?" Grenville asked.

"No."

He nodded, then said, "Very well, I believe I will look in on my house in Clarges Street."

He meant that he would visit Marianne Simmons, an actress who had lived upstairs from me in Grimpen Lane until recently. Grenville, whether wisely or not, had taken her to live in luxury in a townhouse he owned in Clarges Street.

Their relationship was stormy and problematic. I did not believe either of them understood what they wanted from the arrangement. In Berkshire a month ago, Marianne had revealed to me a secret that she had sworn me to keep. I'd advised her to tell Grenville, but I knew by the cynical twist to his lips as he spoke of her now, that she had not.

"Greet Marianne for me," I said. "And please send word when you've obtained an appointment with Mr. Turner's father. It might be decent of us to attend the funeral."

"Cheerful," Grenville grimaced. But he agreed, and we parted.

Lord Gillis's quiet and efficient footmen led me out of the house. Berkeley Square was wet with rain, but the bitter chill of winter had gone, and my breath did not hang in the air.

I had expected to have to hike from the house a way to find a hackney, but a carriage waited at the door, and a footman I recognized as Brandon's hopped down and approached me.

"Good evening, sir," he said. "Mrs. Brandon said we was to have the town coach for you, sir. Will you get in?"

• • •

THE Brandon house stood in Brook Street, a pale brick edifice in which I'd endured many an evening with the hostile
Colonel Brandon. When we'd first returned from the war,
Louisa had seemed to think we could take up our easy com-
panionship in suppers and chatter, but the days of laughing
in the Brandon tent late into the night had gone.

I missed that life. I missed it sharply. Even with the ever-
present danger of battle and death lurking over us, it had
been a good life. I had been a whole man, fit and vigorous,
enjoying my friends and comrades.

The same footman assisted me from the coach and
opened the door to the house. He took my greatcoat and hat
and gloves but left me my walking stick.

"She's upstairs, sir," he told me.

I knew the way. I climbed the stairs, noting that the
house was dark, cold, and silent. If the servants were up and
awake, they were staying out of sight.

I did find two maids in the room with Louisa, both looking upset and alarmed. Lady Aline Carrington, a stout,
white-haired woman with a booming voice, was seated on
a divan next to Louisa.

Louisa herself reclined with a blanket over her knees.
Her maids had loosened her hair and it hung down her back
in a golden swath. She looked tired and old, far beyond her
forty-three years.

When she saw me, she exhaled in relief. "Gabriel."

Lady Aline creaked to her feet. "Lacey, my boy," she
said. "Dreadful business, this. You will find out what really
happened, won't you?"

"That is my intention," I answered.

"Louisa was a bit worried you wouldn't trouble yourself," Lady Aline said, always frank.

Louisa flushed. "Aline, will you please allow me to
speak to Gabriel alone?"

"Of course." She sounded surprised that Louisa needed
to ask. "Come along," she told the maids. "Your mistress
will not crumble to dust without you. At least not for ten
minutes."

The maids, who had been straightening Louisa's blanket and holding a cup of tea for her, made every show of reluctance as they rose and left the room. Lady Aline drove them out before her, then closed the door.

"Louisa," I began as soon as we were alone, preparing to launch into my speech of comfort.

Louisa pushed aside the blanket and left the sofa to fling herself into my arms.

This was so unusual for Louisa, that I stood still, nonplussed for a moment, before I closed my arms around her.

Once, three years ago, Louisa had come to me for comfort. On that rainy, hot night in Spain, her husband had told her of his plan to end their marriage. She'd come, weeping, to my tent in the middle of the night, and I'd held her as I held her now, stroking her golden hair and whispering words of comfort.

"I will do everything I can, Louisa. I will help him. Never fear that."

She laid her head on my shoulder. It was unlike her to crumble, but tonight she had endured much. I wondered whether she had known about Mrs. Harper before this, and I silently cursed Brandon for raining everything upon her at once.

I held her for a long time. The coal fire flickered quietly on the hearth, and rain pattered against the dark windows.

A long time later, Louisa lifted her head and wiped her eyes with her fingertips. "Forgive me," she whispered. "But I feel as if I cannot even breathe."

I smoothed my hand over her hair. "Louisa, I know a few magistrates; I even know a man whom magistrates fear. Your husband will be released and brought back home to you. I swear this."

She looked up at me. Her gray eyes were luminous with tears and contained resignation, and a strange finality. I realized with a jolt that she believed Brandon guilty.

"Louisa," I began, and then I felt a draft on my cheek.

The door had opened, and Lady Breckenridge stood on the threshold.

The widowed Viscountess Breckenridge was thirty years old. She was slender but not overly thin and had thick black hair and dark blue eyes. She was quite attractive and knew it, and I had let that attraction entrance me more than once.

Lady Breckenridge was outspoken and acerbic but could show touches of kindness, such as when she had purchased me a new walking stick when my old one had been ruined. She also enjoyed bringing new and worthy artists and musicians to the attention of society, and she enjoyed her somewhat privileged status as widow of a wealthy and titled gentleman and only daughter of another wealthy and titled gentleman.

She had claimed once that she wanted friendship from me, but I never quite knew how to take her overtures.

Lady Breckenridge paused one silent moment on the threshold, taking in Louisa in my arms, then she swept into the room, gesturing to the footman bearing a tray behind her to follow.

"Lady Aline suggested drink stronger than tea, Mrs. Brandon," she said. "I sent your servant to find your husband's cache of brandy and whiskey."

Louisa stepped away from me and moved back to the sofa.

Lady Breckenridge instructed the footman to leave the tray on the tea table. She was still in her ball gown, a creation of deep blue velvet. The hem was lined with a stiff gold lace that rose in an inverted V in the front to be topped with a bow somewhere near Lady Breckenridge's knees. Her sleeves were long, but the ensemble left her shoulders bare. She'd draped a silk shawl over her arms, but did not bother to pull it up to warm her skin.

Lady Breckenridge gave me a sharp stare, as if daring me to ask her what she was doing there. I was grateful to her for helping Louisa home, but I wondered at her motives. Lady Breckenridge loved gossip, the more salubrious, the better. She would certainly have plenty to spread when she made her calls tomorrow afternoon.

I was grateful to Lady Aline for suggesting the brandy. I

poured a dollop into Louisa's teacup and pressed it into her hands. "Drink this."

Obediently, Louisa lifted the cup to her lips. I sloshed whiskey into one of Brandon's precious cut crystal glasses for myself, and sipped it. The liquid burned a nice warmth through my body.

"Brandy, nothing better," Lady Aline said as she came back into the room. "Lacey, pour me some of that whiskey, and do not look shocked, I beg you. I am much older than you and can drink what I like."

I hid a smile as I obliged her and poured the whiskey. "May I give you tea, Donata?" I asked Lady Breckenridge. "Or will you be daring and drink whiskey as well?"

Lady Breckenridge hesitated one moment, then made the smallest negative gesture. "Nothing for me, thank you."

Louisa gave me an odd look. Lady Aline raised her brows and drank her whiskey.

I realized all at once that I'd betrayed myself. I called very few women by their Christian names; to do so was to acknowledge an intimate friendship. I addressed Louisa by her Christian name, and Marianne Simmons, who had filched my candles when she'd lived upstairs from me. I should properly address Lady Breckenridge as *my lady*.

I decided that trying to correct myself would condemn me further, so I said nothing.

Lady Aline tossed her whiskey back as well as any buck at White's and told Lady Breckenridge to go home. "I will stay with Louisa tonight, poor lamb," she said. "I will call on you tomorrow, Donata, dear."

"Thank you, my lady," Louisa said to Lady Breckenridge from the sofa. "It was kind of you."

Lady Breckenridge raised her brows. "Not at all. Good night, Aline, Captain." She made a graceful exit from the room.

I could not leave it at that. I excused myself from Louisa and Lady Aline and followed her out.

When I caught up to her at the head of the stairs, she

gave me a faint smile. "I am capable of finding the front door, Captain. Mrs. Brandon's servants are most obliging."

She began to descend, not waiting for me. She'd dressed her hair that night in tightly wound curls looped through a diamond headdress. The coiffure bared her long neck, which I studied as I followed her down the stairs.

At the door, one of the maids helped her don a mantle, a heavy velvet cloak with a hood.

"Thank you," I told Lady Breckenridge. "For helping Louisa. It was kind of you."

"You are wondering why I did," she said bluntly as she settled the hood. "I am not known for my helpfulness."

"I know that you can be kind—when you wish to be."

A smile hovered about her mouth. "High praise, Captain. I helped her, because I knew she was your friend. And Lady Aline's." Her eyes were a mystery. "Good night."

I touched her velvet-clad arm. "May I call on you tomorrow? I would like to hear your version of events tonight, if you do not mind discussing them. You were there, and likely much less agitated than Mrs. Brandon."

"Of course." She inclined her head. "I will tell you all I can. Call at four o'clock. I intend to laze about tomorrow and be home to very few. Good night."

I released her arm and bowed to her. She acknowledged the bow with a nod, then swept out into the strengthening rain under the canopy that the obliging footmen held over her.

BY the time I returned to the sitting room, Louisa had regained some color. The blanket was tucked around her again, and pillows cradled her back. Lady Aline sipped a full glass of whiskey, her rouged face now bright pink.

"I should have been more gracious," Louisa was saying.

"Nonsense," Lady Aline retorted. "Donata Breckenridge is a woman of sense, despite her ways. She enjoys playing the shrew, and who can blame her? Her husband was appalling to her from beginning to his very nasty end. She has a good heart, but she hides it well."

"All the same," Louisa murmured. I realized that she was embarrassed. A viscountess, a member of the aristocracy, had witnessed her husband's humiliating arrest and confessions.

"She will say nothing, Louisa," Lady Aline assured her.

Louisa sank into silence. I pulled a chair close to the sofa. "Louisa, I will have to ask you questions about tonight," I said gently. "Can you bear to answer now? Or would you rather wait?"

"She needs her rest, Lacey," Aline interrupted.

I looked at Louisa's drawn face, and my heart bled. I'd spent most of my adult life wanting to make things better for her, and I never had been quite able to do so.

"I would rather do it at once," Louisa said. "I want to put it behind me."

I glanced at Aline. She gave me an almost imperceptible nod.

"Let us start from the very beginning, then. Why did you attend Lord Gillis's ball tonight?"

"We were invited," Louisa answered readily. "I received the invitation a week ago. I decided to accept because we could fit it into our night." She paused. "No, that is not entirely true. I was flattered to be asked. Aloysius had met Lord Gillis during the war. I was pleased that Lord Gillis had remembered us."

"And he was willing to attend?" Colonel Brandon went to social occasions because of a sense of duty, not enjoyment. When he reached the gatherings, he immediately sought the card room or his circle of friends and left Louisa to enjoy the event on her own.

"As willing as he usually is," Louisa said with the ghost of a smile.

"Tell me every detail you can remember," I urged. "Begin with leaving your house tonight. What was Brandon like? Did he behave in any way out of the ordinary?"

"Much as usual, I think." Louisa sighed. "I admit that I

was not paying attention. I was much more worried that my gown would be not quite right, and what would Lady Gillis think of me? It seems so silly now."

I could not imagine Louisa looking anything but radiant, but I did not say so. The way ladies viewed other ladies, I had come to learn, was much different from the manner in which gentlemen viewed them. A woman would notice that the braid on another woman's bodice was two years out of date; a man would note how the color of the braid brought out the blue of her eyes.

"You looked splendid, Louisa," Lady Aline said. "I told you so, I believe."

Louisa gave her a wan smile. "You were very kind, I remember."

"What time did you reach the Gillises' home?" I prompted.

"About ten o'clock, I think. Other people arrived about that time, as well. I remember that the square was packed with carriages."

"When you walked into the house, did you note who was around you? Who went in before and after you did?"

Her brow furrowed. "I am not certain. I cannot remember, Gabriel. It seems as though it took place in another life."

"Why is it important, anyway, Lacey?" Lady Aline interrupted. "Surely, it's only important whether Brandon went near the fellow."

"I am thinking along the lines of the knife. Brandon said he did not even know he had it with him. Perhaps he is lying, perhaps not. In either case, what if someone picked his pocket and obtained the knife that way? In the crush at the front door, with people milling about trying to enter the house all at once, a hand could easily slip into Brandon's pocket and purloin the knife."

Aline gave me an incredulous look. "Do you mean to say that a guest of Lord Gillis's was an accomplished pickpocket? All of Mayfair would swoon."

"Not necessarily a guest. Footmen and maids surround

their masters and mistresses, Lord Gillis's own servants usher in the guests and take their wraps."

"Well, good lord," Lady Aline said. "Then everyone in the house, from the master to the scullery maid and everyone in between, could have murdered Mr. Turner."

"Yes," I said, feeling gloomy. "They all *could* have. We need to pare down the number to the ones most likely, and from there we will find the culprit."

"You make it sound alarmingly simple," Aline remarked, a wry twist to her lips. "How can we?"

"By asking rude and impertinent questions. Something I excel at."

Both Louisa and Lady Aline looked slightly amused. I was not known for my patience, especially in situations with dire consequences, like this one.

I returned to the question. "Do you remember, Louisa? Who did you speak to when you were entering the house?"

She sat silently for a moment. I knew it would be a difficult task for anyone to remember exactly who they spoke to and what they did every minute of one particular evening, and the events that followed would make it doubly difficult for her. But I had to try.

"Mrs. Bennington, the actress," Louisa said at last, naming a young woman who had recently taken the crowned heads of Europe by storm.

From what I'd heard, Claire Bennington—Claire Matthews before her marriage—was English, but had been raised on the continent, taking the stage in Italy as a girl. She had become a success there, then returned to London, where she had quickly won over audiences. She was still quite young, only in her early twenties, and married to an Englishman whom she'd met on the continent. This season, it was quite popular for hostesses to have Mrs. Bennington attend one of their events and give a short performance for the guests.

"She seems a rather vague young woman," Louisa went on. "I have seen her perform and enjoyed it very much. I remember remarking on the contrast, how brilliantly she

plays a part, to her blank stares when anyone greeted her
tonight."

"I noted that, myself," Lady Aline said. "Probably she
plays others so well because she has no thoughts of her
own."

"I can hardly imagine her picking my husband's pocket,
however," Louisa said.

"Who else was nearby?"

She closed her eyes briefly, as though shutting out the
room to remember the streams of people entering Lord
Gillis's house. "I suppose I remember Mrs. Bennington because she is so famous. Oh, yes, Mr. Stokes was behind us.
He is rather loud. I could not mistake him."

I glanced at Lady Aline. "I do not know Mr. Stokes."

"Basil Stokes," Aline answered. "Knew him since I was
seventeen, and he tried to look up my skirts. Said he only
wanted to see my ankles. I boxed his ears. Still likes to look
up a lady's skirt, the devil."

"Would he have a motive for murdering Mr. Turner?" I
wondered.

"I have no idea. Don't see why. I could ask him, I suppose."

I mused that Lady Aline's idea of investigation was more
like interrogation by enemy soldiers. "That might not be
necessary," I told her. I turned back to Louisa. "What happened when you entered the house?"

Louisa plucked at the blanket's edge. "The usual sort of
thing. The footman took my wrap. My maid and I went to
a retiring room, where she brought my slippers from their
box and helped me put them on. Then she repinned my hair.
Lady Breckenridge was in the retiring room with her maid,
as well. We greeted each other."

"Where did you rejoin Colonel Brandon?"

"Near the entrance to the ballroom. He was speaking to
Mr. Grenville, and looking impatient. He so dislikes the
ceremony of balls. I have no idea who else spoke to him
while I'd been in the retiring room."

Brandon was not the sort of husband to say breezily to

his wife, "Oh, my dear, I've just been talking to Mr. God-win and Lord Humphreys about our ride in the park the other day." Brandon kept his mouth closed unless asked a direct question. Louisa had by this time mastered the technique for prying information from him when she needed to, but she'd have had no reason to on that occasion, unfortunately.

"No," I agreed. "Go on."

"I entered the ballroom with him. We were announced, though no one took much notice." She smiled ruefully. "Not of an obscure colonel and his wife."

"But we know your true worth, Louisa," Lady Aline patted her hand.

I frowned. "I dislike to ask you to tell me about everyone you talked to after that, but I am afraid I will have to. That and to whom you noticed your husband speaking. Did he stay with you, or flee as soon as the formalities were over?"

"Fled, of course," she said with a tired smile.

"To the card room? Or the billiards room?"

"No. I had stopped to speak to ladies of my own acquaintance, and when I turned around again, he was approaching Mrs. Harper." Her voice faltered. "I did not know who she was. I remember feeling surprised because he began speaking to her as though he knew her and did not have to be introduced."

"They stood alone?"

"No." Louisa's lips tightened. "Mrs. Harper appeared to be with Mr. Derwent and Lady Gillis. Mr. Turner was also nearby, and joined them."

"What did you think?" I asked as gently as I could.

"I did not think anything, not then. I did not know that the lady was Mrs. Harper—I'd never seen her before. But when Aloysius turned and walked away with her, I wondered if she might be the woman called Imogene Harper. You see, Mrs. Harper had been sending Aloysius letters."

My brows rose. "Had she? Did he tell you of them?"

"Goodness, no. One morning at breakfast, I'd finished

and started to leave the table while Aloysius was still read-ing his correspondence. I paused to kiss his cheek, and I happened to see the signature on the letter he was reading. 'Imogene Harper.' I knew no one of that name. I must have startled him, because he immediately turned the paper face-down. He looked relieved when I merely wished him good morning and continued on my way."

What sort of man read letters from his mistress at break-fast with his wife? Knowing Brandon, I would assume that the woman had simply written him a letter about some busi-ness interest—but then Brandon had admitted to being Mrs. Harper's lover.

"You said *letters*," I observed. "She wrote more?"

"Yes," Louisa nodded. "Several days after that, I saw a letter by his plate at breakfast, written in a woman's hand. Aloysius had not yet entered the room, so I picked it up." She flushed, as though ashamed of herself. "It smelled of a woman's perfume. It was then that I began to suspect."

Tears swam in her eyes. I rested my hand on hers. "Louisa, I am sorry."

"If the connection was innocent," she resumed, "why should he not mention it? Mrs. Harper's husband, it seems, was a captain who died at Vitoria. Why not tell me, or ask if I remembered her?"

Why not, indeed? The evidence and admission were there. And yet, it still seemed unbelievable for Brandon. His sense of moral exactness had always been strong. Or had he simply been moral because he'd never been tempted? It is easy to reject sin when one has no interest in it.

"When he walked away with Mrs. Harper tonight, where did he go?" I asked.

"To an alcove. There were several such niches that opened around the ballroom where the guests could adjourn to talk."

"So he walked into a private alcove alone with Mrs. Harper for everyone in the ballroom to see? The bloody idiot."

"Yes," Lady Aline nodded. "He does not seem to be gifted in the ways of discretion."

Louisa put her hand to her mouth. "Forgive me," she whispered. "Gabriel, I cannot talk of this any longer."

Lady Aline's grim look softened. "You poor darling. You must be put to bed. Captain Lacey can ask his questions in the morning."

Tears slid down Louisa's face and pooled on her lips. I itched to know everything immediately, to run through the streets of London putting everything aright, but I knew that Lady Aline was correct. Louisa was exhausted and upset and needed to rest. I had rarely seen her this wretched.

I silently vowed that when I saw Colonel Brandon, I would make him pay for every one of Louisa's tears.

CHAPTER 3

❧

A LINE signaled me to wait for her as she led Louisa into her bedchamber, so I paced Louisa's feminine sitting room while she and a maid tucked Louisa into bed.

The room reminded me of Louisa. She liked yellow, because she said it brought the sunshine to her and made her feel cheerful even on the gloomiest days. Tonight, the cheerfulness did nothing for me. The cream and yellow striped wallpaper, the white drapes with gold tassels, and the matching gilt and yellow silk chairs and sofa could not chase away the darkness.

I had known Louisa Brandon for twenty years. She'd been a fresh young woman of twenty-two when Brandon had proudly introduced her. I, already married at twenty, had marveled at her forthrightness and good sense, as well as her prettiness. My own wife, Carlotta, had been an ethereal beauty, all gold ringlets and soft white skin. Louisa had a wide smile, a crooked nose, and shrewd gray eyes that noted everything.

I hadn't understood that Carlotta, shy as a mouse, had been intimidated by her, and I had not helped by holding up

Louisa as a model for Carlotta to follow. Carlotta, after we'd been married for six years, had left me, deserting me for a French officer. I had been furious and blamed her entirely, but as the years passed, I'd shifted the blame squarely to myself. I'd been an appalling husband.

Lady Aline returned through the white and gold door to Louisa's bedchamber and closed it behind her. She was shaking her head. A pure white curl came loose from her coiffure and fell to her shoulder.

"She's overset." She wiped a tear from her eye, smearing the kohl she'd applied liberally around it. "I am not certain what has horrified her more, the fact that her husband has been arrested for murder or the fact that he betrayed her with another. *All gentlemen take mistresses*, she said to me, *a wife must learn to bear it*. What rot. Men fill women's heads with that nonsense so that they can do what they like. Don't you think so, Lacey?"

"I agree," I said.

She gave me a look of vast surprise, then of disbelief. "Well, well. If that is the truth, then you are the most remarkable gentleman I have ever known. Ring for the maid, please. We need more tea."

I crossed the room to tug a bell pull.

"I've given her a drop of laudanum," she said. "That and the brandy should ensure that she sleeps well into the morning. I will stay with her until she's stronger. I do hope you clear up this mess quickly, Lacey."

"I appreciate your faith in me."

Lady Aline folded the blanket Louisa had used and drew it onto her own lap. "You have impressed me so far. You cleared up the murder at the Sudbury School in Berkshire, discovered who killed Lydia Westin's husband and that barrister's wife. And I much prefer having you look into the matter than Bow Street. So unsavory."

"It is unsavory no matter who looks into it," I pointed out. I gathered up the tea things to give my hands something to do.

"Perhaps, but this is Louisa's life. Her husband. Their secrets. You can at least be gentle."

"I can be gentle with Louisa," I agreed. "I am certain I'll throttle Brandon when I see him. As far as I can discern, he's been a complete idiot."

The maid entered with a fresh pot of tea on a tray. She removed the dirty cups and saucers and departed. I noted that the maid's eyes were red with tears.

Lady Aline poured tea in a businesslike manner. She sloshed a dollop of brandy into my cup without asking me if I wanted it and handed it to me.

"Now then," she said, lifting the teapot to pour her own. "I will tell you the entire nasty tale."

I lifted the steaming tea to my lips and let her begin.

"I arrived at the Gillis's ball not long after the Brandons did," she said. "I entered, in fact, in time to see the damn fool colonel lead Imogene Harper from her friends to a private alcove. Louisa watched them go with a look of dismay. Tongues around me began to wag on the instant. Mr. Bennington, the husband of the actress, drawled to me, *I say, he's no model of discretion, is he?* He sounded delighted to be entertained, I'm afraid. Others speculated about who this Harper woman truly was. She is a friend of Lady Gillis's, I gather, though she claimed to me that she'd known the Brandons during the war."

"And yet, Louisa says she does not remember her."

"Precisely. At any rate, Louisa's friends took her under their collective wing and went on as though nothing had happened. Colonel Brandon and Mrs. Harper stayed in that alcove for a very long time. They did not emerge, in fact, until the dancing began. Brandon stayed near Mrs. Harper, and whenever I happened to glimpse him, he did not look best pleased. I saw Mr. Turner approach Mrs. Harper, possibly to ask her to dance. Colonel Brandon more or less shooed him away. Mr. Turner looked unhappy, but he went. But later on, I happened to be standing near when he approached again.

"Mr. Turner claimed that Mrs. Harper had promised him

the waltz. Mrs. Harper looked a little confused, then she said, 'Oh yes, of course.' Colonel Brandon turned bright red. He said, 'Mind your manners; the lady does not wish to waltz.' Mr. Turner said, 'You are mistaken, sir. She promised.' Colonel Brandon said, rather loudly, 'If you do not cease pestering her, I will thrash you.' People began to stare at that, I do not have to tell you. Mr. Turner smiled a bit and said, 'No, you won't.' He bowed to Mrs. Harper and wandered away.''

"Damn," I said, exasperated. "Brandon made himself the very picture of a jealous rival."

"Yes, it was not well done," Lady Aline replied. "Soon after that, supper was called. Leland Derwent escorted me in, sweet boy. Colonel Brandon immediately stuck out his arm to Imogene Harper. Never mind that Louisa was standing near to them. I know it's not the thing for a husband to always escort his wife, but the snub was apparent. Brandon was red and uncomfortable. He knew what it looked like.''

"And Mrs. Harper? Was she uncomfortable as well?"

"Not a bit of it." Lady Aline clicked her cup to her saucer. "She smiled sweetly at him and took his arm. He led her to the supper room and seated himself next to her, stayed glued to her throughout the meal. Louisa was not far from him, trying not to look mortified, poor lamb.''

I clenched my hands. "What the devil was he thinking?"

"Precisely what Mr. Bennington asked me. He was seated on my other side. 'My wife runs about where she pleases,' he said with a cynical smile. 'But she pretends to be the very picture of devotion. Of course, that is what makes her a celebrated actress,' he went on. 'Perhaps the colonel chap could take lessons from her.' ''

"Dear God," I said. "Brandon's made himself and Louisa a laughingstock."

"I know," Lady Aline replied sadly. "That was not the worst of it."

I drank down my tea, the bitter liquid burning my tongue.

Lady Aline resumed the tale. "After supper, Colonel

Brandon led Mrs. Harper out again. He monopolized her, kept her near him. They did not dance, but she did not dance with anyone else. When Mr. Turner approached again, Brandon snarled at him. Mr. Turner laughed and walked away. I heard Mr. Turner say, 'Soon, sir. Very soon.' What that meant I have no idea, but Mrs. Harper looked distressed, and Brandon grew even redder."

"Did anyone else approach them?" I asked. "Or Mr. Turner, for that matter?" I knew I needed to tamp down my anger at Brandon and his behavior in order to decide what had happened. Anyone near Brandon might have stolen his knife, including Mrs. Harper herself.

"Basil Stokes spoke to them. I saw him laughing about something in that bluff way of his. Colonel Brandon and Mrs. Harper endeavored to be polite. Leland Derwent spoke to them, but then young Mr. Derwent is a stickler about making the polite rounds. He is too shy to be much of a conversationalist, but he knows to ask about one's mother or ailing sister or to remark upon the weather." Lady Aline put her forefinger to the corner of her mouth. "Let me think. Lady Gillis herself approached them. The irritating Rafe Godwin. He is an annoying young man, tries to imitate Grenville, but Grenville has nothing to do with him, and so he should not."

"What about Mr. Turner? Who did he speak to?"

"Oh, a good number of people. He circulated the room, danced with a few debutantes, whose mothers should have known better, but he is an earl's cousin, after all. He spent much time with Leland Derwent. I believe they knew each other at school, though I would not think that innocent Leland was much Henry Turner's type. But Leland suffers from overpoliteness and likely doesn't have the manners to tell Turner to go to the devil."

I thought over the people Lady Aline had named, some of whom I knew, some I did not. I would have to talk about them with Grenville later, to obtain his opinion. One person, I noted that Lady Aline had not mentioned. "What about Lady Breckenridge? Who did she speak to?"

Lady Aline opened her mouth to answer, then she closed it again and eyed me shrewdly. "Lacey, my boy, what is exactly between you and Donata Breckenridge?"

I blinked, taken aback. "Between?"

"Yes. I am not a fool. I know you are not courting her, and yet . . ."

She left it hanging. My face heated as I touched the handle of the walking stick Lady Breckenridge had given me. "We are friends," I said. But I had kissed her lips on more than one occasion, and she had helped me when I needed it. I had not liked her when I'd first met her, over a billiards game in a sunny room in Kent. I'd found her abrupt, abrasive, and overly forward. "Perhaps more than friends," I finished.

"She had a wretched marriage to Breckenridge," Lady Aline said, a rather unnecessary statement. I had met Lord Breckenridge and knew exactly what kind of man he'd been. "Marriage to him would have killed a woman with lesser strength than Donata's."

"I have no desire to make her wretched," I said.

That was the truth. On the other hand, I had not the means to marry her, either. My own wife, I'd discovered, was still alive, and in France, with my daughter. I had been given her exact whereabouts a few weeks ago, and I had been contemplating traveling across the Channel to find her.

I would go sooner or later, but I was having difficulty steeling myself to meet her again. The only thing that drove me to do it was the thought of seeing my daughter again. Gabriella would now be seventeen.

Even if I came to some arrangement with my wife, even if Grenville helped me with a divorce or annulment, I'd have little to offer Lady Breckenridge. I was a poor man, though I was gentleman born. Lady Breckenridge marrying me would be a sad misalliance for her.

"And I have no desire to see her wretched," Lady Aline said. "But you treat her gently, and she is grateful for that."

I raised my brows. "She said so?" I could not imagine Lady Breckenridge expressing such a tender thought, especially out loud to Lady Aline.

"Of course not," Lady Aline replied. "She does not need to. But I've known her since she was in leading strings. Her mother is a great friend of mine."

"I am pleased she has such an ally in you," I said. "But you haven't answered my question. To whom did Lady Breckenridge speak this evening?"

Lady Aline gave me a tiny smile. "Not to Colonel Brandon and Imogene Harper. Donata spoke to me and to Lady Gillis—although she does not like Lady Gillis very much. She finds her too washed out and tiresome. She danced much, of course. She always does. She even danced with Mr. Derwent, who asked her out of painful politeness. She seemed most amused."

I imagined she had. Leland Derwent was the epitome of innocence, and Lady Breckenridge had a rather worldly outlook. I hoped she had not shocked Leland too much with her pointed observations.

I studied the head of my walking stick, which was engraved with the inscription *Captain G. Lacey, 1817.* "Now, we come to the event of Turner's death. Take me to that and tell me what happened, exactly."

Lady Aline pursed her lips. "I remember very precisely that I was talking to Lady Gillis. We both had seen a patterned silk at Madame Mouchand's and admired it. I was explaining that it would look fine on her, but not me, because I am too stout to carry it off. All at once, we heard a horrible scream. It pierced the air, cutting over the music, which was quite loud. Everyone stopped, of course, even the musicians, as we looked for the disturbance. And there was Imogene Harper, near the stairs with the anteroom door open behind her, screaming frantically."

I leaned forward. "Did you see Colonel Brandon? Was he near her?"

"No. At that moment, I saw him nowhere in the room. He did reappear, however, when I made my way to Mrs. Harper. The colonel came from behind me and shoved his way through. We reached her at about the same time."

"What did he say?"

"Nothing very much. In general, men are useless in a crisis. Except Grenville. He very sensibly took Mrs. Harper by the hand and led her to a seat and called for brandy. Then he entered the room with Lord Gillis. The rest of the guests could only gape. I stayed with Louisa, of course. She took it very well, until Lord Gillis sent for Bow Street. Then she nearly swooned. Louisa believes her husband truly did kill Mr. Turner, you see."

I recalled the resigned look in Louisa's eyes. "Pomeroy obviously thinks he did also. But is there anything that points concretely to his having stabbed Turner? Two gentlemen can exchange sharp words without one murdering the other. Or if they do, they call each other out and make a formal outing of it."

Lady Aline sighed regretfully. "Ah, Lacey, the problem of it is, there were so many people in the ballroom. Who knows who entered that room with Mr. Turner, or who was there already when he entered it? Had he slipped inside for peace and quiet, or did he mean to meet someone? No one saw. We were concentrating on dancing and gossip and disparaging other ladies' gowns, you see. The usual thing."

"One does not expect a member of the *ton* to be murdered at a ball," I agreed. "And yet, these are violent times."

"The rioting, you mean?" Lady Aline asked.

Since March, with the hanging of a seaman called John Cashman for the crime of getting drunk and stealing a few weapons, the people of London had rioted. Some protested the unjust killing of Cashman, some the fact that British soldiers, back from the war, often had no money, no employment, and no prospect of payment for the blood they'd given in battle. Others rioted simply because it focused their anger and disgust at something other than the tediousness of their own lives.

"Rioting, and the men who put down the riots," I said. "Murder in general. It is as though the war allowed us some measure of venting that side of man's nature, but now that avenue is gone."

Lady Aline's plucked brows rose. "Surely the threat of

Napoleon's invasion and the loss of ten thousand men at Waterloo is not better than a few riots."

I gave her a rueful smile. "Never mind. I am melancholy about this entire business."

"As am I. Poor Louisa."

She glanced at the closed door, behind which Louisa rested.

"Is there anything more you can tell me?" I said. "Anything you might have noticed? I do not know what."

Lady Aline shook her head. "I will think on it. I admit, Lacey, that I am rather stunned by it all. When Mr. Pomeroy arrived, he was inclined to believe that Mrs. Harper had killed the man. She may have. I don't know. But then Colonel Brandon stepped forward to protect her, and Pomeroy switched his attentions to him." She sighed. "This will be scandal, vicious scandal."

"Perhaps Louisa would be better off somewhere other than London," I suggested.

"Indeed. I could take her with me to Dorset. That is sufficiently distant, for now, I think."

"She will refuse, of course," I said.

"I will persuade her. If nothing else, I'll feed her laudanum and drag her off while she sleeps."

I smiled at the thought, but I knew Lady Aline was capable of doing just that.

She deflated. "Tonight Louisa came face to face with the idea that her husband might be in truth a very dreadful man."

"Yes," I said absently. I was nagged with the feeling that Brandon's vice in this was mere pigheadedness, not evil. Something did not make sense. I, who should have been ready to believe the worst of Brandon, could not now that it had come to it.

Behind the door, Louisa cried out in her sleep. I sprang to my feet, jolted by the heartrending sound. She must have awakened herself, because we heard a muffled moan, and then the unmistakable sound of weeping.

I was halfway to the door before Lady Aline stopped me. "Not you," she said sharply.

I halted, my heart beating rapidly. The need to comfort her struck me hard.

Lady Aline shook her head at me. Then, gathering her skirts, she strode past me to the door of Louisa's bedchamber and let herself inside.

I quit the house. I could not bear to be there any longer, listening to Louisa cry and knowing I could not help her. I took a hackney coach across rainy London and arrived at my lodgings in Grimpen Lane, near Covent Garden, just as dawn broke the sky.

Bartholomew waited in my rooms for me, awake and as fresh as though he'd slept all night, though I knew he hadn't. He had warmed the sitting room and bedchamber and he helped me to bed.

I closed my eyes, but I could only see Louisa, pale and drawn, her gray eyes full of conviction that her husband had committed murder and adultery. More than that, I could feel Louisa's soft body against mine as she clung to me, needing me. I was not quite certain how I felt about that.

I did doze a few times only to dream of Henry Turner's still, dead body and the sound of Imogene Harper's screams.

Bartholomew woke me at ten that morning. Pomeroy had told me last night that Brandon would be examined by the Bow Street magistrate at eleven o'clock, and I intended to be there. I bathed my face and let Bartholomew shave me.

"Do you think the colonel did it, sir?" Bartholomew asked as he scraped soap and whiskers from my chin.

"I do not know," I answered. "He certainly was not very helpful."

Bartholomew nodded. "Want me to come along, sir?"

"No. I have the feeling that trying to keep Colonel Brandon out of Newgate will take much time. No need for you to waste your day in the magistrate's office."

"Mind if I poke around a bit?" he asked. "Get chummy with Lord Gillis's servants, I mean? See if they witnessed the event?"

He sounded eager, ready to begin the game of investigation.

I told him to enjoy himself. Bartholomew could be a mine of information on what went on not only below stairs, but above stairs as well. He had certainly helped me solve the murders at the Sudbury School and the Glass House.

Before I left my rooms, I wrote a short letter to Sir Montague Harris, the magistrate of the Whitehall Public Office, informing him of my thoughts on the death of Turner.

Bartholomew agreed to post the letter for me, and I walked from the narrow cul-de-sac of Grimpen Lane to Russel Street. I turned left onto Russel Street and traversed the short distance to Bow Street, my knee barely bothering me.

The spring day was warm, and people thronged the lanes. Women with baskets over their arms and shawls against the damp threaded their way among the vendors, working men hurried about with deliveries or on errands, and middle-class women strolled arm-in-arm with their daughters looking into shops.

Bow Street was crowded. Rumor of a murder in elegant Mayfair had reached the populace, and many waited for a glimpse of the murderer that Bow Street had apprehended. I had not looked at a newspaper yet, but I imagined their stories would be lurid. As time went on, every snippet of Brandon's life would be splashed across the pages of the *Morning Herald*.

I let myself inside the magistrate's house and asked one of the clerks for Pomeroy.

"Ah, there you are, Captain," Pomeroy bellowed across the length of the house. He shouldered his way down the corridor, pressing aside the assorted pickpockets and prostitutes who'd been arrested during the night. "Come to see the colonel committed, have you?"

CHAPTER 4

I became aware that every person in the vicinity pricked up their ears and watched us eagerly. Several men gave me impudent grins.

"He must be examined, first," I said.

"Oh, aye, him and the witnesses. I called in Lord Gillis and Mr. Grenville. Lord Gillis because it was his house and he'd likely know what went on in it, and Mr. Grenville because he makes a decent witness. And he was first on the spot when it happened. I wanted to call Mrs. Harper, but the magistrate said wait until she's a bit less distressed." He shrugged. "He's the magistrate."

I wanted very much to meet Mrs. Harper myself, but I agreed that traveling to Bow Street and enduring the scrutiny of last night's crop of prostitutes might be beyond her. "Lord Gillis is coming?" I asked.

"No. It's not the thing for an earl to come to the magistrate, Sir Nathaniel says," Pomeroy said, naming Bow Street's chief magistrate, Sir Nathaniel Conant. "Sir Nathaniel will go to him later today. But Mr. Grenville should be arriving at any time."

Grenville liked to be in the thick of things. I knew he would not mind walking among the muck of Bow Street in his perfectly shined boots if he could indulge his curiosity. I would be happy to see him, though. He'd been on the spot, and he was quite good at noticing things out of the ordinary. A decent witness, as Pomeroy had called him.

Grenville arrived as Pomeroy and I started for the stairs. His fine phaeton stopping in the street outside caused some commotion as those inside craned to look out windows at the most elegant horses and rig in town. He leapt down and handed the reins to his tiger, a young man whose sole purpose in life was to look after Grenville's horses when he was not driving them.

Grenville swept inside, removing his hat, and was instantly bombarded by a mass of humanity.

"A farthing in me palm, milord. Wouldn't say no," an elderly man with few teeth breathed at him. "Spare a penny for an old man?"

"Eee, yer a fine one," a young woman with smeared rouge said slyly. "Remember sweet Jane when she's done with the magistrate, won't you?"

Grenville blushed and ignored her suggestive smiles. He sprinkled pennies to the others until Pomeroy lumbered forward and shouted, "Clear off. Let him through."

"Good morning, Lacey," Grenville said, as though we were meeting at a club. "Mr. Pomeroy."

Grenville apparently had not slept much the night before. His face was impeccably shaved, but his cheeks were pasty white and dark smudges stained the hollows beneath his eyes.

We did not speak further as Pomeroy took us up the stairs and to the room where the chief magistrate waited.

Sir Nathaniel Conant, an elderly man who had presided over the Bow Street court for four years, sat behind a table on which waited a sheaf of paper and a pen and ink. The room felt damp and smelled faintly of unwashed clothes, an inauspicious place to decide the fate of a man's life.

Colonel Brandon sat near Sir Nathaniel, but he got abruptly to his feet when he saw me.

Brandon looked terrible. His usually crisp black hair was disheveled, although he had made some attempt to smooth it. His chin was covered in black stubble, and his dark and elegant suit was rumpled and stained. He gazed at me with blue eyes that resembled cold winter skies.

Sir Nathaniel glanced up at us. "Good, Pomeroy. We can begin. These are your witnesses?"

"Mr. Grenville is." Pomeroy introduced him. "He was at the ball when the murder took place. This is Captain Lacey."

Sir Nathaniel peered at me, his watery eyes taking more interest. "I have heard Sir Montague Harris speak of you. He regards you as intelligent. Why have you come? Are you also a witness?"

"I was not at Lord Gillis's ball," I replied. "But I know Colonel Brandon. He was my commander in the army."

"Ah, a character witness. Sit down, if you please."

"Sir Nathaniel," Brandon said stiffly. "I do not want Captain Lacey here."

Sir Nathaniel looked surprised. "Do not be foolish. At this point, Colonel, you need all the friends you have. Sit."

He pointed his pen at the chair Brandon had vacated. With another belligerent glare at me, Brandon resumed his seat.

Colonel Aloysius Brandon was a handsome man. At forty-six, he had black hair with little gray, a square, handsome face, and an athletic physique that had not run to fat. I had often wondered why he seemed oblivious to the attentions women wished to bestow on him, although, as evidenced with this business, perhaps he was not so oblivious after all.

I took a straight-backed chair next to Grenville. Pomeroy sprawled across a bench, and we waited for the procedure to begin.

At least, I thought, as Sir Nathaniel scratched a few words on his papers, Brandon did not have to suffer the indignity of standing in the dock before the sitting magistrate downstairs, with thieves and prostitutes and other poor unfortunates awaiting their turn. Sir Nathaniel had obviously kept in mind Colonel Brandon's standing, as well as the fact that murder was a bit more serious than the usual goings-on in London's back streets.

"Colonel Brandon," Sir Nathaniel began. "This is an examination, not a trial, in which I will determine whether you should be held in custody for trial for murder. Do you understand?"

Silently, with an angry glint in his eye, Brandon nodded.

"Excellent," Sir Nathaniel said, as though Brandon had agreed to accept a cup of tea. "Now, Mr. Pomeroy, please present the evidence that made you bring in this man for the murder of Mr. Henry Turner."

Pomeroy climbed to his feet and plodded forward. He took from his pocket a wad of cloth, and unwrapped the dagger that had killed Turner. He clunked it to the table.

"This knife was plunged into the chest of Mr. Henry Turner, coroner says near to midnight last night. The body was found at twelve o'clock, and witnesses saw the deceased alive and well at half past eleven, so there's not much doubt about the time of death. When I arrived, I asked who the knife belonged to. Colonel Brandon told me that the knife was his. His wife, Mrs. Brandon, said that she could not remember whether the colonel had such a knife, but he was pretty certain."

"It is mine," Brandon said, tight-lipped. "I never denied that."

Sir Nathaniel gave him a sharp look then made a note. "Any other evidence?" he asked Pomeroy.

"No, sir. I examined Colonel Brandon's gloves and found that they were clean. The colonel denied having killed Mr. Turner, and denied having gone into the anteroom, where he was found, at all. But a few witnesses, Mr. Grenville included, saw Mr. Turner and Colonel Brandon enter the room at eleven o'clock together. However, they emerged almost immediately, after five minutes, and went their separate ways. No one I can find remembers either Mr. Turner or Colonel Brandon entering the room after that, but Mr. Turner must have done, because there he was, dead, an hour later."

"I must ask you, Colonel," Sir Nathaniel said quietly, "why you lied to Mr. Pomeroy about entering the anteroom at all?"

Brandon looked uncomfortable. "Because it was none of his affair. And it had nothing to do with Turner being killed."

"That remains to be seen," Sir Nathaniel said. "Please tell me the nature of your conversation with Mr. Turner in the anteroom."

Brandon sat up straighter. "I do not wish to."

Sir Nathaniel raised his gray brows. "Colonel Brandon, you might well be tried for murder. Were I in your place, I would try my best to establish that my business with Mr. Turner had nothing to do with his death. Now, what did you discuss?"

Brandon's neck went red. "I called him out."

"Called him out. Do you mean you challenged him to a duel?"

Brandon nodded.

Sir Nathaniel made a note. Even the scratching of his pen sounded disapproving. "Dueling is against the law, Colonel."

"I know that. But Mr. Turner was being offensive to Mrs. Harper. He needed speaking to. In any event, it is a moot point now."

I stifled a sigh. Brandon might as well build the scaffold and tie the noose around his neck himself.

"Indeed, it is," said Sir Nathaniel. "And you were annoyed with Mr. Turner's behavior because Mrs. Harper is your mistress?"

Brandon hesitated. I saw his eyes swivel to the paper, above which Sir Nathaniel's pen poised. One thing to say the words to Pomeroy, another to have them written down in black ink.

"Yes," he said slowly.

This was nonsense. It had to be. And yet, what had he to gain from protecting Mrs. Harper?

"Very well." Sir Nathaniel's pen moved. "After you and Mr. Turner made an appointment to meet, what did you do next?"

"We never made the appointment," Brandon said. "He refused me. I told him he was a coward and left him."

Grenville glanced sideways at me. I gave him a grim look in return. If Brandon could convince the magistrate that he'd planned to meet Turner honorably, he might have a chance to prove he'd never kill him *dis*honorably. But Brandon's words put paid to that defense.

"I see." Sir Nathaniel redipped his pen. "Well, then, Colonel, please go on. Tell me what you did from the time that you left Mr. Turner until his body was discovered."

"I've told Mr. Pomeroy," Brandon said in a hard voice.

Sir Nathaniel looked at him with deceptively mild eyes. "Now, tell me."

Brandon's shoulders sagged the slightest bit. "I walked out of the anteroom, as I told you. I went back to find Mrs. Harper, and we adjourned into an alcove so I could speak privately with her. I told her what Mr. Turner had said. She was naturally upset that I had challenged him, and it took some time to calm her down. She asked that I find her some sherry, and I went in search. I could not find a footman with a tray—never about when you need one, footmen—so I was obliged to leave the ballroom. I searched the supper room and found all the decanters empty, so I went out to the hall to find a servant. I had no success, and was about to tramp down to the kitchens myself, when I heard Mrs. Harper screaming. I pushed my way through the crowd and saw her standing outside the anteroom, and Turner dead inside."

Sir Nathaniel scribbled away. Presently he asked, "Did you see anyone in the supper room or the hall outside who can be a witness that you were there?"

"No," Brandon growled. "As I said, I found no servants, no sherry. God knows where they all were. When I came back inside, everyone was watching Mrs. Harper. I do not think anyone noticed me."

I broke in. "That does corroborate what Lady Aline Carrington told me. She said that Colonel Brandon came from behind her."

Sir Nathaniel made a note without thanking me. "Even better," he said, "would be a witness who saw you in the alcove with Mrs. Harper between the time you left Mr. Turner and twelve o'clock."

Brandon shook his head.

"Mr. Pomeroy?" Sir Nathaniel asked. "Have you found any witnesses to swear where Colonel Brandon was at the time?"

"No, sir," Pomeroy said. "Most unhelpful, that."

"Indeed," Sir Nathaniel said. "Now then, Mr. Grenville, what can you add or subtract from Colonel Brandon's statement?"

Grenville cleared his throat. "I did see Colonel Brandon and Mrs. Harper enter the alcove after Mr. Turner emerged from the anteroom. I cannot say when they departed it. I was dancing after that, giving all my attention to my partners. I was very near the anteroom, however, when Mrs. Harper entered it. I saw her go in. After a minute or two, she rushed out, screaming at the top of her lungs. I looked inside and saw Mr. Turner slumped against the table. I settled Mrs. Harper on a chair, then entered the room with Lord Gillis. Lord Gillis pulled Mr. Turner upright. I saw the knife in his chest and knew that he was dead."

He fell silent. The quiet scratch of Sir Nathaniel's pen made a strange contrast to the violence Grenville described.

"Did you see Colonel Brandon come back into the ballroom?" Sir Nathaniel asked him.

Grenville shook his head. "I did not see him, no."

"Well, he wouldn't, would he?" Brandon broke in. "He was looking at Turner, not searching the ballroom for me."

Sir Nathaniel gave him another sharp look. "Quite so, Colonel. Captain Lacey," he said. "What evidence do you have to add?"

Brandon glowered at me. He did not want me to speak, did not want me there at all. I wondered at his resistance. He might not like me, but he ought to at least realize that I could help him.

I replied, "I served under Colonel Brandon from the time I was twenty years old until the time I was thirty-eight. The fact that Colonel Brandon stands accused of this crime surprises me very much indeed."

"Not accused," Sir Nathaniel said quickly. "This is a preliminary examination, as I said."

"I am surprised that he is under suspicion at all. Colonel Brandon has always acted with honor." At least, I added silently, he'd acted with honor except where I was concerned.

"You were in the wars together," Sir Nathaniel said. "A man learns to kill during a war. Otherwise, he'd make a poor soldier."

"Fighting a battle and cold-blooded murder are two different things," I pointed out.

"I concede that," Sir Nathaniel said. "I know some officers who are the gentlest of men. That does not mean your colonel has not done murder." He gave me a nod. "Though I commend your loyalty."

Brandon's face went a bright, cherry red. The last person he wanted to stand up for him was me.

But if I could save the wretch for Louisa, I would. I still had difficulty believing he'd stabbed Turner. Brandon was guilty of something here, but of what, I was not yet certain.

Presently, Sir Nathaniel lifted his head. "I would like to speak with the ladies who were present," he said in his dry, respectable voice. "Mrs. Harper and Mrs. Brandon."

"No," Brandon said at once. "I do not want my wife involved in this."

"My dear sir, this is murder. Did you believe it was a private matter?"

"As a matter of fact, I do," Brandon said stiffly. "This is not France, where the police survey our every action. Our committees call for police reform. Ha. We shall all be scrutinized whenever we leave our houses, if that happens."

His speech did not please Sir Nathaniel, whose nostrils pinched. "That's as may be, Colonel. At present, I need to investigate a murder and determine whether or not you should be tried for it. Your wife, in fact, may be able to produce evidence that you did not do it. You would like me to find that, would you not?"

Brandon said nothing. His eyes glittered with stubborn fury.

I wondered what the devil was the matter with him. He behaved as though he did not want to be proved innocent.

Perhaps he was throwing himself to the wolves, knowing that Mrs. Harper had killed Turner. But why on earth should he feel so compelled to go to the gallows for her? Brandon was, all in all, a selfish man. Why he'd suddenly become heroic for another person was a mystery to me.

Brandon growled something in reply to Sir Nathaniel's question. Sir Nathaniel straightened his papers.

"Very well, I have made my decision. Colonel Brandon, I am committing you to trial for the murder of Mr. Henry Turner on the night of the fifth of April. The evidence against you is stronger than the evidence for your innocence. You will go to Newgate prison and remain there until my Runner gathers the evidence needed for the trial. Thank you, Mr. Pomeroy. Please have Colonel Brandon escorted to the prison."

Pomeroy looked slightly taken aback. I imagined he'd regarded arresting his former colonel as a good joke, assuming I'd quickly get him off. But Sir Nathaniel looked severe, in his understated way.

Pomeroy rose. Grenville and I stood up with him.

"Sir Nathaniel," I said. "Must he stay in the prison? It will be a blow to a man of his standing."

"I am sorry, Captain Lacey, but there are laws. Colonel Brandon will live in Newgate until he stands in the dock. The wait will not be long, and he will have a private room. He will not live in the common cells with the rabble."

No, Brandon was a rich man, and could afford a room with furnishings and good meals. His physical comfort would not be impaired, but he'd be a ruined man.

"Colonel," Pomeroy said reluctantly.

The only one who did not argue was Brandon. He rose, his face set, and let Pomeroy lead him from the room.

NEWGATE prison stood north of the junction where Ludgate Hill became Ludgate Street, not far from lofty Saint Paul's Cathedral. The dome of the cathedral hung against the leaden sky as Grenville stopped his phaeton in the crowds of Ludgate Hill at my request.

"I can drive you all the way," he offered.

"No." I smiled. "Your high-stepping horses and polished rig are for Hyde Park, not the gallows yard at Newgate."

Grenville nodded his understanding. He held the horses steady while the tiger hopped from his perch on the back and helped me to the ground. "I am sorry for all this, Lacey," he said. "I was not much help, was I?"

"You told what you saw. Brandon would be free if he were not so damned stubborn." I adjusted my hat. "Will you take a message to Mrs. Brandon? Tell her what has happened, and that I am here to settle Brandon's needs. Tell her I will come as soon as I can."

Grenville regarded me a moment with enigmatic dark eyes. Already people were taking notice of him and the elegant phaeton. "It's that Mr. Grenville what's always in the newspapers," someone murmured. "I never. What's a posh gent like 'im doing 'ere?"

Grenville took the hint, shot me a wry smile, tipped his hat, then signaled his horses to move on.

Newgate prison itself was a depressing building of gray block stones. Windows, barred and forbidding, lined its walls. In the open area outside the gate was the gallows, empty today. Hangings took place on Monday for the public; those waiting their turn inside could watch. Today was

Sunday. The condemned would attend chapel and emerge tomorrow to their dooms.

When I'd been a small lad, the hangings had taken place at Tyburn near the end of what was now Park Lane. Once, when I'd come to London with my father, I'd sneaked away to witness a hanging there. I still remembered the fevered press of bodies, the excitement and dismay radiating from the crowd, the buildup of frenzy as the prisoner rolled past in his cart, ready to face the gallows.

Thinking back, the hanged man must have been less than twenty years old, though he'd seemed older to me at the time. He'd stood up in the cart, nodding to the crowd like an actor pleased by his audience. The guards with him had led him up the steps to the scaffold, where he'd stood and addressed us all. "Friends, today I die for the crime of being honest. I honestly stole those clothes from me master's shop."

The crowd had laughed. He'd grinned along with them, and gone on. "Do not cry for me, I go to a better place." He'd looked around. "Any place is better than Newgate in the damp."

Again, they'd laughed. The hangman had cut off his words by jamming a hood over his head and a noose around his neck.

I'd crept to the very edge of the scaffold while he'd joked with the crowd. I'd seen his face before the hood had gone down. He'd been gray, his lips trembling. He might have made light of his punishment to others, but he was terrified.

When they hauled him from his feet, he gave a startled cry, which was cut off in midbreath. I'd watched in fascinated horror as he kicked and struggled mightily to live, then just to breathe, while the crowed cheered or mocked him.

They'd cut him down, stone dead, and then sold his clothes to the people there.

I'd run back to the townhouse my father had rented and was sick all night.

I'd witnessed hangings since then, in the army, in India, and deaths more terrible, but the hanging I'd seen as a child of six had seemed the worst terror I could have faced. I'd dreamed for weeks that I was that man, having my vision cut abruptly off by the hood, feeling the burn of the rope about my neck, hearing the crowd laughing and cheering.

Passing the gallows now, I felt a qualm of that old dread, the ghost of the noose that had killed the young thief.

Pomeroy and Brandon had already arrived. I caught up to them just as they passed beneath the gate, following them into a courtyard that smelled of urine.

Pomeroy went to the keeper's room, a square office with a bench and a table and a window giving onto the courtyard. The keeper was alone with another turnkey, the two men both portly from beef and ale.

Pomeroy released Brandon officially, then said, "He's a posh gent. He'll want the finest rooms you have."

"Oh, is 'e?" the keeper guffawed. "A duke, is 'e?"

"He's a colonel and a gentleman," Pomeroy said severely. "He's to be treated fine, or I'll hear of it."

The keeper seemed a bit in awe of Pomeroy, probably with good reason. Pomeroy was a powerful and strong man, not shy about using his fists when necessary. In addition, he was a Bow Street Runner, one of the elite force that policed London and beyond. Keeping on the friendly side of a Runner was always wise.

The keeper told Brandon, in a slightly more respectful tone, "Aye, if you pay me well, sir, you'll have no troubles here. Send for one or two of your own servants, and you'll live as well as you would at home. A gentleman is always welcome."

Brandon looked from Pomeroy to the keeper in fury. "Do you mean, Sergeant, that you want me to bribe this man?"

"You have to pay for room and board, sir," Pomeroy said in a patient tone. "And buy your bedding and fuel and things. Stands to reason. The more you pay, the better you live."

"For God's sake," Brandon began. "I do not even have much money with me."

"I will settle his affairs," I broke in as the keeper took on a belligerent expression.

"No you will not," Brandon retorted. "You will mind your own business."

"I do not believe they will let you visit your man of business at the moment," I answered impatiently. "I will visit on your behalf. Or would you rather bed down on hay with a flea-ridden street girl?"

Brandon blanched. Street girls made him nervous in any case. "I take your point, Lacey. I only wish to God I had someone else to help me."

I knew he did. The turnkey grinned impudently at me, and led us into the bowels of the building.

CHAPTER 5

THE room Brandon obtained was not elegant by any means. A tall tester bed stood in one corner, with a heavy mahogany cupboard on another wall and a table and chairs in the middle of the room. A small fireplace, cold, lay opposite the door.

The turnkey barked at a lackey to build a fire. Gloom-faced, the servant looked neither at me nor Brandon while he worked, then he shuffled out.

Pomeroy, with a cheerful "Good day, sirs," left us alone.

Brandon looked out of a window to the courtyard three floors below. He remained silent, his back in his soiled coat still and sullen.

"Sir," I began. Even after all the years I'd known him and all we'd been through, I still could not bring myself to address him in any way than as an officer who outranked me.

"I suppose," he said coldly, addressing his words to the window, "that as soon as you heard what had happened, you went at once to my wife."

"Of course I did. I knew she would be distressed once I learned what a pig's breakfast you'd made of everything."

"How fortunate that she has a friend as kind as you," he said, biting off every word. "A friend who will stay with her in times of trouble."

"Lady Aline Carrington stays with her."

Brandon swung around. His face was carefully neutral, but his eyes glittered. "You must be delighted, Gabriel. Watching me be arrested and tried for murder. My wife will need much comfort during this ordeal, and there you will be. Perhaps the turnkey will allow me to hang a pair of horns above my door, so that all who pass will know that herein lies a cuckold."

I was tempted to march out of the room and leave the idiot to his fate, but I knew Louisa would never forgive me if I did. "You are a fool and a bloody hypocrite. Your wife has never betrayed you. Yet you claimed, with her standing next to you, that this Mrs. Harper was your mistress. If Louisa leaves you, it will be as much as you deserve."

"Ah, yes. I can learn from you how to be an abandoned husband."

I stared at him in astonishment. In all our quarrels, he had never cast up to me that my wife had deserted me, as though that topic was impermissible. Now he glared at me, his broad chest rising and falling, defiance in every move.

Through my black anger, a hint of understanding reached me. "Why are you deliberately provoking me?" I asked. "You know you need my help. Why are you tempting me to tell you to go to the devil and stay there?"

"Because this is none of your affair!"

"It hurts Louisa. And is therefore my affair."

"Affair," he sneered. "A fine choice of words."

"Your word, sir." I stepped close to him. "Do you *want* to die in ignominy? Hanging is a nasty death, and you know it. Louisa will have to live her life as the wife of a condemned murderer."

"Lacey, for God's sake, stay out of this."

"Why?" I asked him. "Never tell me you really did kill Turner."

He avoided my gaze. "I do not wish to speak of it."

"Did Imogene Harper kill him? Why are you protecting her?"

"I will not answer."

We stood face to face, his ice blue eyes staring into my brown ones. "I will ask her," I said.

"You will leave her alone," he snapped in reply.

"You are no longer my commanding officer. Your own actions made that so. I no longer must obey you."

I expected him to argue, to rage, to bluster. But he said nothing. After a time, he turned away, his shoulders slumped in defeat.

"You are a fool, sir," I repeated.

He turned back to me, a strange light in his eyes. "No, Gabriel. You are the fool."

I knew I would gain nothing more from him, so I turned away and left him alone.

I visited Brandon's man of business before leaving the City, and explained the situation. He was distressed, with good reason. A respectable solicitor wants a respectable clientele, and a client held in Newgate to await trial for murder was most distressing indeed.

However, he put in motion the errands needed to ensure that Brandon spent his time in prison in as comfortable accommodations as possible.

I returned to my lodgings and ate a hasty meal of bread at Mrs. Beltan's bakery below my rooms. I bathed and changed my clothes, giving them over to Bartholomew to clean, but I could not shake the stench of Newgate from me.

I took a hackney back to Mayfair and to Brook Street. Lady Aline met me at the door to Brandon's house. Grenville had been and gone, she said, and had broken the bad news.

Louisa was up, pacing her sitting room in agitation. Her

face was white, her eyes sunken into hollows. She held herself rigid when I went to take her hands and kiss her cheek.

I explained that I'd seen Brandon settled and that he
could have a servant or two to look after him. Lady Aline
said she'd dispatch Brandon's valet at once, and bustled off
to do so. As soon as the door closed, Louisa clasped my
hands tightly. "What will happen now?"

"Pomeroy and his patrollers will gather evidence against
Brandon. If they find nothing that firmly points to his guilt,
then he will be acquitted."

"His knife in the man's chest is not firm evidence?"

I tried to keep my tone reasonable. "Anyone may steal
another's knife and use it. Were I to murder someone, I
would use a weapon easily identified as belonging to another man. Why bring suspicion to myself?"

"If you were angry, you would not think of that," Louisa
countered. "You would snatch up the first thing you saw
and stab."

"Perhaps."

Her observation gave me an idea. What if Brandon had
left the knife in the anteroom when he was there earlier
with Turner? Why he should, I didn't know, but he might
have done. The murderer could have quarreled with Turner,
noticed the knife, and in a fit of pique, snatched it up, and
driven it into Turner's chest.

"Louisa," I said. "He is being stubbornly cryptic, but I
will discover the truth. I will bring him back to you."

Louisa's eyes were bleak, and she walked away from
me. "Gabriel, have I been a fool all my life?" she asked
softly. "I stuck by him through thick and thin. Through
everything he did. Even after . . . When he came looking for
me in your tent that night, I went back to him. Then he tried
his best to harm you, and even then I stood by him."

I remembered. Colonel Brandon had decided one day
soon after Vitoria that he no longer wanted a wife who
could not give him children. He told Louisa he wanted to
find some way to annul the marriage so that they could be

parted without scandal. Then he'd departed to who knew where.

Louisa, seeing her world crumbling around her, had fled to my tent and told me the entire, tearful tale. Brandon had returned the next morning and had found Louisa sitting on my lap in a camp chair, her head on my shoulder.

He'd assumed the worst.

Not long later, Brandon had sent me out with false orders into a pocket of French soldiers, who had caught and tortured me. I'd managed to escape and survive with the help of a Spanish farmer's widow, who'd dragged me the long way back to camp.

I remembered lying on the bunk of the surgeon's tent, hideous pain leaking through the haze of laudanum, my body sweating with fever and infection. When Louisa had come and discovered what Brandon had done, she'd shouted at him long and hard. I had lain in my stupor and laughed.

I smiled briefly. "I recall that you told him quite loudly what you thought of him when you found out what he'd done to me."

"Oh, yes, I was furious. You might have died because of him. I could have left him, then. I should have."

"There was not much you could do, Louisa." When a woman left her husband, she could only return to her family or elope with another man—one was a recipe for disgrace, the other, complete ruin.

"I know. But I remained his wife, in all ways. I wanted to prove, I suppose, that I had not betrayed him. I saw the good in him, still. I loved him." She lifted her arms in a limp gesture. "This is my reward."

"And it is all decidedly odd," I said. "I am not saying that your husband is guiltless in the matter of Mrs. Harper, but the situation seems wrong somehow. I would think that if Brandon were pursuing her, even he would not be so obvious. He prides himself on being the perfect gentleman, the perfect husband, the perfect officer."

Louisa gave me a wry look. "Well, he isn't, is he?"

"But would he let the world see that? There is something very wrong, Louisa. Can you tell me nothing more of this Imogene Harper?"

"No. When I dared ask him, Aloysius grew furious and told me to mind my own damned business. He has never been that harsh to me."

"No," I agreed, "he usually saves that for me. I ask your leave, Louisa, to go through his desk and his letters. I want to read what Mrs. Harper wrote to him, if he has not destroyed the letters. She is key to this murder; perhaps she even killed Turner herself."

Louisa shook her head. "She never went into that anteroom. At least, not until she found him. Believe me, Lacey, I had my eye on her. The only time she disappeared from view was when she went into private corners with my husband."

"And I am going to find out why he did," I promised.

She stood rigidly, her face gray, her eyes tired. "I have resigned myself to the fact that he was having an affair with her. You do not have to try to prove he was not."

I was silent a moment, then I said, "Do you know, I believe I am the only person in London not happy to believe in his guilt."

Her eyes flashed. "*Happy?* Do you believe I am happy to know that my husband has been betraying me?"

"Ready to believe his guilt, then. Perhaps I used the wrong word. But it seems as though everyone wants him to be guilty, including Brandon himself."

Louisa watched me, her gaze deliberately calm. The muscles of her delicate neck were tense, as though she strained simply to hold up her head. "You are kind to try to give me hope."

"And I do wish that both you and your husband would stop trying to assign me motives," I said in irritation. "I am looking into this problem because it distresses you and because I do not believe that Brandon killed Turner. I believe he *could* have killed him, but I will be quite glad to find evidence to prove otherwise."

Louisa sank to the sofa as though my words had weakened her. "Perhaps I simply want it to be over. Perhaps I do not want to wait and hope that you find something. I want it to be over, even if I lose him forever."

"Have you so little faith in me?"

"I know you, Gabriel. You believe a thing is so, therefore it must be so. You stubbornly burrow through things to prove yourself right, no matter who you hurt."

I stilled. "And I've hurt you?"

"No." She smiled a little. "But you are so impetuous, and you will run afoul of the wrong person. It would hurt me so to lose you. I never would have survived all these years without you."

We studied each other. I knew, too, that my life would have been much harsher without her in it.

I could have said something then that might have changed everything between us. I think she wanted me to say it, waited for me to say it. Perhaps I was foolish to keep my silence. But I kept it.

"Louisa, I will do everything in my power to help your husband. And you. I swear this."

A light went out of her eyes. She looked away, and then she nodded. "Ask his valet for the key to his desk. He will know where it is. Tell him I said to give it to you."

"Thank you," I said quietly.

She looked up at me, but her eyes held no hope. I bowed to her briefly, then left the room.

I found the harried valet and requested Brandon's key. He hurried off to find it, seeming relieved to escape Lady Aline's strident demands. Louisa was always gentle with her servants; Lady Aline must have seemed like an unexpected hurricane.

"Lacey, my boy, I do wish you luck," Aline said as she passed me on her way back to Louisa's sitting room. "If you can find an answer to this murder, I will bow before you."

The thought of the large Lady Aline bowing her bulk

amused me somewhat. I told her I could only do my best, and took myself to Brandon's private study.

I'd been in this room only a few times, because Brandon rarely invited me. He put up with me in his dining room and his drawing room for Louisa's sake, but he disliked me in the more private rooms of the house.

In one corner stood a screen of gold-leaf and ivory that he'd obtained in Spain. I'd always wondered where he'd found it, and if it had in fact been looted. Wellington—Wellesley then—had declared looting to be a hanging offense—the English army had gone to liberate the Spanish from French rule, not to rob from them. Brandon had claimed he'd purchased it from monks who needed money, and the story was plausible. But his belligerence whenever he spoke of it always aroused my suspicion.

The desk stood near the screen, a secretary with a closed bookcase. I sat down in the mahogany chair before it, put the key in the lock, and pulled down the sloping cover that formed the base of the desk when opened. Two pieces of wood slid out of slots on either side of the drawers to support the desk's top.

Inside I found neat ledgers and folded papers and small drawers full of letters. None of the letters were from Imogene Harper, nor were the papers.

I searched the drawers and even the ledgers, and then unfolded all the letters to see if another letter had been tucked between pages. I found nothing. I hadn't thought I would.

I remembered Grenville showing me a secretary that he'd purchased in France, a beautiful piece of golden satinwood with rosewood inlay. Grenville's delight in it, however, were the secret drawers. He'd made me try to discover the drawers myself, while he'd hovered gleefully at my shoulder.

I had found two, but he'd showed me four others that I'd missed.

I lifted the small drawers out of the middle of Brandon's desk and felt the recesses behind them for hidden catches. I found one rather easily, which extruded a drawer from the left side of the desk. Rather obvious, I thought. Many desks had such drawers.

I found no letters in the drawer, just a stray button. Perhaps Brandon had no use for secret drawers and had simply burned Mrs. Harper's letters.

I found a second secret drawer that again had nothing inside it. I searched for the catches that Grenville's desk had, but either I missed them, or the designer of this desk had given up after he'd created two.

I slid the main drawers back in, and was about to put the first secret drawer back, when I noticed that its bottom did not fit correctly. I lifted the button and found that its shank just fit into the slight gap. I worked it back and forth, and then suddenly pulled up a thin slice of wood from the bottom of the drawer.

Three letters lay beneath it.

I lifted them out and unfolded them. They were written in a woman's hand, and signed, *Imogene Harper*.

As I perused them, it struck me as strange that if Mrs. Harper had been Brandon's mistress, she'd written him only three letters, brief ones at that. I'd always imagined that mistresses wrote their lovers long and detailed letters.

I supposed it depended on the mistress. Marianne Simmons had never written a word to Grenville, and I doubted she'd ever send a lover a scented missive filled with passionate phrases. I also suspected that Grenville and Marianne's relationship had not progressed beyond tight, tense conversations.

These letters were not dated, but I made sense of the timing after I'd read them. The first was hesitant, as though she'd been timid to contact him again.

I learned your direction from Colonel Singleton, whom my husband also knew during the Peninsular campaign. I make so bold to write to you to remind you of the circumstances of our last meeting. Perhaps I am the last woman on earth from whom you wish to receive correspondence, but I find it necessary to write to you. If you would speak to me, I will be riding in Hyde Park at five o'clock on Wednesday next. I will wait near Grosvenor Gate for you to come. I have need to see you, my dear A. Please come.

She signed without any closure.

The second letter opened with relief. *How glad I was to see you and think that perhaps I might be relieved. You are a gentleman of honor, and I have always known you to be. To see you riding to me, as tall and strong and handsome as you were four years ago, brought pleasure to my heart. I did not know how much I longed to see you again until that moment. The friendship we shared returned to me, with a warmth that I will never forget. I hope that when we meet again on Saturday, I will have good news for you. Until then, God bless you.*

I set aside the second letter and scanned the third again. The tone was quite different. *My dear A. What shall you do? You refer to your wife, but shall I suffer alone? If I must pay, then you must. We are both guilty, and I cannot take the blame alone. He said he would be at the Gillis' ball on Saturday night, and that he would ensure that you were invited—with your wife. I have played upon my connections of friendship and wheedled an invitation for myself from Lady Gillis. We will meet there and decide what to do. He must not reveal all. And if he does, he will reveal your sins as well as mine. You know this. You must come.*

The letter was signed, *Imogene.*

I sat back, my thoughts racing.

Who was "he"? Turner? Had Henry Turner threatened to reveal Mrs. Harper's affair with Brandon? To whom? In any event, Brandon had betrayed it himself; he'd not needed Turner to do it for him.

The letters read very much like a woman wanting to rekindle an affair begun years before, then angry because Brandon had indicated he did not want the relationship to resume. The threat in the last letter was blatant. She would not face Turner alone. If she was exposed, she would expose Brandon.

I wondered, had Turner threatened to blackmail the two of them, and had Mrs. Harper killed him before he could?

Mrs. Harper had gone into the anteroom and found Turner's body. She'd gotten blood on her glove, and according to Grenville, it was a minute or two before she screamed. Time for her to snatch up the knife—which Brandon had possibly left for her—stab him, then rush out and begin her screaming. Her horror at the blood on her glove had no doubt been real.

Was it that simple? That Brandon and Mrs. Harper had feared Turner's knowledge, and so had conspired to kill him?

Louisa had been right about one thing. Many gentlemen took a mistress after they were married. It seemed almost expected. Society marriages often occurred because two families wanted to increase their power or wealth. A poor aristocrat married a rich nabob's daughter; the daughter of an impoverished baron married a wealthy merchant. Even better, wealthy nobility married each other.

Once the nuptials were complete, the ladies busied themselves setting up their nurseries and hosting parties, and gentlemen adjourned to their clubs, horses, and mistresses. Husband and wife might live very separate lives, seeing each other only occasionally.

Brandon's marriage had been different. He'd married Louisa by choice, not for gain. Brandon came from a wealthy gentleman's family in Kent. Louisa's family had been as gently born, but poorer. Her father had considered a cavalry captain with a personal income to be a good catch for Louisa.

I understood perfectly well why Brandon had married. Louisa at twenty-two had been a beautiful woman. Not only did she have golden hair and brilliant gray eyes, but she'd had fire, an adventurous spirit coupled with grave intelligence that would make her a fine life companion. I'd regretted from the moment I'd met her that I'd not found her before Brandon had.

But until this business with Mrs. Harper, I never believed that Brandon had sought another lady's bed. Now I wondered. Mrs. Harper's husband had been killed at Vitoria. Shortly after that, Brandon had declared his intention to end his marriage with Louisa, because she could not give him children.

I wanted very much to meet Imogene Harper. I wanted to know what sort of woman could draw Brandon from Louisa's side.

I folded the letters together and tucked them into my pocket. I carefully reassembled the drawer, dropped the button back inside it, and slid the drawer into its recess.

I sighed as I closed the desk. Brandon, as usual, was not making things easy.

AFTER taking leave of Louisa and Lady Aline, I met Bartholomew in the tavern in Pall Mall where I often conferred with Grenville when I investigated things. Bartholomew was there before me, enjoying an ale with his brother, Matthias.

I had hoped that Grenville would be there as well, so we could talk things over together. Grenville would have a more objective sense of this case than I could. But I was curious to hear what they had learned from speaking to the Gillises' servants.

Bartholomew and Matthias looked much alike, both big and broad-shouldered and blond-haired. The pair of them had been footmen for Grenville for a time before Bartholomew had announced his intention of becoming a valet, and Grenville had sent him to train with me. The bargain was that I got someone to wait on me while Grenville paid his wages. I had a wardrobe that would make the best valet shudder, but Bartholomew kept my few coats and trousers and regimentals cleaner than they'd been since new.

The brothers jumped up when they saw me, and I waved them back to their seats. The landlord brought me an ale, and I sat down and joined them.

"An interesting morning I've had," Bartholomew said. His eyes sparkled. "The servants of Lord and Lady Gillis, though a bit high and mighty, were glad to give me a meal and a bit of a gab. Didn't hurt that I'm slavey to Mr. Grenville."

Being employed by Grenville carried much weight in Bartholomew's world. The higher the master, the higher the servant could hold his head.

"They didn't mind talking about the night of the ball," Bartholomew said. "The thing is, Captain, several of the servants said that Lady Gillis was in a rare state most of the day. They admitted to hearing a flaming row coming from the private rooms early in the afternoon. Lord and Lady Gillis, about someone who was invited to the ball that Lord Gillis did not want there."

"Turner?" I asked.

Bartholomew took another sip of ale and wiped his mouth. "They could not say, in fact. None of the servants heard a name."

That disappointed me, but there was nothing to be done. I asked Matthias, "During the ball that night, did you by chance chat with Mr. Turner's valet?"

"That I did, sir," Matthias answered readily. "When he was brought the news that his master was dead upstairs, you would have thought that Mr. Turner died just to upset him. He was quite mournful about it, saying didn't he have enough to do already without Mr. Turner up and getting himself killed?"

"That is interesting," I said slowly. "You don't happen to know where Mr. Turner's rooms are, do you?"

Matthias started to answer, but Bartholomew broke in cheerfully, "In Piccadilly, sir. Near the Albany. In fact, Matthias says that once the valet realized that his master was gone, he was quite keen that we should come and help him drink up Mr. Turner's claret."

"I believe you should oblige him," I suggested.

Bartholomew winked while Matthias glared at him. "Right you are, sir. You would like to come along?"

"Please," I rose, took up my walking stick, and let the lads lead the way out.

CHAPTER 6

❦

WE took a hackney coach around St. James's Street to
Piccadilly. Mr. Turner had lived in rooms near Burlington House and the Albany. The Albany was the former res-
idence of the Duke of York, which had been sold and
converted into flats for the very rich man-about-town. I
noted that Henry Turner had taken lodgings as close as he
could to the house without having to pay the exorbitant rent
to live there.

Turner's rooms consisted of a sitting room and a bedchamber, one room in the front, one room in the rear. I lived
in similar accommodations, but Mr. Turner's rooms held a
comfort and warmth that mine would always lack.

Mr. Turner, in fact, lived in a bit of decadence. His furniture was either made of costly satinwood or thickly
gilded. I noticed Bartholomew and Matthias look around in
some distaste. Working for Lucius Grenville had given the
two of them experience with the best that money could buy,
plus the taste and moderation that made a thing worth having. Mr. Turner seemed to have been the sort of young man

more interested in what a thing cost than in taste or moderation.

We found Mr. Turner's valet in the bedchamber. He had emptied the armoire and spread Mr. Turner's clothes over the bed, chairs, and every other available surface. He looked up as the landlord ushered us inside.

The valet wore drab black pantaloons that bagged around his knees and ankles in preposterous wrinkles. His coat was of good cut in last year's style, probably one of Turner's castoffs. His long chin was covered with stubble, and his brown eyes were morose.

"Oh dear," he said upon seeing us. "What now?"

Matthias reminded him that they'd had a chin-wag at the Gillises' ball, and that he and his brother worked for none other than Lucius Grenville. He introduced the man to me. The valet's name was Bill Hazleton.

Hazleton glanced at me, categorized me, and dismissed me. I would not be likely to hire a valet out of work, and he knew it.

"I would like to ask you a few questions about your master, if I may," I began.

Hazleton looked sorrowful. "Are you a magistrate? I never killed him, and I don't know who did."

Bartholomew opened his mouth, probably to inform the man that I was in thick with Bow Street, but I forestalled him with a look. "Nothing like that. Mr. Grenville and I are simply curious."

Hazleton regarded this explanation dubiously. But he nodded, as he folded strips of linen, disposed to listen to my questions.

"How long were you Mr. Turner's manservant?"

"Seven years." He sounded depressed. "All through his long Oxford years I looked after him. It was me what had to lie to the proctor when he'd been out all night, me what had to roll him out of bed in the mornings and get him to lectures. And what did he do? Wager my pay on horses, he did. And any other thing he could think of. Always kept good drink, though."

He trailed off wistfully. Servants' posts were difficult to obtain, and no matter how irritating the master, most preferred employment to the prospect of having to look for work. Also, a personal manservant would regard other forms of menial labor as beneath him.

"And then," Hazleton continued, "he went and got himself done in and left me high and dry. Typical."

"Getting himself killed is typical?" I asked.

"Leaving me to bear the brunt of his problems is. After all I've done for him."

I pondered my next questions with care. A manservant could know more about his master than his master did himself. But a manservant could also have fierce loyalty to his gentleman and never reveal that man's secrets. I picked a question that would seem neutral.

"Was Mr. Turner ever hurting for money? If he had to wager your pay on the horses."

Hazleton nodded readily. "He got an allowance from his pater, but he was always in need of funds. Had to be, hadn't he? He had to dress and keep rooms and go to White's and Tattersall's. Spent all his pater's money, but he did used to win on his wagers. Sometimes quite a lot, but then the money would be gone to high living." He glanced at his master's clothes strewn about the room. "Little good it's done him, though, eh?"

I ran my hand over one of the coats. The cloth was fine; the coat as costly and elegant as one Grenville might wear. Indeed, Turner probably had many of his clothes made to imitate Grenville's. Most young men-about-town did.

"His father continued to give him money?" I asked. "He did not cut him off with a shilling, as angry fathers sometimes do?"

"No, no. Mr. Turner's family are respectable people. Too respectable for the likes of my master. Must have been an embarrassment to them, he was. His father kept up the allowance, but sent him pleading paternal letters to mend his ways."

I wondered if Hazleton knew this because he'd read his

master's mail, or if he'd known Turner well enough to guess exactly what the man's father would say to him.

"Had he recently received more money than usual?" I glanced about the room as I asked the question, as though only half-interested in the answer.

Hazleton looked blank. "Not that I know of, sir. Least-wise, I saw no sign of it. Of course," he continued, his face getting longer, "he'd not be likely to give any money to me."

I wondered what Turner would have done with any money Brandon or Mrs. Harper had given him, Would he hoard it or give it to his tailor or pay his gambling debts? Was he experienced at blackmail, or had he simply seen and seized upon an opportunity?

I sent Bartholomew a meaningful look. I wanted to have a look at Turner's rooms without Hazleton hovering over me.

Bartholomew took the hint. "Well then, Hazleton, what about this claret?"

Hazleton perked up, at least as much as Hazleton would ever perk up. His mournful mouth smoothed the slightest bit. "Ah, yes. His pa told me to put his things together and send them home. But a bottle of claret wouldn't travel very well now, would it?"

I thought it would make no difference to the bottle of claret, but I welcomed the chance to clear Hazleton out of the way for a few minutes. Bartholomew told him to lead the way, and he and Hazleton and Matthias clattered out.

Left alone, I searched the bedchamber, but unfortunately I found very little. I went through the pockets of the coats strewn throughout the chamber, then checked the cupboards. I found nothing. Turner, or perhaps Hazleton, had kept these rooms very neat.

I left the bedchamber and entered the front room, where I went through the small writing desk and its few drawers. Remembering Brandon's secret drawer, I went carefully through the writing table, but found nothing hidden.

Turner had kept no correspondence, no dunning notices

from his creditors, none of the tearful letters from his father. In short, Mr. Turner seemed to have no personal papers in his rooms at all.

As I closed the last drawer in disappointment, I was startled by the sound of the door opening. I knew how long Bartholomew and Matthias could linger over a glass, and they both knew that I'd wanted time to search the rooms.

But neither the tall footmen nor the long-faced Hazleton stood in the doorway. Instead, a woman I did not know walked inside. She did not see me until she closed the door behind her, then she froze, the color draining from her face.

She abruptly reached for the door. Moving with a speed I'd not known I had, I made it to the door and pressed my hand against it before she could open it. She looked up at me with brown eyes that were rather too small and sparsely lashed.

We stared at one another for a full silent minute. The room was chill, because Hazleton had not bothered to start a fire. The woman had wrapped a cashmere shawl about her, but the skin on her neck stood out in gooseflesh, and her lips were thin and almost bloodless.

"I beg your pardon," she said stiffly. "I seem to have entered the wrong room."

I did not think so. In wild surmise I said, "Mrs. Harper."

Her eyes widened. But to her credit, she did not faint or grow hysterical. Her assessment was one of surprise, not fear.

"Who are you?" she asked, as though I were the intruder.

"My name is Gabriel Lacey."

She did not know the name, or if she did, she hid it well.

"Yes, I am Mrs. Harper. Mr. Turner—" She broke off, uncertain of what to tell me. Perhaps she'd prepared a story for the servants, but not one for the likes of me.

I answered for her. "You were looking for a letter or paper that belonged to you that you thought Mr. Turner had."

Now, some fear did enter her eyes. "Why do you say so? Exactly who are you?"

"I am a friend to Colonel Brandon."

She looked me up and down with new scrutiny, her lips tightening. I saw that she was still not sure whether to categorize me as friend or foe. A friend of Colonel Brandon could be for him and against her.

I returned her look with the same slow curiosity. Brandon might have been having an affair with this woman; indeed, he might well have tried to leave Louisa for her, but she was not beautiful. She wore a brown dress trimmed with black braid, and black buttons making a neat line down the bodice. The cashmere shawl was also a rich brown, setting off the gown. She did know how to dress tastefully, and her bonnet, brown straw trimmed with creamy brown silk ribbons, was of a very late fashion.

The hair that straggled from under the bonnet was brownish yellow, the color to which some blond women found their hair turning, much to their despair. Her face was round, her nose straight, and her eyes, as I had observed, were small, though a pleasing shade of brown. She was not by any means a radiant beauty, although she was not ugly. I would describe her overall as pleasant.

I gestured to the sofa, which was upholstered in crimson damask and had gold claw feet. "Shall we sit down, Mrs. Harper, and talk about Mr. Turner?"

She searched my face, her eyes wary, but at last she inclined her head and walked gracefully to the sofa.

She settled herself, adjusting her skirt and her gloves and not looking at me as I limped across the room and sat next to her, resting my hands on the handle of my walking stick.

"You knew Colonel Brandon," I began, "on the Peninsula."

She nodded. "Yes, he was very helpful to my husband and to me."

So might any woman express gratitude toward a friend who had lent assistance. "Your husband was killed at Vitoria, I believe," I said. "I was there. The battle was devastating. We lost many."

She looked up at me. "My husband had often been

praised for his valor. He died trying to save others." She made the statement flatly, as though she had said it many times.

"Quite heroic of him. Brandon had been a friend of his?"

"Yes." Her eyes held more than defiance. She had a quiet confidence about her, something I might admire under other circumstances. Her apparent ease at dealing with me, someone she had not expected, made me wonder. If she were this cool-headed, why had she become hysterical at the sight of Turner, dead?

"If you are a very close friend of Colonel Brandon, Mr. Lacey—"

"Captain," I broke in. "And yes, I am very close to the Brandon family."

"Captain," she corrected herself. "Then you know more about me than you appear to at present."

I inclined my head. "I do not wish to be rude, Mrs. Harper, but it will help me if you tell me exactly what your relation was and is to Colonel Brandon."

"I believe you've already guessed," she said. She looked at me with calm eyes. "There was an affair when we were on the Peninsula. When my husband died, I was alone and afraid, and Aloysius helped me. Small wonder that I turned to him." Again her voice held that flatness.

"Not surprising under the circumstances. I know from your recent letters to Brandon that Turner somehow found out about the affair and threatened to expose you."

She flushed. "You are quite well informed, Captain."

"You came to London and wrote to Brandon for help. Turner told you to meet him at Lady Gillis's ball, and you asked Brandon what to do. What did he suggest?"

"That we meet him. That we try to persuade him that it was all in the past and did not matter anymore."

"Then I take it that you had no intention of resuming the affair?"

She hesitated. "I'm not certain what my intentions were. At the moment I was worried about Turner and his revelations."

"What did you fear? That Turner would go to Brandon's wife with the information? Turner had no need to tell her. Brandon's actions at the ball and even beforehand shouted it loud and clear. It was most tactless of him."

"I cannot help Brandon's behavior," she said, tight-lipped. "We agreed to speak to Turner. I'm afraid I was quite agitated last night, or I might have noticed that we were making cakes of ourselves. My only concern was speaking to Turner."

"And Turner, very conveniently, turned up dead."

At last, Mrs. Harper looked distressed. "I do not know why you say *convenient*. It was the most horrifying thing that ever happened to me."

"More horrifying than the casualties of the battlefields?"

"Yes," she said defiantly. "I followed the drum long enough to expect the carnage. Even when my husband died, I cannot remember feeling terribly surprised. I think I knew it was only a matter of time before it was his body brought back from a battle. But last night was different. You certainly do not expect to find a corpse sitting in a chair in your friend's house. It frightened me. More than that, it appalled me. London is supposed to be civilization. To see something like that in such an elegant little room was unnerving."

"More than unnerving," I observed. "In fact, witnesses say you screamed quite a lot. You were quite upset and had to be taken home—leaving Brandon to face arrest by himself."

She reddened. "I am not stupid, Captain. You believe that I killed Mr. Turner, then feigned hysteria in order to gain sympathy and let Aloysius take the blame. But I assure you, I did not murder Turner. He was dead when I entered the room."

"How quickly did you understand that he was dead?"

"Not right away," she answered. "I thought him drunk. He'd been quite foxed when he spoke to us earlier, so I was not surprised to find him unconscious. But when I touched his shoulder, I saw that his face was gray. It was quite hor-

rible. Then I saw the knife, and lost my head. I did scream.
I cannot remember much after that. I know I made a great
fool of myself."

"How did the blood come to be on your glove?"

She looked startled. "On my glove?"

"Mr. Grenville told me that you stared at your glove in
horror, and that it was crimson with blood. But if you only
touched Turner's shoulder, you could not have gotten blood
on your glove. You can have only gotten the blood on your
glove if you had touched the knife or the wound."

Mrs. Harper stared at me, her lips parted. But she was
not dazed. I sensed her thinking rapidly, considering argu-
ments and discarding them before she chose her answer. "I
believe, that I touched the back of the chair," she said at last.
"I rested my hand on it. The blood must have been there."

I had not seen blood on the chair, dried or otherwise. She
lied, but I was not certain why. She had either truly murdered Turner, or she had touched him for some other reason
that she did not want me to know.

One thing I did notice was that she had not suggested
that Brandon did not murder Turner. I said, "Colonel Brandon was committed to trial for killing Turner, and now he is
in Newgate prison."

"I know," she answered.

She looked neither angry nor distressed. She spoke in
the same calm voice, looked at me in the same resignation.

"You do not defend him?"

She made a gesture that was almost a shrug. "What
would you have me say? Colonel Brandon was quite upset.
He was livid with Turner. I had never seen him in so much
of a temper."

"You had not seen him in a long time," I remarked. "Had
you?"

"No, I had not seen him since I left Spain four years ago.
Do you believe me?"

"More unsettling to me is that you believe he did kill
Turner."

"I really have no idea what happened," she said in a hard

voice. "I walked into that room, and Turner was dead. No, I did not see Colonel Brandon actually kill him, but I have no idea who else would want to."

"Colonel Brandon seems to believe that you killed him." Her color mounted. "He said that?"

"No. He did his best to incriminate himself and not you. Which made me realize that he believes you killed Turner. If he'd thought a passing footman had done the deed, he would have been outraged to be arrested, and ready to call in every favor from every man in a high place to acquit him."

She looked astonished. "He truly believes that I would do such a thing?"

"You believe that *he* would. In either case, it will be Brandon who pays. He is being gallant, and you are condemning him to hang."

She pressed her hands together, gloves sliding over very thin fingers. "You have not told me what *you* believe, Captain Lacey."

"I believe the colonel is innocent. I have not yet decided who else would want Turner dead. There were quite a few people at that ball. Who knows, one of them may have been his mortal enemy. I only know that you are ready to send Brandon to the gallows, and I do not want him to go there."

For the first time since she had entered the room, she looked at me in real fear. "Did you plan to give me to the magistrates?" Her pale lips trembled, and I saw her strive to keep them steady. "Without knowing me, without proof that I went into that room and stabbed him?"

"There is the blood on your glove," I reminded her.

"Which I have explained. I touched the back of the chair."

"What I think you actually did, Mrs. Harper, was put your hand inside Mr. Turner's coat. You checked his pockets, did you not? You were looking for the letter or whatever evidence he had of your affair with Colonel Brandon. I assume that you did not find it, because you came here today to look for it. So did I."

She stared at me, eyes wide. I saw her reassess my character. She must have first thought me simply a hanger-on of Colonel Brandon, a hearty cavalry captain left over from the war. Colonel Brandon was a man who did not always think before he acted. He was brisk and decisive but sometimes did not bother with critical thought. Imogene Harper had assumed that my character would be much the same.

"You have found me out, Captain." She met my eye, but her jaw was hard. She seemed to realize that bursting into tears or breaking down would not alter my stance. "Yes, I looked for the letter. I must have gotten blood on my glove when I did so. I searched his pockets quickly, but found nothing. At least, not the letter. He had a snuffbox, a few coins, and a scrap of lace, but no letter." She opened her hands. "You are correct, I came here to look for it."

"A scrap of lace," I mused.

"It looked as though it had come off a lady's ball gown."

"That is interesting. Could you happen to tell me which lady?"

"I am afraid I paid very little attention to the lace. I cared only for the letter."

"I will assume that Pomeroy took the contents of Turner's pockets from him." I could ask Pomeroy for the lace, although I would prefer to allow him to run through London trying to match it to a lady's dress. "What puzzles me, Mrs. Harper, is why you and Brandon were so afraid of Turner. Your affair ended four years ago. Brandon moved back to England and went on with his life, and that was that. I read the letters that you wrote to him. You were not certain that he would remember you or would want to remember you. So I believe you when you say that the affair was over."

I saw her try to remember exactly what she had written in her recent letters. A worried look settled in her eyes, but she spoke briskly. "It is hardly something that you would wish to see made public."

"Is that what Turner threatened? To make it public?"

"I do not know what he threatened. I only know that he had a letter and that he would make us pay to have it back."

"But how easy it would have been to dismiss his threat," I pointed out. "You could claim the letter was a forgery, written by Turner himself, or perhaps written by another of your lovers in a fit of jealousy, to punish you. Louisa Brandon would be hurt by the revelation—indeed she *is* hurt—but she would hardly take her husband to court over it. She prizes discretion."

Mrs. Harper flexed and closed her hands. "We did not think. How could we? When Mr. Turner approached me about the letter, it was horrible. In panic, I wrote to Colonel Brandon, and he suggested that we do what Turner said in order to get the letter back. If we were foolish, then we were foolish."

"Have you considered the possibility that Mr. Turner did not have a letter at all? That he somehow got wind of your affair and, always liking cash, decided to capitalize on it? I have searched these rooms thoroughly, but I found nothing."

She gazed at me first in surprise, then something else flickered through her eyes. Relief? Why relief? Perhaps she worried that I, too, might blackmail her, or perhaps she simply did not want me to read a love letter she'd written to Aloysius Brandon.

"The idea had not occurred to me," Mrs. Harper said. "Why should he say he had the letter if he did not?"

"He did not show it to you?"

"No."

"You and Colonel Brandon have behaved like a pair of fools," I said in exasperation. "You took it on faith that Turner had a letter that would betray you. If you were experienced at being blackmailed, you would know to insist that the blackmailer show you what he has to sell you first."

The curls on her forehead trembled. "Perhaps we were fools, Captain. But we did not want to chance that he did not have the letter. We did not think of that possibility, I confess." She looked at me a moment, clearly not happy.

"What will you do with the letter if you find it? Give it to the magistrates?"

"I have not yet decided. It is possible that I will burn the foul thing." I fixed her with a stare that had made the men under my command quiver. "I do not intend to let Colonel Brandon hang for this crime."

She lowered her gaze. "I know you will not believe me, Captain, but I wish no harm to come to him, either. He was good to me. He helped me when I could turn to no other."

"You knew he was married," I stated flatly.

"I did." She raised her eyes. The defiance had returned. "I needed him. At the time, that was all I could consider."

She rose to her feet. I got to mine as well, because that was the polite thing to do. She said, "I admire you for standing by your colonel."

She was not offering me any help to save him. Perhaps she still believed him responsible, or perhaps she was pushing the blame on him to save herself.

I bowed to her. "May I call on you if it proves necessary?"

"Can I stop you, if you think I can bring evidence to bear?"

"I am not a magistrate, nor am I a Bow Street Runner. I simply wish to clear Brandon's name, so that his wife does not have to watch him hang by the neck until dead."

At last, Mrs. Harper looked ashamed. "Please tell Mrs. Brandon that I am deeply sorry for the trouble I have caused her. I have been a fool in so many ways. I never realized how much grief a person can bestow when they are fixed on one course."

She did not elaborate on what that one course might be. I imagined loneliness, but looking back later, I realized that the entire conversation seemed wrong somehow. Imogene Harper did not tell me much more than I already knew. Unfortunately, I was not to realize that fact until other things emerged. I did not know then how murky things would become for me and for Brandon.

I ushered Mrs. Harper out the door and closed it behind

me. I stood at the head of the stairs, watching her descend, in order to discourage her from returning to search the rooms again. I had found no letter—Turner's rooms had presented nothing but innocence and badly matched furniture—but she might not have believed me.

Mrs. Harper glanced back at me once, her expression veiled, and she walked out of the door and into the rain.

I collected Matthias and Bartholomew from the kitchens below stairs. Hazleton, the valet, held up his glass and slurred a greeting to me. One bottle was empty, on its side, the other, upright, but half-empty. By the look of things, Matthias and Bartholomew had stuck to only one or two glasses each, allowing Hazleton to imbibe the rest. From Hazleton's earlier state, I imagined he had already partaken of a bottle or two before we arrived.

Bartholomew and Matthias said farewell to him, wishing him luck, and we departed.

Imogene Harper had long since vanished. Matthias took leave of his brother to return to Grenville's house, while Bartholomew prepared to make the journey back to Covent Garden with me. Matthias told us good-bye, touched his forelock to me, and trotted off in the direction of Green Park.

Bartholomew and I took a hackney back across London to Covent Garden. I returned to my rooms in Grimpen Lane, while Bartholomew strolled among the vendors on Russel Street and Covent Garden to scare together our next meal.

Therefore, he was not present to help me when I was attacked in my rooms.

CHAPTER 7

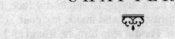

THE attacker was not waiting for me; he followed me up the stairs at a dead run. He was a man of my height with a wiry build, a thin face, and wide dark eyes. He had little hair on his head, as though he habitually cropped his hair close.

I started to ask him who he was and what he thought he was doing, when he hurtled into me and pushed me back inside my rooms.

Many men have made the mistake of thinking me feeble because I hobble about with a walking stick, but I was still fit and strong. I brought up the walking stick, slammed it into his chest, and shoved him away.

He, too, was a strong man, his slim build disguising powerful muscles. He also knew how to fight. He kicked my bad knee hard. As pain engulfed me, he took advantage of my weakness and pummeled me in the face.

I fought back. We struggled, each of us emitting only the occasional grunt as we vied to best one another. I dropped my walking stick and got my hands around his throat, my thumbs reaching for his windpipe. He kicked my bad leg again, scooping my feet out from under me.

I went down, trying to take the fall with my shoulder. He kicked me again in the ribs. He snatched up my walking stick and struck me repeatedly across the chest and shoulders. I tried to roll away, but the pain in my leg swallowed my strength.

As I rocked on my back, trying to shield my face, he let off on the blows. He thrust his hand inside my coat, searching my pockets. Before I could stop him, he found and drew out the three letters from Mrs. Harper that I'd taken from Brandon's desk.

I snatched for them. The man punched me across the jaw. In fury and in pain, I lunged at him. He brought up the walking stick and again beat me thoroughly and deliberately. My father, an expert at beating his son, would have admired him.

At last, I could only lay there, groaning and cursing. As soon as he thought me no longer a threat, he flung away the walking stick and began to open all the drawers and cupboards in the room, searching as I'd searched Henry Turner's rooms.

"It is not here," I croaked. "I could not find it, either."

The man ignored me completely. He sifted through the contents of my writing table and chest on frame and dumped everything onto the floor.

While he worked, I got painfully to my hands and knees and begin to crawl toward my walking stick. Inside the stick was a sharp sword, and I was anxious to begin poking it into my intruder.

He saw me. He swung around, took a pistol from his greatcoat, and trained it on me. I froze.

"I will not be long, monsieur," he said. His accent was thick.

I wondered in the back of my mind why he'd bothered to beat me if he might have simply shot me dead, or at least threatened me with the pistol from the start.

"At least tell me who the devil you are," I snapped. "Or are you taking revenge for San Sebastian?"

He did not answer. Instead, he flung open a final drawer and tossed aside the expensive snuffboxes that Grenville had given me. One box broke open, fragrant snuff drifting through the air. Other than that, the drawer was empty. The Frenchman, with a snarl, threw the drawer down.

I heard a gasp from the hall. "Lacey, what the devil?"

Marianne Simmons stood in the doorway, her eyes wide as she took in me on the floor and the Frenchman rifling my belongings.

"Get out!" I cried to her.

The Frenchman pulled out his pistol. "Tell her to show her pockets."

Marianne would have none of that. She began screeching obscenities that would make the most hardened soldier flinch. I shouted at her to hold her tongue, fearing the Frenchman would shoot her in anger.

The Frenchman strode to Marianne and slapped her face. Marianne screamed in rage, grabbed his hand, and sank her teeth into it.

I struggled to my hands and knees, finally reaching the walking stick. The Frenchman struck Marianne again. I wrapped my hand around the walking stick and withdrew its sword.

The man fumbled at Marianne's dress, trying to search her, while she screamed and struck out at him. I got shakily to my feet and came at him with my sword.

The Frenchman realized finally that he could not fight us both. He took a step away from Marianne and pointed the pistol at her head.

I stopped. She tried to kick him.

"Be still, Marianne, for God's sake!"

The Frenchman, his face scratched and bruised, gave us both a look of fury, then he turned and ran out of the room. Marianne started after him. I shoved her aside, told her to stay put, and followed him.

The man hurtled down the stairs and out of the house. I

gave chase as quickly as I could. Outside in the tiny cul-de-sac of Grimpen Lane, rain and mist shrouded the street. I heard the Frenchman running away toward Russel Street, then he disappeared into the fog.

I knew I'd never catch him. Angry and hurting, I made my way back upstairs.

Marianne helped me inside. "Who the hell was that?"

"I don't know. I have never seen the man before." Whoever he was, he'd just run off with Imogene Harper's letters to Brandon.

"Well, he made bad work of you." She gave me a critical look. "Sit down. You look terrible."

"Thank you very much." I obeyed her and sank to a chair before the hearth, where this morning's fire had died to smoldering.

Marianne took out a handkerchief and touched it to my face. I winced as she found my bruises. "I should ask what you are doing here," I said.

Marianne now lived in luxury, but she could not bear confinement. She liked to confound Grenville as much as she could by leaving the house without word and returning when she pleased. At first, Grenville had tried to restrict her, but he had not counted on Marianne's pride and her love of freedom.

In the end, she'd worn him down, and a few weeks ago, after she'd disappeared to Berkshire without warning, he'd wearily told her that she could come and go as she liked. The blue silk gown she wore was the finest I'd ever seen her in, although it was now mussed and torn from the fight.

"I came to talk to you," she said. "To ask your advice." She bit her lip. Marianne so hated to ask for advice.

"About your son?" I asked.

I'd found out about Marianne's son by accident when I stayed in Berkshire. I'd told her to confide the entire story to Grenville, but I knew she had not.

Marianne gave me a hard look. She had an almost child-like face with a pointed chin and big blue eyes and curls made more golden by artifice. Her looks kept her employed on the stage at Drury Lane, or so they had before she had taken to living in Grenville's house. But her little girl prettiness belied a shrewd mind and a very sharp tongue. Marianne, having to live by her wits all her life, took a severe and cynical view of the world.

"No, not about David. And I will thank you to keep that to yourself."

"I promised to keep silent. And though I think you a fool, I will keep my promise. But if you came to ask my advice, you should be a little more polite to me."

"That's a fine thing to say from someone I just found brawling." Her voice softened as she spoke, and she dabbed blood from my face. "You had no idea who he was? He could not have been here to rob you. You have nothing to steal. He must have been looking for something specific."

Marianne, as I said, was too shrewd for her own good. "I believe I know what he was looking for. But for the life of me, I do not know why."

"Has it to do with your Colonel Brandon getting himself committed to trial?"

"Very likely. Did Grenville tell you about it?"

She gave me a sour look. "No. I heard it in the usual way. Gossip among the servants. I have not seen *Mr. Grenville* in many days."

I looked at her in surprise. "But last night he said—"

She shot me a cynical look. "It was not me he visited last night. If he told you that, he lied. That is why I came to see you, his dearest friend. He tells me nothing, but you will know what is what."

She cleaned my cuts in silence for a few moments, her nostrils pinched and white. I recalled Grenville telling me the previous night, with a self-deprecating smile, that he'd go to Clarges Street from Lord Gillis's. I wondered whether he'd lied or simply changed his mind on the way—and in either case, why he'd done so.

"Grenville does not answer to me. I did not see him today; possibly something happened that prevented him from visiting you as he planned."

"Of course," Marianne said in a hard voice, "The 'something' was Mrs. Bennington."

"Mrs. Bennington?" I repeated, puzzled.

"Mrs. Bennington, the celebrated actress."

"Yes, I do know who she is."

Mrs. Bennington had gone to give a performance at the ball last night. Grenville had not mentioned her at all; I'd heard of her presence there from Louisa and Lady Aline. Grenville had never indicated interest in her, at least, not to me.

"He has become quite fascinated with her," Marianne went on. "He has seen many of her performances since his return from Berkshire. He cannot say a bad word about her. Now, he has taken to visiting her."

I listened in growing disquiet. "She is a fine actress, Marianne. You know that he is fond of patronizing the very best artists."

Marianne gave me a pitying look. "She is already so popular that she has no need of *his* patronage. And I know that he is fond of lady violinists and actresses and dancers. His interest in me is rather unusual."

I could not argue with her. I had seen Grenville with his previous mistresses, all of whom had been famous in some way or other. Marianne had never had many parts other than in a chorus or a short walk-on, and she was by no means well known. I do not believe even Grenville understood what had brought about his fascination with Marianne.

"He has expressed no particular attraction to Mrs. Bennington," I said. "And he has told me of no special visits to her."

"That confirms it then. If he had nothing to hide, he would have confided in you."

"Or, he has nothing to confide, " I said.

"For God's sake, Lacey, I am not a fool. I know when a gentleman is tiring of me. Usually I am wise enough to leave when I see the first signs. This time, I've held on and hoped that I was wrong. I do not know why." Her words grew slower, sadder. "Perhaps because he is so wealthy."

I knew that was not her reason. Her relationship with Grenville was complex, and I by no means understood it, but I sensed that beneath Marianne's hard-bitten cynicism, she cared for him. I had seen evidence of that when Grenville had been hurt earlier this year. Marianne had come to me, anguish in her eyes, and begged me to let her see him. She'd sat at his side, holding his hand, until he awakened.

I also knew that Grenville was a man easily bored. He might have grown tired of Marianne's willfulness and unpredictability and decided that he could find a less complicated woman elsewhere.

I took the now-bloody handkerchief from her—a fine piece of lawn that Grenville must have provided—and dabbed at the abrasions myself.

"Have you given him a chance, Marianne? You are keeping secrets from him yourself. You never let him give you what he wants to give you."

"What he wants to give me is an entirely different life," she said. "Without asking if that is the life I want. Without so much as a by-your-leave."

"Many a penniless actress would be pleased by the prospect."

She snorted. "And many a penniless captain would be pleased at his offer to let you share his house or travel with him. And yet you decline."

I could not deny that. I was as proud as she was. "I do have my own income, tiny as it is. But you have even less. Perhaps you had better reconsider."

"You mean that I should share his bed so he'll look after me. I should let him make me into the woman he wants."

"I mean that you should stop antagonizing him. He helps you because he feels charitable, and yes, he does pity you. And you punish him for it."

"Ha. I have discovered this day that you men will always defend one another. You say that he is looking to Mrs. Bennington because I am angering him. Of course, it is all my fault."

"I said nothing of the sort. You will drive me mad. The fault lies in both of you. You both have stubborn pride." I touched my face hesitantly, feeling the bruises. "He has said nothing to me about leaving you for Mrs. Bennington. However, if he does try to cast you into the street, I will stop him."

She cocked her head and observed me with childlike blue eyes. "You can do nothing against him. He is a powerful man. When he makes a pronouncement, even royalty listens. You may hold his interest now, Lacey, but when you lose that, you will be nothing to him."

I could not deny the truth of this, but I perhaps had more faith in Grenville than she did. "I have seen evidence of his kind heart," I said. "He is not as callous as you would have him be."

Her eyes were as cool as ever, but I knew Marianne well, and I sensed the hurt in her. I could reassure her until my breath ran out, but both she and I knew that Grenville did what he liked for his own reasons.

"If I discover anything, I will tell you," I promised. "I agree that he should not keep you in the dark about Mrs. Bennington."

"Well, thank you for that anyway."

"I do not blame him if he grows exasperated with you. You are a most exasperating woman."

"He has power," she said simply. "I have none. I am only getting back a little of my own."

The door banged open. I leapt to my feet, and so did Marianne, both of us expecting the return of the Frenchman. But it was only Bartholomew, balancing a covered dish and two tankards. He caught sight of me, and his jaw sagged.

I sprang forward and rescued the plate. "Do not drop my dinner, Bartholomew, for heaven's sake. I am hungry." I put the platter safely on a table and took the tankards from him as well.

"Good lord, sir." He looked me up and down, then glanced at Marianne. "Did she have a go at you?"

Marianne looked affronted. "Of course not, you lummox."

I quickly told Bartholomew about the Frenchman. Bartholomew, growing excited, wanted nothing more than to dash out and scour the city for him then and there.

I stopped him. "He did not find what he came to find, so he will no doubt show himself again. He has a distinctive appearance. We will find him."

I did not say so, but I had the feeling that Imogene Harper knew good and well who the Frenchman was. If he'd taken her letters to Brandon, he must have had good reason to do so. He could be her friend or a lover—even her husband. Mrs. Harper had left the Peninsula four years ago, after all, and had only recently come to London. She could have done many things during that time.

"Do run to Bow Street," I told Bartholomew as I uncovered the beefsteak he'd brought me. "Tell Pomeroy to watch out for a lean Frenchman with close-cropped hair. He may next try to search Mrs. Harper's rooms, or even Turner's father's house in Epsom."

"Of course, sir." Bartholomew's eyes were animated. He loved to chase criminals, despite the fact that one had shot him last summer and laid him low for weeks. But he was young and resilient and eager.

He tugged his forelock and ran off, leaving me with Marianne and a quickly cooling dinner.

I shared the beefsteak with Marianne. Never one to forgo a free meal, she ate but did so in silence. We did not mention Grenville or Mrs. Bennington again.

Marianne went away before Bartholomew returned. She did not tell me where she was going, and I did not ask. She was angry and worried, and somehow, I did not blame her.

Marianne was correct when she said that Grenville could wash his hands of me and that I could do nothing against him, but I did not care. The threat of losing his patronage would not hold my tongue if he had been betraying Marianne. I had seen men change mistresses before, but I felt somehow protective of Marianne, perhaps because I knew how vulnerable she truly was, despite her hard-nosed approach to life.

I finished my meal and, as it was nearing four o'clock, remembered my promise to call upon Lady Breckenridge.

In my bedchamber, I looked at myself in the dusky mirror above my washstand and winced. The left side of my face was puffed and bruised, and a cut creased my right cheekbone. My lip had split, and dried blood stained my chin. I was sore and stiff, and my knee felt as though it was wrapped in bands of fire.

I was in no fit state to visit a lady. I soaked a handkerchief in water and continued to clean my face. It was a slow, tricky business, because every touch stung.

I made myself ready for the visit anyway. I very much wanted to put together the pieces of Turner's murder before Brandon could be tried. When the wheels of justice turned, they turned quickly. Brandon's trial could come up before a week was out, and only days after that, he could be hanged or transported. Louisa would be shamed and disgraced, and likely abandoned by everyone she knew, myself and perhaps Lady Aline excluded.

I refused to let Brandon bring that sorrow upon her. I would find the killer and release Brandon, whether he liked it or not.

My other reason for resolving to visit Lady Breckenridge as planned was that I simply wanted to see her.

Since our first discordant meeting in Kent, Lady Breckenridge and I had become friends of a sort. She had helped me during the affair of the Glass House and had given me a new walking stick when my old one had been lost. I had kissed her in the privacy of her box in Covent Garden and had very much enjoyed it.

She had taken to inviting me to gatherings in which she launched musicians or poets into society and had made it clear that I could add her to my list of afternoon calls. I rarely made calls, but I had twice since my return from Berkshire sat in her drawing room sipping tea while other members of the *ton* stared at me and wondered why I had turned up.

I bade Bartholomew accompany me back to Mayfair, and we made our way to South Audley Street, where Lady Breckenridge's house lay. I used Bartholomew as a scout to discover whether Lady Breckenridge had received anyone else that afternoon. If she had guests in her drawing room, I would take my battered face away.

Bartholomew returned with the news that the lady was alone. Relieved, I descended from the hackney coach and went inside.

Lady Breckenridge's butler, Barnstable, looked at me in shock. "Sir?"

I gave him a smile that pulled at my sore face. "Will I frighten her ladyship, do you think?"

"No, sir." He continued to stare at me. "Her ladyship is made of stern stuff. I have just the thing to put on those bruises, sir. Take them down in no time."

Barnstable, it seemed, had remedies for everything. He had, a few months ago, treated my sore knee with hot towels and a penetrating ointment, which he'd graciously sent home with me. I had begun to believe in Barnstable and his remedies.

One of Lady Breckenridge's footmen, looking no less shocked at my state than the butler, led me up the stairs. He did not take me to the drawing room, but led me up another flight to Lady Breckenridge's private rooms. When I entered, I realized that I'd been brought to her boudoir.

Lady Breckenridge's entire house was very modern, and this room was no exception. A Roman couch faced the fireplace; windows elegantly draped in light green silk complemented the cream-colored walls. The carpet was thick under my boots, warming the room.

I did not have to wait long for Lady Breckenridge; she entered only a few moments after the footman left me.

Today she wore a peignoir of gold silk, and had threaded a wide, ivory-colored bandeau through her dark hair. When she saw my bruised face, her reaction was predictable.

"Good God," she said, stopping on the threshold.

"Forgive me," I answered. "I decided to participate in a boxing match before making my calls today."

She came all the way into the room and closed the door behind her, but her expression did not alter. "Who did you anger this time, Gabriel?"

"A Frenchman searching for something he could not find."

She raised her brows. I explained the incident. As I spoke, Barnstable bustled in with a steaming bowl on a tray. He politely waited until I'd finished then bade me to sit on the Roman couch.

I did so and stretched my aching leg to the fire. Barnstable dipped a cloth in the liquid and touched it to my face. It hurt like fury and at the same time soothed me.

"You ought to be a physician, Barnstable," I said.

"Indeed, no, sir." He sounded affronted.

Lady Breckenridge watched the proceeding without speaking. She wandered to a small rosewood table, pulled a black cigarillo from a box, and lit it with a candle.

"Are you certain this robbery was connected with Turner's death?" she asked, as thin smoke wreathed her face.

"I am certain of nothing." I inhaled the heady-smelling steam that Barnstable waved beneath my nose. "If he were a mere robber, he would have taken the snuffboxes, which were costly. But he held on to the letters he found in my pocket."

"Why would a Frenchman be interested in letters written by Mrs. Harper?"

"That I do not know. I do not know anything." I seethed in frustration, as Barnstable calmly patted my bruises and cuts. Colonel Brandon was being uncommonly stubborn, I had only vague accounts of what had happened at the ball, and both Louisa and Mrs. Harper had convinced themselves that Brandon had murdered Turner.

"If your line of thinking is that Mrs. Harper stabbed Turner before she screamed, you will be wrong," Lady Breckenridge observed, breaking my thoughts. "She did not. At least, not then."

"How do you know?"

She took a pull of the cigarillo. "Because I saw her. When Mrs. Harper went into the anteroom at twelve, she left the door ajar. I could look right in and see her."

I sat up straight, pressed Barnstable's hand aside. "Why did you not say so?"

Lady Breckenridge shrugged. "I did not have the chance. Your Mr. Pomeroy had already turned his attention to Colonel Brandon, and I had not the time to tell him."

Yes, Pomeroy could fix on one purpose and ignore everything else in his path.

"What did Mrs. Harper do?" I asked.

Her eyes narrowed in thought. "I saw her bend over Turner, then she gave a little start. I suppose that's when she realized he was dead. She patted his chest, or moved her hands over him. I could not see exactly, because she blocked my vision. Then she straightened up. She looked at her glove, which was red with blood. She recoiled from it, and that was when she began to scream."

"If you could not see exactly, how do you know she did not press the knife into Turner's chest when she bent over him?" I did not think Mrs. Harper had done so, but I wanted to know what Lady Breckenridge supposed.

"Because I did not see a knife in her hand as she went in. Nor did I notice her picking it up from the desk. She went nowhere else in the room. Besides, she would have had to put quite a bit of strength behind the blow, would she not? She did not raise her arm, and likely Turner would have seen her and fought her. Unless he was drunk and senseless." She shook her head. "No, I do not believe she stabbed him. It was as though she searched him for something— love letters perhaps? Although I cannot imagine her writing love letters to Turner. But supposing he had letters from her to someone else?"

She was a perceptive woman. "Perhaps," I said cautiously.

Lady Breckenridge glanced at her butler. "Barnstable, will you leave us?"

Barnstable rose at once and handed me the linen pad. "Of course, my lady. Keep that pressed to the wound, sir. It will take the ill from it."

I promised I would see to it. Barnstable bowed and took himself from the room, closing the door behind him with every show of deference.

"He looked a bit disappointed," I observed.

"Of course he is. He is as interested in this business as I am. But he will not listen at the door. He considers it beneath him."

I smiled slightly. "I am certain that my man, Bartholomew, will tell him all he wants to know below stairs."

Lady Breckenridge did not return the smile. "I sent him away so that we might speak frankly. Because your colonel was arrested for the crime, I assume that Mrs. Harper was looking for letters she had written to Colonel Brandon, or he had written to her. That would explain their mutual antagonism toward Mr. Turner."

"You guess well," I said.

She sank to the sofa next to me, crossing her legs in a graceful move. "You must remember I was there last night. I observed the very strange behavior of Colonel Brandon and Imogene Harper. Did they forget how much the *ton* gossips? Believe me, today, the polite world is grateful to Lord Gillis for providing them with something new to discuss. We were growing tired of who would race what horse at the Derby and what an appalling frock Lady Jersey wore last Thursday. Mind you, it would be much more interesting if Colonel Brandon were one of us, but it will have to do."

She spoke with her usual acid tones, but I took no offense. She was directing her sarcasm at her own circle, not Colonel Brandon.

I removed the linen pad from my face, defying Barnstable's instructions, and laid it across my knee. The warmth of it felt good there. "And what is the *ton* saying today?"

"Well, I will know more tonight, of course, but I have already received a note from Lady Seville, a girlhood acquaintance who attended the ball. She was terribly excited at having attended a gathering where something actually *happened,* even something so low as murder. Lord Gillis is to blame, she says, for having so many military men for his acquaintance. They are violent, she believes, and not always from the upper ten thousand. Lady Seville puts much on pedigree."

"Colonel Brandon comes from a fine family."

"But not a peerage." She emphasized her words with a jab of the cigarillo. "And that is the only thing that counts with Lady Seville. She is a horrible snob. She would approve of you, however."

I looked at her in surprise then glanced at my rather threadbare trousers, made worse by my scuffle with the Frenchman. "Good lord. Why?"

"Because you have pedigree of the right sort. Your family is older and more connected than your colonel's. At least it was."

"I would be interested to learn how you know all this."

She took another pull from the cigarillo then laid it on the edge of the table. "I am not the only person who likes to investigate things. Your family was quite important during the time of Charles the Second. They were given land, and even offered a title, one declined by your proud ancestor. Some Lacey then married a peeress, rendering you quite respectable."

"Until my father and grandfather impoverished us," I said.

She waved that away. "Money is not as important as breeding. You know that, my dear Captain. That is, until someone sets their sights on marriage. Then money is quite important, but it would never do to let on, would it?"

I smiled. "You are a most cynical lady."

"Indeed. I learned very early that the world is not a kind place. Your position in it determines all. For instance, were I born into the servant class, my sharp tongue would earn me many blows. As it is, I am smiled at because I am the daughter of an earl and the widow of a viscount."

I had to concede the truth of this.

"And so Colonel Brandon suffers," she concluded. "If he were a peer, there would be much scandal and sensation, but I doubt he would be cooling his heels at Newgate."

"He might be," I said. "He is mostly there because of his pigheaded stubbornness."

She hung her arm over the back of the sofa, dangling a well-shaped hand near my head. Slim gold rings hugged her fingers, one embedded with a topaz, the other with twinkling sapphires.

I found myself thinking that I could never afford to give her jewels. For instance, if I wanted to give her a strand of diamonds to hug her slim wrist, I could not do it. It stung a man's pride not to be able to give a lady a gift, even one as wildly inappropriate as a diamond bracelet.

I reached over and drew my thumb across the inside of her wrist where the bracelet would lay.

Her eyes darkened and grew quiet. I waited for her to drawl sarcasm or to snatch her hand away, but she did neither. I rubbed her warm skin, comforting myself in the small feel of softness. She moved closer to me and rested her hand against my chest.

I had kissed her before, once in her private box at Covent Garden Theatre. She had not minded. I leaned to her and kissed her now. My sore lip pulled a little, but I did not care. She kissed me long and well, then she lifted my hand and kissed my fingers.

She was a lovely woman, and I needed comfort. We were alone in her private rooms. Only the servants would know what we did here. I wondered how loyal they were to her or whether they would give the *ton* something new to talk about tomorrow.

"Stay for a time, Captain," she said, as though reading my thoughts. She smoothed her palm across my chest. "Your heart tells me that you wish this."

Indeed, my heart beat fast and hard beneath her fingers. I kissed her again, tempted, so tempted to take her hand and lead her to the bedchamber, despite the pain in my body. Her eyes were moist; her lips, soft.

I smoothed back a strand of her hair. "It could cause you scandal if you had a liaison with me."

She studied me with a mixture of curiosity, disappointment, and resignation, as though she'd made a wager with herself what my reaction would be to her offer. I wondered whether she'd won or lost.

"It is not only scandal that you think of," she said.

I regarded her in surprise. "Indeed, it is."

"No. You forget. I saw exactly how you looked at Louisa Brandon last night when you comforted her in her sitting room."

I sat up. Her hand dropped away from me. I remembered Lady Breckenridge entering the room while I had held Louisa. At the time, I'd tried to ignore Lady Breckenridge's shrewd glance, but she had seen all and forgotten nothing.

"Louisa Brandon and I have been friends for twenty years," I said. "She loves her husband, and I will help restore him to her."

Lady Breckenridge folded her arms across her silk peignoir, assuming a neutral expression. "So that is the way of it."

"The way of what?"

She did not move but I felt a distance grow between us. "Do you know, Captain, I am trying to decide whether I am too proud to take another woman's leavings."

I stared. "What do you mean?"

"I know what I saw. You love Louisa Brandon. But you are a man of honor. You would never stoop to offering her the shelter of your arms while her husband waits in prison.

You would never violate your honor or hers in that way."
She drew a breath. "And so, you seek solace elsewhere."

Her voice shook, but she lifted her chin. Lady Breckenridge had her own code of honor. She would never let me
see her hurting.

"No," I replied in a hard voice.

"Why not let him hang? She will no doubt turn to you
once the deed is done."

Brandon had said much the same thing. The devil of it
was, Louisa *would* likely turn to me for comfort if Brandon
was hanged—at first. Eventually, she would want to put all
reminders of the sordid business behind her, including me,
no matter how many years of friendship we'd shared.

I realized that my compulsion to clear Colonel Brandon
might have more significance than my simply trying to discover the truth. Perhaps I believed Brandon innocent because I needed him to be innocent. If I could not save him,
I knew that I would lose Louisa's friendship—forever.

Lady Breckenridge was wrong, however.

"It is not solace I seek from you," I told her. "I would not
insult you so."

"What do you seek, then?"

She sounded curious, not offended.

I touched her cheek with the backs of my fingers. "What
you said you sought from me."

She looked at me for a moment with her dark blue eyes,
but she did not pull away from my touch.

"You put me in a difficult place, you know," she said at
last. "Your heart is already beyond reach. Any victory I
have with you must be hollow. If I lose, you lose nothing.
If I win, I will never win you completely."

She stood up, cutting off anything that had begun between us. "Please go now, Captain. I am attending the theatre tonight, as well as an at-home, where I and the rest of
London will talk incessantly of the murder. I need time to
prepare myself."

I rose, surprised to find myself shaking a little. "Donata."

"Go, Lacey. While I can still cling to the shards of my dignity, please."

I wanted to admonish her or to take her into my arms and prove that she was wrong, but my common sense told me that either course would be unwise.

I buttoned my coat, took up my walking stick, and crossed the room in silence. At the door, I turned back. "You are not completely correct as to where my heart is engaged." I bowed, while she watched me speculatively. "Good afternoon."

I departed. She held herself stiffly, watching me go.

CHAPTER 8

THE next afternoon, Grenville and I journeyed to Epsom to attend the funeral of Henry Turner.

Grenville drove his phaeton, the weather being fine. His larger traveling coach followed us, bearing his servants and our bags southward. The phaeton was light and fast, and we soon drew clear of the city and headed across green downs for Epsom.

Grenville's persona today was that of the horse-mad dandy. He sat upright, his gloved hands competently holding a complex configuration of reins. He occasionally touched his whip to the horses, encouraging them to hold a smart pace. In his black suit, knee-high boots, and fine hat, he was the epitome of the fashionable gentleman. His horses were perfectly matched grays, the phaeton nearly new and shiny black, the wheels and points picked out in gold.

Before I'd departed that morning, I'd written to Sir Montague Harris in Whitechapel, keeping him up to date of what I'd learned, and asking him if I might speak to him further when I returned. I wanted very much to know what he made of things.

Grenville navigated us swiftly through other vehicles and over the rutted roads. I held tightly to my hat with one hand and the seat with the other.

Remembering his motion sickness inside carriages on previous journeys, I remarked, "The movement does not bother you when you drive?"

"No," he said, his gaze on his horses and beyond. "Don't honestly know why. Probably because I must concentrate on something other than my stomach."

Grenville evidently liked to focus on obtaining the speediest journey possible. I braced my feet on the foot board and concentrated on holding on.

When I'd mounted the phaeton this afternoon, Grenville's reaction to my bruised face was less than others', because Bartholomew had already told him the tale. He quizzed me on the particulars as we rode south.

"Are you certain the Frenchman had connection with the Turner murder?" he asked. "Perhaps he was looking for something else."

"He had an inordinate interest in Mrs. Harper's letters," I answered. "Why take them? No, depend upon it, he has something to do with Mrs. Harper, and probably with Turner."

We rode silently a few moments, the rattle of the wheels over the road and the clopping of the horses' hooves making talking impractical.

"What I most wonder," Grenville said, when he slowed to drive through a village, "is why Marianne was there."

He shot me a glance. I grew uncomfortable.

"She'd come to talk with me," I said. "She happened to get in the way of the Frenchman's fists, which she would not have if she'd run away like any sensible woman."

"She was hurt? Bartholomew did not tell me that."

"She was not much hurt," I said. "I made certain of that. And she gave back as good as she got."

Grenville rarely grew angry, unlike me, who was easily

goaded, but he grew angry now. "Why the devil was she there to get in his way at all? If she wanted to speak to you, why not send for you to visit her?"

"She still feels a bit confined."

His mouth set. "I have told her she can come and go as she pleases. She can do what the devil she likes. I have ceased trying to hold her."

"*Constrained,* I should have said. Your servants would no doubt mention a visit from me to you, possibly telling you what they heard us discuss."

"Dear God," Grenville shouted at the countryside in general. "The woman will drive me mad. It is my own fault; I remember you warning me against her. I wish I had listened."

"You wanted to help her. It was kind of you."

He gave me a sideways glance. "Helping her was not my only reason, and you know it. Well, I suppose I have paid the price for my folly."

If he'd imagined she'd be forever grateful and fall into his arms, he had certainly read Marianne's character wrong.

I wanted to ask him about Mrs. Bennington, and Marianne's speculations, but we exited the village and picked up speed, and I did not fancy bellowing questions to him. Time enough for that later.

I did tell him when we slowed again near Epsom about my encounter with Imogene Harper in Turner's rooms and the rest of my investigation until this point.

I had imagined we'd put up at an inn in Epsom and journey to Turner's father's home for the funeral the next day, but to my surprise, Grenville drove to a red-brick, Tudor-style manor house a little outside the town, which he said belonged to Mr. Turner.

When the phaeton finally rattled to a halt, a groom sprang out of nowhere to greet us and hold the horses. Grenville said, "When I wrote to Turner to express my condolences, he invited me to stay. You are welcome, as well."

A footman appeared at the door and led us into a narrow, dark-paneled hall that was lined with doors. At the end of this hall, a staircase, its wood black with age, wound its way upward to a gallery.

We did not meet Mr. Turner, but were taken upstairs to bedchambers that were low-ceilinged and dark, though warm and comfortable. The footman brought us hot coffee and hock and left us alone.

"I've stayed here several times," Grenville said. "Turner does fine house parties for the Derby. They are quite popular, and Turner is a good host."

I looked out the window across green downs toward the dusty road on which the Derby race was held. I had no doubt that house parties here were filled with gaiety and excitement. Sad that such a place would now have to be the site of so dismal an undertaking.

We settled ourselves and then the baggage arrived with the coach and Matthias and Bartholomew. Soon after that, our host sent for us, and Grenville and I descended to meet Mr. Turner in a study. Large windows overlooked a lush back garden where spring flowers pushed themselves up in the beds. The sun shone hard, rendering it a lovely landscape. On any other occasion, I would stop to enjoy the sight.

Henry Turner's father, Mr. Allen Turner, looked much like his son. His hair was straight and close cropped, but he had the same rather soft features and had probably been quite handsome in his youth. He was not very tall, standing only about as high as Grenville, and he had to look up at me. He shook my hand politely, showing no resentment of my intrusion.

"You are that captain who works with the magistrates sometimes, are you not?" he asked.

I admitted that I was. "My condolences on the loss of your son, sir."

He nodded, as though resigned. "It came as a bit of the shock. When your only son dies, it is as if you lived your life for nothing. All this"—he gestured to the room, and I took him to mean the entire house and the estate, as well—

"Henry will not have any of it now. It will go to my second cousin and his son, and that will be the end of it."

His eyes were sad, but his back was straight, as though determined to face the future, no matter how bleak it was. I remembered the frustration Brandon sometimes expressed that he had no son to carry on his name and his line, no one to inherit his money and his houses. I personally was happy not to have a son to whom to leave the ruin of the Lacey house in Norfolk, but Brandon and Mr. Turner had much more to lose. An Englishman without a son was almost like a man without an appendage.

Brandon had been disappointed at Louisa's failed attempts to produce his hoped-for heir, but I believe Turner suffered worse. He'd had a healthy and robust son cut down in the prime of his life. No matter what Henry Turner's character had been, he might have lived a long time and produced many sons so that his father might see his line stretching to eternity. Now that possibility was gone.

Mr. Turner placed his hands behind his back. "I have offered a large reward for the conviction of the felon who killed my son. I understand from Grenville that you believe there is some doubt that the colonel they have arrested actually committed the murder."

"I'm trying to ascertain whether he truly did, but I am skeptical," I answered. "This might seem a strange question, sir, but could you tell me if there is anyone who could have been angry enough to want your son dead?"

He shook his head. "If Henry had been called out and died in a duel, I would understand it better. This—the senseless killing—while he sat in a chair, at a society ball of all places, confounds me. No, Captain, I do not know whether he angered anyone in particular. My son had a wide circle of acquaintances, and he was not always the most polite young man, unfortunately. The young seem to find extreme rudeness to be fashionable."

He glanced once at Grenville, as though speculating whether Grenville's famous disdain were to blame for the rudeness of young people today.

"Did he speak of anyone with particular emphasis?" I asked. "Or did he fear anyone? What I mean is, he must have known the person who killed him. He died without much struggle. The only comfort I can offer you is that he died almost instantly. It took him by surprise. He certainly would not have had time to feel fear or pain."

Mr. Turner's eyes were moist, but his mouth was tight. "I am afraid that he did not speak much to me about his acquaintance. His friends will attend his burial tomorrow. Perhaps they know whether Henry was afraid of anyone."

Grenville and I again gave him our condolences. Mr. Turner excused himself and Grenville tactfully suggested that he and I walk in the garden since it was such a fine day. We strolled along the flower beds, and the head gardener, who looked as morose as his master, pointed out the garden's more unique characteristics designed by Capability Brown, the brilliant garden designer from a century ago.

By the time the gardener had taken us to the folly and had us admire the formal walks and fountains, the dinner hour had arrived. Mr. Turner joined us for the meal, although his wife did not appear. He was still quiet and apologized for his lack of conversation, as though his quietness stemmed from unsociability rather than the death of his only son. Grenville and I assured him that we understood. We did not press him to join us for brandy, saying we would entertain ourselves.

Mr. Turner seemed distressed that he could not rise to the occasion and be the host he should be, but he also seemed grateful that we understood and would leave him be.

It was not until Grenville and I had returned to his bedchamber to drink brandy that I could mention Mrs. Bennington.

I ventured surprise that Grenville had told me he would be visiting Marianne when in fact he had gone to see Mrs. Bennington. His dark brows furrowed. "Does it matter?"

"It mattered a great deal to Marianne."

Grenville's eyes glittered. "My visit to Mrs. Bennington

is my own business." I knew he resented my intrusion, but I did agree with Marianne on one point. Grenville did have far more wealth and power than either of us, and if he chose to use us ill, there was not much we could do. However, I intended to prevent him from using Marianne ill if I could.

"I doubt it meant anything to Marianne," he went on. "She was simply trying to plague you. I doubt she cares whether I live or die."

"Not true. She was quite distressed when you were hurt in Sudbury."

He snorted, an inelegant sound.

I tried another tack. "I remember when you took me to Covent Garden to see Mrs. Bennington perform. You did not sing her praises as everyone else in the theatre seemed to."

"What are you talking about? I said much that was complimentary."

"No, you simply did not disagree with what others said. That is a different thing."

He gave me a tense glance. "Why this sudden interest in my opinion of Mrs. Bennington?"

"I am merely curious. She was at the Gillises' ball, and afterward, you sought her company. At her house?"

"Well, if you must know the entire story, no. As I journeyed home, I happened upon her—her carriage had broken an axle, and she was wild to get home. I took her there in my carriage and stayed with her until she'd calmed down. Then I went home. That is all."

I drank brandy in silence for a moment, while he grew red in the face. He was annoyed, and trying to stifle it.

"I would like to meet her," I said eventually.

"What the devil for?"

I raised my brows. "If nothing else, to ask her what she observed at the Gillises'. If she saw something that would point to solving Turner's murder, I certainly want to hear it."

"I tried to ask her," Grenville said in a more even tone. "She is a rather vacant young woman, unfortunately."

Louisa Brandon had said much the same thing. "What did she notice?" I asked.

He shrugged. "Next to nothing. She believes she saw her husband speak to him, but she cannot be certain."

"Did she?" I pushed my feet closer to the fire. "Who is Mr. Bennington? Is he known for anything but marrying a famous actress?"

Grenville seemed to relax now that I'd moved to another topic. "Bennington is one of those Englishmen who enjoy living perpetually in Italy. Both she and Bennington are a little vague about how they met, but from what I understand, he saw her perform one night in Milan and asked her to marry him the next day."

"It was a love match?"

"I do not think so," Grenville said slowly. "The marriage was sudden, but I cannot believe love had anything to do with it. He is sardonic about Claire Bennington if he speaks about her at all, and she never mentions her husband or even notices when he's in the same room with her. I imagine that the truth is that they came together for mutual convenience. They each had something the other needed."

"Money?" I speculated.

"Who knows? Bennington seems well off. Perhaps she needed money, and he wanted something pretty to look at." His mouth twisted in distaste. "Although he does not dance attendance on Claire nor seem inclined to be possessive of her."

"Is it an open marriage, then?"

"I do not know why you should think so," Grenville began, then he seemed to catch himself. "Admittedly, they live nearly separate lives. I imagine that they appeared at the Gillises' ball at the same time entirely by accident."

I had begun to construct a scenario in which Mr. Bennington killed Turner in a fit of jealousy when Turner made up to his young wife, but at Grenville's answer, I discarded the idea. If they married for convenience and lived separate lives, Bennington might simply look the other way at his wife's affairs, and she at his.

"Did Mrs. Bennington know Henry Turner?" I asked.

"She says not," Grenville answered. "She has no reason to lie about that."

"After he was found murdered? She is an actress. Perhaps her first instinct would be to lie."

Grenville gave me an unfriendly glance. "I know what you are doing, Lacey. You need a suspect other than Brandon. Do you plan to suspect everyone at the ball?"

"Every person in that house had the opportunity to murder Henry Turner. Including you."

He nodded grudgingly. "True. I was close to the room when he was found. I could have slipped in and out without anyone much noticing. Although most people notice what I do. *Some* person usually has their eye on me, which makes things dashed difficult at times. I cannot take a private walk across a remote country meadow without it being reported in full in every London newspaper the next day."

"The curse of fame," I said dryly.

"You wonder why I travel to the corners of the earth. Escaping newspaper men is one motive. But you are correct, I could have killed Turner. I had no reason to murder him, however, except that his cravat knot was appalling. But I am reasonable enough to simply look away and swallow when I see such abuse of a cravat."

He spoke lightly, but I sensed his tension. I also noted that he'd turned the conversation rather neatly away from discussion of Claire Bennington.

"Who else would have reason to murder him?" I asked. "Either because of his cravat, or something else?"

Grenville's eyes at last began to glow with interest. He dropped his dandy persona and went to the writing desk to search for paper and pen and ink.

"Suppose I make a list of all present at the ball who knew Turner and who might have reason to dislike him."

"That would be helpful," I said cautiously.

Grenville began writing, his pen scratching softly. "The most obvious person, of course, is Imogene Harper. She found Turner, she admitted that she searched his pockets for her love letter to Colonel Brandon, and Lady Breckenridge confirms that she saw Mrs. Harper doing so. Turner was apparently blackmailing Mrs. Harper about the letter, which gives her quite a strong motive."

"Yes, but why kill him in so public a place as a ballroom?"

Grenville waited, pen poised. "Because she was angry and frightened, and in such a place, there would be a chance someone else would be accused of the crime. As indeed, happened."

"Yes," I said sourly. "Who else besides Mrs. Harper?"

"Lady Breckenridge?"

I raised my brows. "She did not know him well."

"So she says. And she was quite close to the room when Mrs. Harper went in. I remember seeing her, standing nearly next to the door. Not speaking to anyone, just looking about the room."

"She is an unlikely murderess. If a gentleman angered her, she would dress him down, in no uncertain terms, no matter who listened."

Grenville chuckled. "The lady has a sharp tongue and a sharper wit. I include her only because she was so near the room. And she told you that she'd seen Mrs. Harper bend over Turner—she might have invented the story to make you more suspicious of Mrs. Harper. I admit, that seems unlikely."

"We are looking for people who knew Turner well," I reminded him.

"Indeed. Lord and Lady Gillis, then. They invited him."

"Lord Gillis says he knew Turner only in a vague way. The friend of a friend of his wife's, he told me."

"Yes, Lady Gillis is the connection there," Grenville said, writing. "You did not meet her. She can be a charming woman when she wishes, and she is very much younger than Lord Gillis. About Turner's own age, I put her."

"Hmm," I said. "And Bartholomew puts her arguing with Lord Gillis earlier that day. I wonder who this other friend of Lady Gillis's is—if she or he even exists."

"We can but ask her."

"Any other names?" I asked.

"Leland Derwent," Grenville said. "He and Turner were at Oxford together. Leland often mentions this, usually in a tone of apology."

"I doubt Leland Derwent would commit murder." Leland was one of the most innocent young men I'd ever met. He looked upon life with the unworldly eyes of a puppy and had the enthusiasm to match. I regularly dined with his family, and he would listen to my stories of the war in the Peninsula with flattering eagerness.

"I would agree with you," Grenville said. "The thought of Leland Derwent as a murderer stretches credulity. I saw him speak to Turner at length that evening, however, angrily, and he was quite troubled when Turner left him."

"I see." I sighed, unhappy. "Very well, write his name, and we will ask him about this conversation with Mr. Turner." I paused. "Mr. Bennington next, I think."

Grenville hesitated, looking annoyed, but he nodded and wrote again.

"You said it was accidental that he and Mrs. Bennington were there together," I said. "Were they invited separately, or together?"

"I do not know, but thinking it over, I wonder why Bennington was there at all. He tends to sneer at social gatherings. 'Where we stand about and pretend interest in the cut of Mr. Teezle's coat and whether Miss Peazle's come-out will be a success,' he says."

"And yet, he arrives at a grand ball and stays most of the night?"

"Precisely. I must wonder why."

"Very well, make a note of him. Any others?"

Grenville tapped his lips with the end of the pen. "It is difficult to say. Turner was not well liked. Snubbed people at Tattersall's and so forth. But he always paid up his debts at White's when he lost and everywhere else for that matter, and always stopped short of mortally insulting a fellow

so that he would not be called out. Not very brave, was our
Mr. Turner."

I half listened to him, while I contemplated all I'd
learned from Lady Aline, Louisa, and Lady Breckenridge.
"What about Basil Stokes?" I asked when Grenville finished. "Louisa and Lady Aline mentioned him, but I know
nothing about him."

"Stokes?" Grenville raised his head in surprise. "Why
would you suspect him?"

"Because Louisa said he stood very close to Colonel
Brandon when they entered the house. I am looking at the
possibility of someone stealing Brandon's knife—picking
his pocket. Louisa said the closest persons to them in the
crush were Mrs. Bennington and Basil Stokes."

Grenville regarded me with his lips parted for a moment.
I could not read his expression. Then he shrugged and made
a note. "Very well, then, Basil Stokes. We will easily find
him at Tatt's or the boxing rooms—he is mad for sport."

"In all frankness, I cannot imagine why he would murder Turner, but I hate to leave any stone unturned."

"If nothing else, we'll get good tips on what horse will
win the Derby or which pugilist is likely to be a champion.
Now, what about this French gentleman who assaulted
you?"

I took a sip of brandy, letting the mellow taste fill my
mouth. "I had not forgotten him. He had a rather military
bearing, an officer, I would say, not one of the rank and
file."

"He was not at the ball," Grenville said. "I would have
noticed a lean man with close-cropped hair, a military bearing, and a thick French accent. I knew everyone there.
There were no strangers."

I cradled my brandy goblet in my palms. "Lord Gillis
likes military men, which was why he invited Colonel
Brandon and the Duke of Wellington. Supposing this
Frenchman was a guest in the house but did not come down
for the ball. Suppose he was someone Lord Gillis had met
and had invited to stay at the house, where they could dis-

cuss military campaigns. The Frenchman spies Turner entering the house for the ball, and kills him—for reasons of his own, which I do not know. He took Imogene Harper's letters, but if he had not looked at them closely, he would not know what they were. Perhaps he thought they were something of his own that Turner had."

"Or the Frenchman has nothing to do with Henry Turner at all. You are only guessing that he does."

"True," I conceded. "But he followed me, after I'd finished searching Turner's rooms, and he was looking for something. Pomeroy is now scouring the city for the Frenchman, and I hope to question him before long." I touched my face gingerly. "And complain of his very hard fists."

If anyone could find the man, Pomeroy could. He had a tenacity greater than that of the Russians who'd driven Bonaparte out of Moscow. Also, the Frenchman would not remain hidden for long. A French officer of such distinctive appearance walking about London would be noted and remembered.

There existed one other reason that a Frenchman might profess interest in me. My wife, Carlotta, had eloped with a French officer. I had never met the man, or even seen him. Why Carlotta's lover would come to London and ransack my rooms, I had no idea, but I had to concede that the connection might be along those lines.

I kept this speculation to myself, however, as Grenville and I continued our discussion. Grenville brought up names and wrote them down or dismissed them, usually because they'd left the ball long before Turner's death. His circle of acquaintance was vastly greater than mine, so I let him speculate on the characters of gentlemen of whom I knew nothing.

By the time we parted to seek our beds, we had come up with a lengthy list. But I had focused on only a few of those as most likely: Imogene Harper, Mrs. Bennington, Mr. Bennington, Basil Stokes, my mysterious Frenchman, and possibly Leland Derwent.

I felt grateful that Grenville did not suggest listing Brandon, but I knew, glumly, that I could not rule him out altogether. He and Mrs. Harper still had the strongest motives, although I hoped to uncover a few more.

I went to sleep in the soft bed in my chamber and dreamed of Lady Breckenridge and her blue eyes.

THE funeral for Henry Turner was held the next morning. The day dawned clear and fine, the air soft, the sky an arch of blue overhead. It was a day made for hacking across the downs on a fine horse, not for standing in a churchyard while a vicar droned the burial service.

"Man that is born of a woman hath but a short time to live, and is full of misery. He cometh up, and is cut down, like a flower; he fleeth as it were a shadow . . ."

I stood next to Grenville, both of us in somber suits. Nearer the tomb stood Mr. Turner and his wife, several young men whom I took to be Turner's friends, and a few older men, who must be Turner's father's cronies. Several people from the town of Epsom also attended, working people who had given Mr. and Mrs. Turner respectful words of condolence as they arrived.

Henry would be buried in a rather private corner of the churchyard where, Mr. Turner had informed me, his family had been buried for generations.

"I thought the next person there would be me," Mr. Turner had said.

I'd had little comfort to give him. Grenville spoke all the right phrases, but I, whose mentor was even now waiting in prison to be tried for the murder, could think of nothing to say.

One of the mourners was Leland Derwent. He had seen me when we all arrived at the church and had given me a smile of greeting. Now he stared down at the grave, his young brow furrowed.

Next to him stood a young man called Gareth Travers. I'd met Travers during the affair of Colonel Westin last summer. He was Leland's closest friend, but he lacked the complete innocence of Leland, having a bit more worldly intelligence.

The vicar launched into the Lord's Prayer. I heard Grenville murmuring along, although most of the other attendants remained silent. A soft spring breeze carrying the scent of new earth touched me.

At last, we turned away from the graveside. In tacit agreement, Grenville and I hung back while Mr. Turner led his wife away. Turner's friends and the townspeople followed slowly.

Leland and Gareth Travers waited for us at the gate to the churchyard. "It was kind of you to come, Captain," Leland said as he shook my hand.

"I am afraid that my motive was not entirely kindness," I said. "I came to obtain an idea of Turner's character, and to find out who would want to kill him."

Leland looked bewildered. "I thought that your colonel had been arrested."

"He has, but an arrest does not mean he is guilty. I intend to bring forth some evidence that he is not guilty before his trial."

I had expected, if anything, for Leland to look interested, but his expression became troubled. "You think someone else committed this crime?"

"Yes, but I'm damned if I know who. You went to school with Henry Turner, I believe."

Leland nodded. "He was two years ahead of us. But yes, we were at school with him." As Grenville had indicated, Leland sounded apologetic.

I gestured to a path that led off in a direction opposite from which the rest of the party had taken. "Will you tell me about him?"

Leland fell into step beside me, and Gareth Travers and Grenville came behind. The path skirted the edge of the churchyard and swung out across the downs.

After a slight hesitation, Leland said, "There is not much

to tell. I do hate to say anything bad about him, now that he's lying in the ground."

"I assure you, I will repeat nothing. But I need to know everything I can about Henry Turner."

Leland settled his curled-brimmed hat against the breeze. "I admit that he was a bit of a bully. I didn't fag for him, but I knew the lads who did. He put them through their paces and was never happy with anything."

"Was he, forgive me for putting this bluntly, a blackmailer?"

Leland looked startled. "A blackmailer? No. No, I do not believe so. I never heard anyone say anything like that."

"Did he ever seem desperate for money?" I persisted.

"He liked money, that is true, but I do not know that he was *desperate* for it. His allowance was plenty, I would think."

I stifled my impatience at his nicety. "Anything you can tell me will help us, Leland. I need details. Did he have lovers? Did he keep to himself? Did he seem to have more money than could be accounted for from a father's generous allowance? Was he a gambler?"

"Yes, he did like to gamble." Leland eagerly seized on my last question in seeming relief. "But he generally won. Chaps always owed him money for some wager or other."

"And they paid him?"

"Oh, yes. Well, you have to, don't you? Pay up your wagers. All in good sport."

"He played cards? Dice?"

"He was not so much a gamer," Leland said. "I do not think he had a head for cards or hazard. No, he would wager on other sorts of things. Something so simple as a horse winning at Newmarket or as obscure as whether one of the housemaids would get well on Wednesday or Thursday. He had an uncanny knack of always being right."

"If he won so often, why did the other chaps wager with him?"

"Couldn't resist." Leland flashed me a wan smile. "One always wanted to best him. And betting whether or not a cat would walk to the left or right around the quad seemed safe. Half on odds. But he still managed to win."

"Perhaps," Grenville said behind us, "he enticed the cat with a bit of chicken or put ipecac in the maid's tea."

Leland gave him a horrified look. "Cheated?" He glanced about as though we'd just accused a heroic man of being a traitor. "I do not think he would have cheated, Mr. Grenville. He was simply lucky."

"Perhaps," I conceded, more to calm him than because I agreed. "Aside from his great fortune at games, was he particularly liked or disliked?"

"I would not say so," Leland answered. "Not particularly disliked—or liked, I suppose. He had his friends, his circle."

"Did you particularly like or dislike him?" I asked, turning my gaze to him.

Leland looked startled. "Why do you ask that?"

"You turned up for his funeral," I said. "Is that because he was a great friend, or did you wish to make certain he was buried?"

Leland gaped at me. "How can you say that? I came out of respect, Captain. I was there when he died—I thought it well that I come to show his father how sorry I was." His face had gone white, his lips, tight.

"I meant no offense. I am simply trying to ascertain why someone would want to kill him. You say he had no particular friends but no particular enemies, that he usually won at wagers but that those he bet against paid up without fuss. You paint a picture of a young man with a gaming streak, but of rather neutral temperament. But this does not bear out what others have told me, nor his appalling rudeness to Mrs. Harper at the ball."

"Well, I cannot help that," Leland said weakly.

"What I am getting at is that someone might have killed Turner because he owed Turner a great debt. Suppose the Frenchman who attacked me was not looking for a letter, but a note of hand, perhaps a ruinous gambling debt. My bruises attest to the fact that the man was capable of violence."

"I saw no Frenchman in the Gillises' ballroom," Leland said dubiously.

"I know." I sighed. "He seems to have been inconveniently invisible at the critical moment. What did you see, Leland? Did you observe anyone trying to corner Henry Turner, perhaps leading him to that little anteroom?"

Leland shook his head. "I am sorry, Captain. I saw nothing."

I hadn't thought he would have, but I had to try. "What is it about Turner that you do not want to tell me?"

Leland stopped walking, his walking stick arrested in midair. "I beg your pardon?"

"Mr. Grenville says that you had a conversation with him at the ball, in which you became angry with him. What did you argue about?"

"Nothing. Nothing in particular. I'd lost a bet with him on a London-to-Brighton race recently, and perhaps he gloated a bit."

"But you paid up your wager, without fuss?"

He flushed. "Of course I did. Why would I not?"

I know I was being hard on the boy, but I was frustrated, and wanted *something.* "You knew him in school, but you did not like him, that is obvious. Why not? What is it about Henry Turner that would drive someone to murder?"

Leland looked at me with wide eyes, disconcerted. "Please, I cannot answer any more questions. The day is too warm, and I am tired. I—" He broke off, flushing. "I must rest. Good-bye."

He spun on his heel and set off back the way we'd come. His long and hurried stride belied his claim that he was tired. He would quickly cover the three miles back to the house at that pace.

Grenville watched him go, brows raised. "Good lord."

I feared I had just spent the last pleasant evening at the Derwents' home. Leland would tell his father, Sir Gideon, that I was a bully, and gone would be the lovely meals and warm conversation I enjoyed once a fortnight. Worse, I feared that Leland's nervousness meant that he truly had murdered Henry Turner. I desperately hoped I was wrong.

I expected Gareth Travers to go storming after him, or to berate me for browbeating his friend, but Travers simply watched Leland go. He leaned on his walking stick, the April breeze stirring the brown curls beneath his tall hat.

"Do not mind, Leland," he said, his voice light. "He is embarrassed, that is all."

"Embarrassed?" I looked after the retreating figure. Leland was putting all his strength into getting away from us as fast as he could.

"There are certain things that Leland does not like to speak about. Henry Turner knew of a few of Leland's peccadilloes at Oxford, and threatened to tell his father. Leland would have died rather than disappoint his father, so he became rather Turner's toady."

Travers' explanation worried me more than it comforted me. I wondered what knowledge Turner had had that Leland feared, and what Leland might have done to keep Turner from reporting to Leland's father.

Travers smiled, but I felt uneasy as we walked back toward the house.

CHAPTER 9

꧁

"WELL, Gareth Travers has given us another motive,"
Grenville observed as we rode toward London in his
phaeton that afternoon.

"Leland, you mean," I said. I did not like to think of Leland as a murderer, but I could not close my mind to the
possibility. "What Travers told us does explain the argument that Leland and Turner had."

Grenville speculated. "If Turner threatened to reveal Leland's indiscretion—with a lady?—then Leland might do
anything to stop him. His father is not a cruel man, but
somehow one wants to look good in his eyes. I imagine
being Sir Gideon Derwent's son is not always easy."

"I cannot say." I stretched my leg, which had become
sore, trying to find comfort on the small seat and tried not
to worry about Leland. "I am playing with possibilities."

I thought of the bedchamber Turner's father had let me
see that afternoon. Mr. Turner was not certain why I wanted
to see where his son had stayed when he was at home, but
he had led me to the chamber without fuss.

Inside, Mr. Turner had stopped, as though realizing all at

once that his son would never inhabit the room again. Numbly, he'd straightened a chair in front of a desk, then he'd turned around and walked out without so much as looking at me.

I'd wandered about the chamber, not certain what I was looking for. The fire had not been made in some days, so the air was cold and still. It was not a terribly personal room. Turner's flat had been filled with his things, as tasteless as some of them were. This room had been a mere place to sleep when he visited the family. I'd found no indication that Turner had had lovers, no love letters from ladies of the courtesan class. In fact, I'd found no letters at all.

The four books in the small bookcase near the fire revealed nothing. Two were treatises on botany, one on rose gardens with colored plates. The rose garden book was nicely bound, but did not look as though it had much been read. The fourth was several volumes of *The Gentleman's Magazine* bound together. The magazines were a few years old. I thumbed through them, but saw little of interest, except an article on the house of one Lucius Grenville in Grosvenor Street. Drawings of the interior of his drawing room and ballroom were presented.

I returned the books to the shelves and left the room, unenlightened.

Now, as I held on to the seat while Grenville let his phaeton fly over the roads, I said, "I keep returning to that damned Frenchman. What did he want? If he was interested in Turner, why have we not seen him here in Epsom?"

Grenville competently steered his phaeton through a ford of a small stream. Water splashed from the wheels, but did not so much as touch our boots.

"Perhaps it was not Turner who interested him," Grenville suggested. "Perhaps it was Mrs. Harper, or Colonel Brandon."

"Mrs. Harper, perhaps," I answered. "I do not know what such a gentleman would have to do with Colonel Brandon. He barely speaks to anyone French, even émigrés who have lived in England for twenty-five years. 'Damn all French,' is his motto."

"I did not say that he and the Frenchman were friends. Perhaps they encountered one another during the war."

"I very much doubt it," I said, "although I will not out-and-out disregard the idea. Brandon and I and Louisa spent some time in France during the Peace of Amiens, but I never remember meeting the fellow who invaded my rooms. Brandon refused to have anything to do with a French person even in France. He talked only to English-men and ate only English food. He was quite a bore about it."

Grenville smiled a little. "I encounter such Englishmen abroad. Cannot abide foreign ways, they say. Give them the *Times* and a joint of beef, and they are happy. I wonder why they bother to leave home at all."

"Travel broadens the mind, I have heard tell," I said.

Grenville glanced at me again and barked a laugh. "You are in a cynical mood today, Lacey. But let us return to France. Did Mrs. Brandon have the same prejudice about all things French? Or did she make friends with French per-sons?"

"She did make friends. She simply neglected to mention them to her husband."

"Could she have met this Frenchman herself? Perhaps Mrs. Brandon is the connection."

I shook my head. "She might not have mentioned her friends to Colonel Brandon, but she told me of them. She never spoke of meeting a French military man, and I never saw her speaking to anyone who looked like him."

"Perhaps she simply did not tell you. I don't wish to be indelicate—I know the lady is a great friend—"

"But you wonder whether she had an affair with him?" I sighed. "It is quite unlikely, but I do not know."

I'd often had the notion that I was Louisa's greatest friend, that there was nothing she would not confide in me, but I knew this was not true. She could very well have con-ducted an illicit liaison at any time in her life without my knowledge. She was wise enough and discreet enough to hide it well, much as I disliked to think so.

"I will have to find this Frenchman and squeeze the truth from him," I said.

We had reached the outer limits of London, rolling fields giving way to houses with gardens and increased traffic of drays and wagons and carriages.

"Do you think your Mr. Pomeroy will have found him by now?" Grenville asked as we closed in behind a chaise and four.

"He may have. Pomeroy is nothing if not thorough. However, if he has not, then I know a gentleman who will definitely be able to put his hands on the Frenchman— whether the Frenchman is still in London or not."

Grenville glanced sideways at me. "You mean Mr. Denis."

I nodded once. "I do."

James Denis was a man who found things, and people, for others for an exorbitant price. The ways in which he found them were not exactly legal—stealing artwork and other valuables was in his line, as well as punishing those who disobeyed him with death.

He and I had lived in uneasy truce since the day a year or so ago when he'd had me kidnapped and beaten to teach me manners. The event had, in fact, *not* taught me manners, but we'd each learned exactly how far we could push the other. Earlier this spring, I had found the culprit who'd murdered one of his lackeys, and Denis had expressed gratitude. In return, he'd told me where in France my wife lived, leaving it up to me whether I sent for her or sought her out or left her alone.

Grenville never approved of my visiting Denis. He knew of my uncertain temper and was convinced that one day I would go too far and induce Denis to rid himself of a troublesome captain once and for all. Grenville was likely right.

"He has told me he will own me outright," I said. "If so, I might as well make use of him."

"The more favors he does you, the more favors he can call in," Grenville pointed out.

"It has gone far beyond that already," I said. And it had. James Denis had said he would snare me in his web, and I already felt that web closing about me.

Grenville drove me all the way to Grimpen Lane. Bartholomew joined me there, descending from Grenville's coach and making his determined way toward the bake shop and my rooms, as though resolute that I'd not be assaulted today.

"Come to the theatre tonight," Grenville said as he gathered his reins. "My box at Covent Garden."

I shook my head. "I am not certain I am in the mood for frivolity. A funeral tends to dampen my spirits."

"Come anyway. I have invited Mr. Bennington and Basil Stokes. I will introduce you, and you can interrogate them."

"That puts a different complexion on things," I said, tipping my hat. "Thank you. I will attend."

Grenville told me good-bye, turned his phaeton in a complicated move, and signaled his team on.

Bartholomew had already lit a fire by the time I entered my rooms. Mrs. Beltan brought me my post and some coffee. She'd been quite distressed at the attack on me, but she informed me that no suspicious person had come near the place while I'd been gone. She'd kept watch specially.

Certainly, nothing had been disturbed. I thanked her, read my post, and wrote my letters for the day. Sir Montague Harris had written that Brandon's trial was scheduled for the fourteenth of the month, one week from now. I gritted my teeth. I needed to find information that would acquit Brandon, and soon.

Sir Montague had also fixed an appointment to meet me the next day. I looked forward to discussing things with him, because too many questions swam in my head. Why had Turner gone into the anteroom just before midnight? How had Brandon's knife arrived in the anteroom, convenient for murdering Turner? Why could I not find the incriminating letter that Turner was using to blackmail Mrs.

Harper and Colonel Brandon? If Mrs. Harper had lied when she'd said she'd not found it when she searched Turner's body, why had she turned up in Turner's rooms?

I sighed and wrote a note accepting the appointment. Next, I wrote to James Denis asking if he knew anything of my Frenchman, and if not, could he find out.

Denis had an uncanny way of knowing about everything I did, so I would not be surprised if he already knew the man's name, where he came from, and whether he enjoyed fishing in the Seine.

I posted the letters, ate the bread and butter that Bartholomew had procured for me, and took a hackney to Newgate prison.

Brandon was not best pleased to see me. He'd grown thinner even in the few days he'd been imprisoned. His cheekbones looked sunken, and untidy bristles covered his chin.

"What do you want?" he growled as I was shown in.

"To save your hide," I answered. "Sit down and let me ask you questions."

He would not sit. He stood stiffly in the center of the room, ever the officer, and eyed me with chill dislike. "If you have come to further impugn Mrs. Harper, you may leave at once."

I dragged a chair in front of the meager fire and sat down. If he wanted to freeze in the center of the chamber, that was his own business. "I have met Mrs. Harper. I believe you are both fools."

His eyes widened. "You met her?"

"Yes. She was attempting to search Turner's rooms for whatever letter he had of yours and hers. What I am trying to decide is, how did the letter come to be in his possession at all?"

"I have no idea," he shot back.

His indignation was so prompt and so adamant that I believed him.

"What I want to know," I continued, "is why you and

Turner entered the anteroom at eleven o'clock and left it together a few minutes later."

"I told you. I called him out. He refused."

"No, that was your lie for the magistrate. You claimed that you resented Turner's intentions to Mrs. Harper. But I want the truth. Why did you enter the room with him? To fix a time and place to exchange money for the letter? Or did you make the exchange then?"

"I do not need to answer you. You are not a magistrate or a judge."

"Damn you, but you are obstinate. I am trying to prove that you had no reason to kill him. If you'd already made the exchange for the letter, then you would not have to kill him. Your dealing with him would be over."

"It is none of your business what I did in that room," he said stiffly.

"Very well. Perhaps they will let you weave the rope for your inevitable hanging, because that is what you are doing."

Brandon looked away.

I grew impatient. "Mrs. Harper believes you killed him, and you believe Mrs. Harper killed him. You are a fine pair. You might be pleased to know that she did not kill him when she found him. A witness saw all she did in that room. While it was true that she searched Turner's coat for the letter—which she did not find—she did not murder him."

He started. I saw it dawn on him that he might be mistaken, that he might be in Newgate prison for no reason at all.

Then he rearranged his expression to one of indignation. "None of this is your business, Lacey. Leave it alone."

"I truly believe that you did go to the anteroom at eleven to make the exchange," I said. "Turner probably did not trust you enough to meet you somewhere too privately. You are a man of uneven temper after all. Mrs. Harper, he might have handled, but you were a different matter. If he meets you in the anteroom, and you try to obtain the letter by violence, he can cry out. People nearby would come to see what was the matter."

"If that is true, then why did he not call out when he was stabbed later on?"

"I have thought of that. I believe he trusted the person who stabbed him. He was not expecting it."

"A woman, then," Brandon said.

"Perhaps. Maybe his lover."

Brandon made a face. "Sordid."

"That lover might be your savior. But let us return to your meeting with Turner. How much money did he want?"

"Five hundred guineas."

My jaw dropped. "Good God." A gentleman could live for a year on five hundred guineas. Many gentlemen, indeed, entire families, lived on far less. "That is a princely sum. You paid it?"

"It is what he asked," Brandon said.

Brandon was wealthy enough to have come up with the money. I would query his man of business, make him tell me if Brandon actually did liquidate five hundred guineas.

"You did not have five hundred guineas in your pocket when you were arrested," I said. "Pomeroy would have mentioned that. So you must have given it to Turner. In return, he gave you the letter."

"So you say," Brandon replied, too calm. "I did not have the letter in my pocket, either, did I?"

"I know." I stood up and faced him. "So what did you do with it?"

He met my gaze, his eyes so cold he froze me through. "I have told you, leave it be."

"That letter could save your life."

"You call me foolish," he said softly. "But you, Lacey, are the biggest fool of all."

"Help me, God damn you."

"I told you, I do not want your help." The muscles of his jaw tightened. "Now go, before I call the turnkey to throw you out."

"It would serve you right if I let you rot," I said savagely.

I wanted very much to throttle him, could feel the satisfaction of my hands closing on his neck. "But I care too much for Louisa to do that."

"I know you care for her," he said. "I am sure you will now go to her and comfort her."

I backed away to prevent myself from striking him. "You do not understand what you have. You never did."

His eyes narrowed, chill and hard. "Get out."

I left him.

I felt unclean as I made my way, angry and shaking, back through Ludgate Hill and Fleet Street toward Covent Garden.

Brandon hated me so much. I'd done everything for him, tried to be the man he wanted to make, and I never could. I'd tried to please him just as I'd tried to please my father, and got nothing for my pains.

Louisa had once told me that what Brandon could not forgive was that I'd taken her side when things had gone wrong between them. I'd stood behind Louisa, and he'd hated me since that day.

I had not tried very hard to heal the breach. I'd been too wounded by him, both physically and inside my heart.

Now he needed me, and he knew it. Why he was being so bloody obtuse, I did not understand. I could not believe that even Brandon would take himself to the gallows to spite me.

As I rolled along in the hackney, I tried to calm myself and look at things logically. I went over my conversation with Brandon in my head, pulling out the facts that I'd learned.

If Brandon *had* made the exchange with Turner at eleven o'clock—the letter for the five hundred guineas—that changed several of my assumptions. Imogene Harper would not have been searching Turner's rooms for the letter if she knew Brandon already had it. She'd let me believe that had been her purpose in looking through Turner's coat, and had not corrected me.

When Pomeroy searched Turner, and Brandon for that

matter, he would never have missed something so obvious as a bank draft for five hundred guineas. If Brandon had actually given Turner the money, then that was what Imogene Harper took from Turner's pocket as soon as she'd seen that Turner was dead.

Why then, my mind prodded me, *did she try to search Turner's rooms?*

Well, Brandon had done *something* with the letter he'd purchased from Turner. He had left the anteroom just after eleven and stepped into a private alcove with Mrs. Harper. Therefore, she was the most logical person he would have passed the letter to.

Or perhaps Brandon had decided to trust no one but himself and refused to give her the letter. Or perhaps Turner had promised to bring him the letter later, and Brandon had paid him the money anyway like an idiot.

I rubbed my temples in frustration. If I could trace the letter and the money, I would be happy, indeed.

Putting my hands on the murderer would make me even happier.

By the time I arrived home, I had calmed somewhat and turned back to my plans. Tonight at the theatre, I would meet and interview Mr. Bennington and Mr. Stokes. If nothing else, they might be able to give me more ideas about what had happened the night of the ball.

I let Bartholomew draw a bath for me, then he helped me dress from the skin out in my dark blue regimentals. As I attached the last of the silver cords across my chest, someone knocked on the outer door. Bartholomew darted out of the room to answer, and returned quickly.

"Mrs. Brandon, sir," he said.

CHAPTER 10

LOUISA was staring mutely into the fire when I emerged. She wore a drab, long-sleeved, high-waisted dress and a woolen shawl that hung limply from her shoulders. A bonnet with green silk ribbon lay on the table.

My usual course in greeting her would be to take her hands and kiss her cheek, but when she turned to me, her white face and haunted eyes made me stop before I reached her.

"I thought Lady Aline was preparing to take you to Dorset," I said.

Louisa gave me a wan smile. "She is. But I could not remain in the house any longer. The walls seemed to press on me. Aline is a dear friend and my servants are loyal, but I believe they mean to keep me prisoner in my rooms." She gave an exasperated sigh. "Why I ever thought yellow was a cheerful color, I have no idea. It glares at me—it laughs at me. Bloody color for a sitting room."

I took her elbow and guided her to a chair. "Well, there is nothing cheerful here, so that should not worry you. You are in sore need of refreshment, and if I know Bartholomew, he's already run off to obtain it."

She sank into the chair gratefully. "I simply could not stay home. I legged it, as my maid would say. Aline will be frantic, and I know it is childish of me, but at the moment, I truly do not care."

"I think I understand."

"Thank you. I somehow knew that you would enter the conspiracy with me instead of scolding me and taking me home."

I smiled. "I will do that later."

Bartholomew banged back in at that moment, carrying a tray of steaming things. He set down the tray and poured out a mug of coffee. "You get that into you, ma'am," he said, handing it to her. "And a few of these sausages. You'll be right as rain."

Louisa fell upon them hungrily. "My maids believe that thin slices of bread and weak tea are all my constitution will abide. And Aline keeps plying the brandy. I shall be in a sad state before long."

"I will send my instructions to fatten you up," I said. "Is that why you fled? In search of food?"

Louisa dabbed her mouth with a handkerchief, and Bartholomew removed the empty plate and the tray. "The magistrate questioned me. The one from Bow Street, along with your Sir Montague Harris."

I grew alarmed. "In the Bow Street House?" I thought of the smell of unwashed bodies in the lower rooms, the dirty, callused palms thrust out for coins.

"No," she answered, to my relief. "They came to me. They asked me all sorts of questions. Had I known that my husband was having an affair with Mrs. Harper? What had he told me about Mr. Turner? Did he behave in a peculiar fashion that night? How did he not remember bringing the knife with him? Did I know he would kill Turner? And other nonsense."

"I will speak to Sir Montague," I said indignantly. "They should not have harangued you."

"No, do not grow angry with him. The pair of them obviously did not think I was an accessory. They see me as the poor, betrayed wife, deceived by her husband." She gave me a bitter look. "Which is what I am."

I took her hand. "Louisa, I will do everything in my power to restore him to you."

Her fingers briefly tightened on mine, then flowed away. "I have been lying awake at night thinking of you trying to save him. And sometimes, in the small hours of the morning, when I am most alone, I am not certain I want you to."

I gazed pensively at her, unsure what to say.

She went on quickly, "Oh, I do not mean that I wish him to die. I would not wish that on anyone. But I believe that I do not want him to come home again."

"Louisa—"

"I know now what you felt when Carlotta left you. I felt sorry for you at the time, but I did not truly understand. To live your whole life for someone, to vow to stand by them and to care for them, no matter what happens, and then to have them betray you, to throw your devotion in your face, is the hardest thing a person can bear. You feel like a fool that you have spent so much time on such an unworthy person, that you have been found wanting—" She broke off, her eyes filling. "And I am so bloody tired of weeping. If you pat my hand, Gabriel, I shall never forgive you."

I took a handkerchief from my pocket and handed it to her in silence.

I knew that Brandon *had* found Louisa wanting. He'd not bothered to hide the fact. Louisa had been forced to stand by the night Brandon was arrested and look at the face of the woman whom Brandon admitted was his mistress. I thought Louisa was holding up well, considering.

"What you do with him after his trial will be your choice," I said, keeping my voice steady. "Leave him, obtain a legal separation—that is for you to decide. I will help you as much as I can, use my few connections to bring about a happy ending for you."

She lifted her head. "Take me to France."

I stared at her. "To France?"

"Yes." She crumpled my handkerchief in her hand. "You told me that you wanted to go to France to find Carlotta. I offered to accompany you. Let us go, and leave London and all of this behind."

Her eyes blazed fire in her pale face. Despite her anguish, she looked beautiful, resolute and glittering, like a diamond.

"Louisa," I said, "if you hie off to France with me while your husband endures a murder trial, you will never live it down."

"What does it matter? We are ruined, I am ruined. Even if Aloysius is found innocent, we shall always be known for it—the colonel who was tried for murder. It will follow us all our lives."

"I know," I said.

She sprang to her feet and began pacing the room. "I want no part of it. Take me to France, Gabriel. I am certain that Paris will be slightly more exciting than a country village in Dorset."

"Suggest a journey to Lady Aline. I will persuade her to take you."

She stopped. She faced me, two dark red spots on her cheeks. "I do not wish to go with Aline. I wish to go with you."

I studied her flushed face, her brittle eyes, her round bosom as it rose and fell. If she had offered me this in 1814, after Napoleon had been temporarily defeated, when France was open again, just before Brandon and I returned to London ignominiously, I would have gone with her in a flash.

I would have taken her to Paris and bought her frocks and drunk wine with her while the English delegation decided what to do with France and the restored Bourbon king. I would have abandoned honor and everything else to be with her, to take her hand and explore the world with her, never to return to England.

I would have done it. I would have done it in 1815, after

Waterloo, when my life was nothing and the continent was free and open once again. I would have fled with her to begin anew.

But not now. Now, I'd begun to build something on the wreck of my life. I'd laid a foundation with my friendship with Grenville, discovered an interest in investigating and solving crime with Sir Montague Harris. I had made friends with the Derwents and Lady Aline Carrington and my land-lady, Mrs. Beltan.

And I had met Lady Breckenridge.

I thought that in Lady Breckenridge I'd found a friend who understood me, one who could keep me from making too great a fool of myself. I remembered her fingers on mine the day before I'd journeyed to Epsom, and how much I'd liked that feeling.

I had forged tenuous things that were new and needed to be explored. I now had something to lose.

I cared for Louisa more than I'd ever cared for myself. But I no longer wanted to give up my entire life for her.

She saw that in my eyes as I gazed up at her. Her expression became one of defeat, and her shoulders drooped.

My heart burned. "I am sorry," I said, as though that would make any difference.

"I ought to have known," she said. "That you would abandon me, too."

I got to my feet. "No, never abandon you. Never that." I gently took her hands. "I will never leave you to face anything alone. You have my word. But if we did dash away together to France, or Italy, or any number of places, you would soon grow ashamed. You would dislike yourself, and you would grow angry at me for not stopping you. You would begin to dislike me, and that I could not bear."

Tears stood in her eyes. "Gabriel."

"In any case, I am horrible to live with. Ask Bartholomew."

She did not smile. She stood looking at me for a moment longer, then she lowered her gaze and walked away from me. She moved to the window and stood looking out at the gray drizzle that had begun.

I did not know what else to say to her. I felt numb.

"I should not have asked you," she said softly. "I'm sorry."

Her back was slim, but straight and strong. She might not believe she could weather this problem, but I knew that she could. Louisa had a core of strength that the stoutest general would admire. Her strength had taken her through the hellish living on the Iberian peninsula, and through the grief that both Brandon and I had put her through.

"Louisa," I said gently. "I swear to you that I will get his charges dismissed. I will bring Aloysius Brandon home. Because as much as I despise him for what he has done to you, I do not believe that the idiot did murder."

"Why not? The rest of the world does."

"What did Sir Montague and Sir Nathaniel tell you?"

She turned around. "They said that Aloysius had reason to kill Mr. Turner. He had been seen growing angry with him, they had gone off alone together where he claims he called the man out, Aloysius named him a coward when he refused, and the knife was his."

"The knife." I paused. "Was the knife truly his, without question?"

"I do not know. I assume he had one like it. I did not know all of his private possessions. And in any case, he admitted the knife was his."

"But he does not remember carrying it to the party. Or at least, so he says."

Louisa clenched her fist and made an exasperated noise. "The two magistrates asked me that as well. As though I go through my husband's pockets before we leave the house. I'm not the sort of wife who dresses her husband. He has a valet for that."

"So if anyone would know about the knife, it would be the valet."

"Yes, they asked Robbins. Interviewed him quite closely. Robbins agreed that the knife belonged to Brandon and said that he placed the knife in the pocket of Aloysius's frock coat. Aloysius did not ask for it, but he liked to have the knife with him, because it was handy. Aloysius insisted he did not notice whether the knife was in his pocket."

"Therefore," I said, "the knife is Brandon's in all likelihood. What we must discover is how it got from Brandon's pocket into the wound."

"Most people think he put it there," Louisa said.

"Well, I am one person who does not. But it would not be difficult to steal the knife from him. Someone could easily dip into his pocket. The most likely person to have taken the knife is, of course, Mrs. Harper."

"You believe she is a murderess, not just a Jezebel?"

"I do not know yet what I believe. She lied to me, that is certain. Brandon is lying, too. Once I clear out the lies of these two fools, I believe the solution will present itself."

Louisa sighed. "I no longer know what to believe."

I went to her and put my hands on her shoulders. "Please trust me. I will do everything in my power to make your world better for you. I love you that much."

The tears that had been threatening to fall now spilled down her cheeks. "I love you, too, Gabriel. I always have."

I kissed her forehead. Her curls were like silk beneath my lips.

It was difficult not to embrace her, not to whisper that the world could go to hell, and we could leave England together.

But I resisted. I stepped back from her and let her go.

In silence, she gathered her shawl and her bonnet. She would not look at me as she tied the green silk ribbon under her chin. "For some reason," she said, trying to keep her voice light, "I feel as though I should be wearing black."

"Have you seen your husband since he has been committed to Newgate?"

"No. How could I?"

I observed her quietly. "Go and see him. Have Sir Montague take you."

She looked at me in anger. But she said nothing. She finished tying the ribbon then she gathered her shawl about her shoulders and walked to the door. "Good-bye, Gabriel," she said.

And then she was gone.

MUCH divided in mind, I set off for Covent Garden Theatre.

The arched piazza leading to the theatre stretched along the northwest side of Bow Street, its soaring columns sheltering theatregoers, game girls, pickpockets, and servants from the April rain and wind. I walked among ladies and gentlemen dressed in the finest style as well as girls dressed in tawdry gowns picked from secondhand stores or parish charities.

A lord descending from a carriage marked with a coat of arms was instantly surrounded by beggars with hands outstretched. The lord scattered a few pennies among them before he lifted his head and swept past them. His footman swatted at the group of grinning men, telling them to clear off. Then he hopped back onto the coach and rattled away to no doubt drink and dice with the coachman.

I stopped to bow to a gentleman I recognized and his wife, a large woman with feathers balancing atop a mass of gray and black curls. I had met the man through Grenville, and the three of us exchanged polite pleasantries. Just as the gentleman drew his wife on toward the doors of the theatre, someone hissed at me from the shadow of a pillar.

"Lacey!"

I waited until the gentleman and his lady had entered the theatre, then I peered into the darkness beside the pillar.

"Marianne," I said. "What are you doing?"

She stepped from the shadow. She wore a fine enough gown, blue velvet trimmed with gold and silver tissue, and a bonnet with a long blue feather. She ruined this semblance of respectability by lurking beneath the column like a street courtesan.

"Is *he* here?" she asked.

"I am to meet Grenville in his box, yes."

Her tone grew bitter. "He has come to see Mrs. Bennington. He suggested to his friends that they meet with her afterward. I heard him as he arrived."

"Did you hide here and spy on him?" I asked incredulously.

"Well, if I did not spy on him, I would never know where he was, would I? He has not come to see me in days. His servants are useless for information of him. He does not even write a letter."

I gave an exasperated sigh. "He and I spent the last two days in Epsom. At a funeral, if you must know. It was not a frivolous outing."

"He might have been plowing a field, for all he'd tell me. And now, he arrives, sweet as you please, to ogle Mrs. Bennington in yet another performance."

I remembered Grenville's evasiveness about Mrs. Bennington. I did not want to lie to reassure Marianne, but then again, she was becoming most obsessed about the subject. "He invited me tonight so that I might have a chance to speak to more of the guests who were at the Gillises' ball."

She stepped close to me and lowered her voice. "If you'd like to know something interesting, *he* seemed quite keen to go to that ball. Kept saying there was something he had to do."

My interest perked. "Did he? He seems to have spoken to you a little, in any case."

"Mrs. Bennington was also there. I can imagine what he had in mind."

"Well, I cannot." I became aware of people glancing at me as they passed, of their raised brows or disdainful looks. "I must go in, Marianne. Go home and cease lurking in the piazza. Someone might mistake your intentions."

"I believe I will stay," she retorted. "It will be interested to see what direction he takes when he leaves—and with who."

"You'll catch cold." I pulled a key from my pocket. "Go and wait in my rooms if you cannot bring yourself to go home. Bartholomew has the fire hot. If he is there, you can interrogate him about Grenville's motives, if you wish, but I imagine he will tell you the same as I."

She scowled, but she snatched the key from my fingers. "Gentlemen so enjoy giving orders."

"I know better than to expect you to obey. Use the key if you want to keep warm; if not, wait out here in the rain and hand it back to me as I leave."

Her expression darkened. She stepped back in the shadow of the pillar, but she leaned there and did not walk away.

Sighing, I left her and entered the theatre.

Grenville's box was located above the stage, where the viewer could look down on the drama below as well as see who waited in the wings. Comfortable mahogany arm chairs stood in two rows, with tables between them for lorgnettes or gloves or glasses of claret and brandy.

The box was filled with gentlemen tonight, not a lady in sight, which made it, to my taste, rather dreary. But I was interested enough in the gentlemen present to tolerate the absence of female company.

An empty chair waited next to Grenville, I assumed for me. Grenville introduced me all around, beginning with Basil Stokes. Mr. Stokes was tall and white haired. As usual with a man of his age, he had a large belly from years of consuming at least a bottle a day of port, but he did not have the usual gout. He had a booming voice, which, when he greeted me, caused heads throughout the theatre to turn in our direction.

Stokes was from Hampshire, which, he assured me, afforded excellent hunting and fishing if I ever wanted to take the trouble. He laughed loudly and made a comment about the large bosom of an actress who had just entered the stage.

The actress, indeed a buxom young lady, heard him. She simpered, and the audience laughed.

Mr. Bennington, on the other hand, contrasted Stokes completely. He was perhaps an inch or two shorter than I, dark-haired, and very lean, as though he ate sparingly and drank little. He had a long face and a longer expression, a young man devoted to sardonic observation. His handshake was rather limp.

"Pleased to meet you, my dear Captain Lacey. Have you come to watch my wife stun the masses of London again?"

He said it with no pride, only a drawl of resignation.

"I have seen her perform," I said politely. "She is a lady of great talent."

"Oh, yes, indeed," Mr. Bennington said, as though much put upon. "Her reputation is well deserved."

I thought I heard a slight emphasis on the word "reputation" but could not be certain.

The other gentlemen in the box were club fodder, gentlemen I'd met in passing while visiting Grenville or going with him to Tattersall's or Gentleman Jackson's boxing rooms. They greeted me with varying degrees of enthusiasm, some warm, some indifferent, each making a polite comment or two.

We settled down to watch the performance, which was already well into the first act. As was usual, the restless audience talked among themselves or shouted to the actors, drank and ate, or jostled each other in the stalls.

In our box, the conversation turned to sport, namely pugilism and the latest prize fighter. Sitting next to Grenville, I apologized under my breath for being late.

"Not at all," he murmured back. "I take it some new twist in the investigation?"

"No. Marianne Simmons."

Grenville stared at me. "I beg your pardon?"

"She accosted me under a column outside, of all places," I said quietly.

Grenville's mouth hardened. "Why the devil is she under a column outside?"

"She might be gone by now. I gave her the key to my rooms. Told her to go there and get warm."

Grenville's body stiffened and his gaze became fixed. He brought one closed fist to his mouth. "Damnation."

Below us, the audience began to applaud, then to stamp,

then to cheer, as the lovely Mrs. Bennington glided onto the stage. She waited, poised and gracious, while London adored her.

Grenville rose from his chair and woodenly made for the door of the box. In alarm, I followed him, excusing myself to the other gentlemen. I heard murmurs below as people noticed Grenville's abrupt exit.

Outside the box, the halls were deserted. Grenville walked away from me swiftly. By the time I reached the stairs, he'd already gone down, flinging himself out of the theatre without stopping for his hat and coat.

I went in pursuit, leaving the relative warmth of the theatre for the cool wind and rain of the night.

Marianne had not gone. Just as I entered the piazza, Grenville yanked her out from behind a pillar. I heard him begin, "What the devil—"

I closed the distance quickly. "Do not begin an altercation in front of the theatre, I beg you," I said, cutting off his words. "It will be all over England by morning if you do. Take Marianne and have things out in my flat. It is a short walk from here."

Grenville swung to me, his eyes narrowing in anger.

"Marianne has the key. Go, Grenville. You cannot be such a fool as to have a falling-out with your mistress in front of Covent Garden Theatre while Mrs. Bennington plays inside."

Grenville drew himself up, but the sense of my words seemed to penetrate his anger. He seized Marianne's hand. "Come along."

She tried to resist. "Go," I told her. "Shout all you want to once you get there. Mrs. Beltan has gone home. The house is quite empty."

Without waiting for them to depart, I turned on my heel and stalked back into the theatre.

By the time I entered the box, Mrs. Bennington had finished her scene and left the stage. The audience was talking loudly, laughing and gesturing, some, I saw to my alarm, at Grenville's box. They completely ignored the new scene and the actors desperately trying to say their lines over the noise.

"How strange," Mr. Bennington drawled as I resumed my seat. "I have never before observed anyone leave a theatre once my wife has taken the stage. And Mr. Grenville, no less. The event will be the talk of the town."

CHAPTER 11

BENNINGTON looked amused, not angry. I wondered suddenly why he seemed to so despise his wife.

"Yes, what happened?" Basil Stokes boomed. "Did the fellow take ill?"

"He was not feeling his best," I extemporized. "I am not certain he will return."

"Ah, well," said a gentleman I'd met at White's. "We must endeavor to endure the finest claret and best seats in the theatre without him."

Several men chuckled.

The play dragged on, a lackluster affair. I found little trouble turning the conversation with Mr. Bennington next to me to the events at the Gillises' ball. "Did you know Mr. Turner well?" I asked him.

"No," Mr. Bennington said, rolling his claret glass between long fingers. "I do not have much acquaintance in London, living so long on the continent. He was rather a rude fellow, and I had no interest in him."

"Did you see him enter the anteroom that night? Just before he was killed, I mean?"

"Oh, yes. He went in about a quarter to the hour. I told the Runner already. The Runner is a friend of yours, I believe. He mentioned you."

"He was one of my sergeants when I was in the army," I replied. "So you saw Turner enter, but no one else?"

"Not really paying attention, I am afraid. I know you wish to get your colonel off, and I commend your loyalty, but I would not be surprised if Brandon really did peg the fellow. He was red-faced and angry with Turner the entire night."

I silently cursed Colonel Brandon, as I had many times since this business began, for being so obvious. "Any man might be angry with another, but murder is a bit extreme, do you not think?"

"Not in this case." Bennington took a sip of claret and assumed a philosophical expression. "Turner was a boor. It was long past time that someone stuck a knife into him. I truly believe that a man should be hung for having appalling manners. They are as criminal in my opinion as a pickpocket. More so. Pickpockets can be pleasant fellows. So charming you do not realize your handkerchief or purse has been lifted until too late."

He smiled as though I should take his words as a joke.

"You believe he was murdered because he was rude?" I asked, also punctuating my words with a smile.

"He ought to have been. I believe our Mr. Turner died because he was obnoxious to a lady. Mrs. Harper, I mean. The colonel defended her. He should not be hanged for that."

As he said his last words, the audience began their cheering and stamping again as Mrs. Bennington returned for her next scene.

Interested, I turned to watch her. As before, she waited until the applause died down, then she began her speeches.

I could not help but be entranced. Mrs. Bennington was young, with golden hair and a round, pretty face. But her girlish looks belied her voice, which was strong and rich. She spoke her lines with conviction, as if the soul of the person written on the page suddenly filled her. She was still Mrs. Bennington, and yet she flowed into her character at the same time. She had a voice of sublime sweetness and a delivery that made one's troubles fade and fall away.

Mr. Bennington poked me with his elbow. "I will procure an introduction if you like."

He was smirking. I knew he needled me, but at the same time, I did want the introduction. "Please," I said.

When Mrs. Bennington finished her scene and left the stage, the magic faded. Apparently, that was to be her last appearance, because the audience began to drift away, uninterested in the rest of the play.

Mr. Bennington rose. "Shall we greet her backstage and tell her how splendid she was?"

I had wanted to stay and become better acquainted with Basil Stokes, but Bennington seemed to be ready to fly to his wife's side. Before I could say anything, Stokes broke in.

"I hear you are all agog for pugilism, eh, Lacey?" he bellowed in my ear. "Come to Gentleman Jackson's tomorrow, and I'll show you some boxing." He grinned and winked, as though he told a joke.

I accepted. I had, with Grenville, attended Gentleman Jackson's on occasion and had even gone a few practice rounds in my shirtsleeves, but to tell the truth, I could take or leave the sport. However, the prospect of questioning Stokes was not to be missed.

I agreed, then let Mr. Bennington escort me out.

"He is so terribly hearty, is he not?" Bennington asked. He had to raise his voice over the other theatregoers who poured out of boxes. "So terribly English. So John Bull. He is what I went to Italy to escape."

He rolled his eyes, oblivious of the disapproving stares he received from the other John Bulls around us.

As we walked, I wondered why, if Bennington had gone to Italy to escape utterly English Englishmen, had he returned?

I followed him down a flight of stairs into the bowels of

the theatre, then through a short corridor to the green room. Mrs. Bennington was there, surrounded by flowers and young dandies.

The gentlemen present could have been cast from the same mold as Henry Turner. They wore intricately tied cravats, high-pointed collars, long-tailed frock coats, black trousers or pantaloons, and polished slippers. They varied only in the type of cravat pin they sported—diamond, emerald, gold—and in the color of their hair. Brown, black, golden, or very fair hair was curled and draped in similar fashion from head to head.

I did not miss the flash of annoyance in Mrs. Bennington's eyes as she beheld her husband. She obviously wanted to bask in the attention of these lads who brought her bouquets and kissed her hand. Bennington ruined the mood.

From the twitch of Bennington's lips, he knew precisely what he had done.

"My dear," he said, drawing out the words as he took her hands. "You were too wonderful this evening. Mr. Grenville was so overset with emotion that he had to flee. He left Captain Lacey behind as his emissary. Captain, may I present my wife, Claire Bennington. Claire, Captain Lacey, a very dear friend of Lucius Grenville."

Mrs. Bennington had been looking at me in a rather vacant fashion, but at the last announcement, her expression changed to one of trepidation.

She had hazel eyes, an indeterminate shade between brown and green. Her lips were full and red, and parted slightly while she gazed at me. As I bowed over her hand, I realized what Louisa and Grenville had both meant when they said she was an empty vessel. Except for that flash of trepidation, she seemed a rather vacuous creature.

Her hand was soft and not strong, the flesh yielding to the press of my fingers. Her hair was artificially curled; close to, it looked frizzled from too many times crimped around an iron, and the color was dulled with dye.

"Greet the good captain, my dear," Mr. Bennington prodded.

She started, as though she was an automaton that needed a push to begin its trick. "How do you do?" she said. Her voice, too, was rather breathy, holding none of the quality of her intonation on stage. "Grady," she said to an older woman who bustled about the room, seemingly the only person with anything to do. "Bring the captain some port."

"None for your husband, eh?" Bennington said, and strolled away.

Mrs. Bennington had not let go of my hand. She pressed it tighter, her nails sinking into my skin. "Captain, I am glad you have come. I must speak with you."

"I am all attentive, madam," I said.

She shot a furtive glance at the dandies, who were eyeing me in jealous dislike. "Not here. Later. Alone. In my rooms. Grady will tell you." She released my hand with a little jerk as her maid approached with a glass of port carefully balanced on a tray. Then she turned away and seized the arm of the nearest dandy.

The young man gave me a triumphant look and led her off. Grady, who had far less vacant eyes than her mistress, handed me the port. As I drank, she gave me instructions. I was to appear at number 23, Cavendish Square, at half-past one and be admitted to her mistress. I was to come alone, no followers, excepting, of course, a servant.

She marched away, leaving me alone with the port and nothing to do but watch the dandies fall all over Mrs. Bennington. Mr. Bennington wandered about making cutting remarks to his wife's face, and looked amused when she did not notice.

I realized, listening to him, that Bennington severely disliked his wife. It was clear in his drawling comments, the looks he shot her when her attention was elsewhere. He viewed her as contemptible, and he despised her.

Why then had he married the woman? He might have stayed on the continent, happily avoiding hearty Englishmen and listening to opera. But he had married Claire Bennington and returned to England. It was a puzzle, but I had other puzzles to solve.

I stayed in the room until I could politely take my leave. When I gave Mrs. Bennington my good-byes, she shot me a meaningful look that was plain for all to see. Her husband saw it. He gave me a beatific smile and shook my hand.

"I hope I have made your visit to the theatre worth-while," he said, his teeth gleaming.

I responded with some polite phrase and departed.

As I walked home through the rain, I let the vivid picture of Bennington killing Henry Turner fill my mind. Bennington made no bones about the fact that he thought Turner deserved to be murdered. The look he'd given me as I'd parted from him had been full of self-deprecating amusement, but also full of anger. He knew bloody well that I'd be visiting his wife later and that he would be expected to keep out of the way.

I longed to tell him that I had no intention of cuckolding him, but I did not think he'd believe me. I would have refused Mrs. Bennington's invitation altogether, but she intrigued me with the worry in her eyes, and also, she'd been at the Gillises' ball.

As I turned to Russel Street, making my way to Grimpen Lane, a few game girls called to me from the shadows. They laughed when I merely tipped my hat and did not respond.

They knew by now that I treated street girls with kindness and did not turn them over to the watch or to the reformers. But they saw no reason why they should not capitalize on my kindness.

"Come, now, Captain," one called. "I'll only ask a shilling. No better bargain in London."

"Tuppence," another girl insisted. Her voice was hoarse, her throat raw from coughing. "Only tuppence fer yer. 'Cause it wouldn't be work for me."

The girls bantered with me often, but I was never tempted by them. The poor things were always wracked with some illness or other, a few of them with syphilis. It was not simply pity and caution of disease that kept me from them, however. Most of them were younger than my daughter, and all were accomplished thieves. Their flats, as

they called the gentlemen they shared, never paid them
enough, and they saw no reason why they should not lift the
handkerchief of anyone passing to sell for an extra bob or
two.

A year or so ago, I'd helped one of their number, Black
Nancy, by taking her to Louisa Brandon. Louisa was used
to taking in strays, and she'd found the girl a place as a
maid at an inn near Islington.

I distributed a shilling to each of them and told them to
go get themselves warm.

"A fine gentleman yer are," one said. She reached out to
stroke my arm, and I backed quickly out of reach. I wanted
to keep my coins.

They laughed, and I tipped my hat again and walked
away.

When I entered Grimpen Lane, I half expected to hear
the altercation between Marianne and Grenville filling the
street. All was quiet, however, even when I opened the door
that led up to my rooms.

In the past, the staircase had been painted with a mural
of shepherds and shepherdesses frolicking across green
fields. Now the paint had mostly faded except for the occasional shepherdess peering out of the gloom. Mrs. Beltan
didn't bother painting the staircase because it would be an
extra expense, and no one saw it but her boarders.

I climbed the stairs slowly, my knee stiff from the
weather. At the top of the stairs, my door, once ivory and
gold, now sullen gray, stood ajar.

I studied it with irritation. If Marianne and Grenville had
departed for more comfortable surroundings, they might
have at least closed the door and kept out the cold.

I heard a soft step on the stairs above me. I looked up to
see Bartholomew descending from the attics, his tread surprisingly quiet for so large a young man. I opened my
mouth to speak, but he thrust a finger over his own lips, urg-
ing me to silence.

Nonplussed, I peered through the half-open door and
saw Marianne and Grenville close together in the middle of

the room. Marianne's arms hung at her sides, but she looked up into Grenville's eyes as he cradled her face in his hands. As I watched, he leaned to kiss her.

I shot Bartholomew a surprised glance. He shrugged. I signaled for him to follow me, and he tiptoed down the stairs and past the doorway. We descended quietly to the street.

"Is the altercation over, then?" I asked.

"I hope so, sir. They shouted for the longest time."

"Hum. Well, let us hope they have come to some accordance. Are you hungry?"

"Famished, sir."

I suggested the Rearing Pony, a tavern in Maiden Lane, and Bartholomew readily agreed. We walked through Covent Garden square to Southampton Street and so to Maiden Lane, where we ate beefsteak and drank ale like every good John Bull.

It was there that James Denis found me.

Denis was still a relatively young man, being all of thirty. But his dark blue eyes were cold and held the shrewdness of a born trader or banker or dictator. If Emperor Bonaparte had met James Denis over a negotiating table, Bonaparte would have ceded everything and fled, considering himself lucky to get away so easily.

I was surprised to see Denis in such a lowly place as a tavern. He kept a wardrobe as costly and fashionable as Grenville's and lived in a fine house in Curzon Street. He did not often venture out to see others; he had others brought to him.

Two burly gentlemen flanked him to the right and left, former pugilists that he employed to keep him safe.

He studied me for a moment or two, his eyes as enigmatic as ever, then he gestured to the seat next to me. "May I?"

I nodded. Bartholomew moved off the bench, swiping up his ale as he went. He sauntered across the room, where he smiled at the barmaid, Anne Tolliver, who gave him a sweet smile in return.

James Denis seated himself. His men moved to nearby benches, which seemed to magically clear of patrons. The barmaid approached with tankards of ale. The lackeys gladly took them, but Denis waved his away. He folded his gloved hands over his walking stick and laid his hat on the table.

"I've come about your Frenchman," he said.

I had assumed so, although, with Denis, one should never assume anything. He did things for reasons of his own, and not always reasons that would benefit the person who hired him.

"I have not much more to tell you about him than what I wrote in my message," I said.

He lifted one perfectly groomed brow. "No need for more of a description. I have already found him."

"Truly? I only wrote you of it this morning."

"I heard of the incident before you journeyed to Epsom," he said, confirming my idea that he knew where I went and what I did at all times. "One of my men saw the Frenchman fleeing your rooms. He followed him across the river, but lost him in Lambeth. That at least gave me a place to begin. We found him tonight, and he is waiting at my house. He is from Paris and answers to the name of Colonel Naveau."

I had never heard of him. But my idea that he had a military bearing seemed to be correct.

"You could simply have written," I said, "fixing an appointment for me to meet him."

"I thought you might be anxious to interview him," he answered, his expression neutral. "I began to call at your rooms, but my man said he'd seen you walking toward Maiden Lane."

And he'd know that I liked to come to the tavern here. I wished I could meet this "man" of his, who watched all my movements and reported them to his master.

"I have an appointment tonight," I said. "As much as I wish to interview Colonel Naveau, I will have to leave it until morning."

"I will accompany you to your appointment," he answered.

I wondered why the devil he was so anxious for me to see the colonel right away. "It is with a lady," I explained.

His eyes flickered in surprise, then slight distaste, as though speaking with a lady should never come between a man and his business. I had never bothered to wonder why there was no Mrs. Denis. James Denis was cold all the way through.

"Very well, then," he said, his expression still neutral. "We will fix an appointment for breakfast tomorrow. Nine o'clock. I will tell Colonel Naveau that he is welcome to spend the night with me."

I was certain that Colonel Naveau would not like that arrangement one bit. I was equally certain that Denis would give him no choice.

I took a casual sip of ale, as though his turning up at one of my haunts did not unnerve me. "You could not tell me, while you are here, who murdered Henry Turner?"

The corners of his mouth moved in what might be an expression of amusement in a more feeling man. "I am afraid not, Captain. I did not anticipate that your colonel would get himself into trouble at a society ball, or I should have had a man in place to prevent it."

I was not sure whether he joked or not. His countenance was blank, as usual, as he rose to his feet. He did not shake my hand, but he bowed and took up his hat. "Until morning, then, Captain."

I nodded stiffly in return. Denis made for the door and exited, placing his hat on his head precisely the moment before he stepped outside. His lackeys fell in with him like trained dogs.

Bartholomew drifted back to the table. "Well, that was what I call interesting," he remarked.

"Yes." I watched the dark doorway that Denis had exited, wondering. "Well, I will know more what he wants tomorrow. Tonight, we will take a hackney coach to Cavendish Square and pay a call." I drank the last of my ale and thumped the tankard to the table. "No doubt Denis's man will follow and tell him exactly who we visited and why."

Bartholomew grinned, a little shakily, and then we left the tavern. The married Anne Tolliver smiled at us both as we went.

THE house in Cavendish Square was no different from its fellows, being tall and narrow with tall, narrow windows and a tall, narrow front door with a polished knocker.

I arrived at half past one precisely, and the maid, Grady, answered the door. She seemed used to dealing with visitors at all hours, because she calmly ushered me upstairs to a small sitting room.

The room was rather anonymous, with fashionable upholstered Sheraton chairs in a salmon-colored stripe and studded wood, salmon-colored swags on the windows, and cream silk on the walls. Nothing personal marred the room, as though the house's inhabitants had ordered the furnishing to be as elegant and innocuous as possible.

I expected Mr. Bennington to pop up at any moment, drawling sarcasm about his wife receiving male visitors in the small hours of the morning. Grady must have noticed me looking about, because she said, "Mr. Bennington is staying at his hotel tonight," and departed to fetch her mistress.

Again, I wondered at the strangeness of the Bennington relationship. They'd married for convenience, that was certain, but what was the convenience? And would a husband truly vacate the house so that his wife could receive a gentleman?

I paced the room while I mulled this over. The room was cool despite the fire on the hearth, its anonymity shutting me out.

I turned when the door opened behind me. Claire Bennington paused on the threshold just as she'd paused on the stage earlier tonight, waiting for the adulation to die down before she spoke her lines. She was dressed in a peignoir, similar to the one that Lady Breckenridge had worn when she'd received me a few days ago.

The difference was that Lady Breckenridge wore her peignoir with awareness of how it enhanced her body. I, as a man, had not been unmoved by the garment. Mrs. Bennington looked like a child in clothes too old for her.

Mrs. Bennington glided to the center of the room. She had no rehearsed lines, and she obviously found it difficult to begin. She wet her lips, but said nothing.

I was struck anew with how young she was. I'd read in newspaper articles that she was barely past twenty, not much more than a child. She might be comely, and she might have seen the sometimes harsh world of theatre, but she seemed far less aware than the game girls to whom I'd distributed shillings earlier that night.

"Mrs. Bennington," I prompted her. "Why did you ask to see me?"

She wet her lips again, then touched the lapel of my coat, her fingers light as a ghost's. "Captain Lacey," she said, "I am so very much afraid."

She let the words roll dramatically from her tongue. But I realized that as much as she embellished the phrase, her eyes held real fear.

"Of what?" I asked. I gentled my voice. "It is all right. You may tell me."

She studied me with round eyes. Then she drew a breath said hurriedly, "I am afraid of Mr. Grenville."

CHAPTER 12

THE statement was so unexpected that I stared.

"Of Grenville? Good lord, why?"

She shuddered, her fingers trembling on my chest. "Please tell him to stay away."

"Grenville is a kind man," I said, puzzled. "He might not show it at times, but he has a good heart. There is no need to be afraid of him."

I felt as though I were trying to still the fears of a child. She swung away from me, the skirts of her peignoir sweeping dramatically. "Yes, there is need. He comes here, and to my rooms at the theatre, and remonstrates with me. He scolds me, grows angry when I speak to young men. Why should I not speak to young men? There is no harm in it. I am young, and Mr. Bennington sees nothing wrong in my speaking with gentlemen of my own age. But Mr. Grenville will have none of it. He shouts at me." Her hazel eyes filled with tears. "He is so jealous that he frightens me."

"Jealous——" I broke off, astonished. I had never seen Grenville behave like a jealous lover. With the exception of his obsession with Marianne, he'd always conducted his affairs coolly, never voicing any approbation of the lady, no matter what she did. When the liaison ended, he departed from the lady just as coolly.

Only Marianne had ever angered him, and that was not jealousy but frustration. Marianne could drive anyone distracted.

But the idea that Grenville drove off Mrs. Bennington's suitors and took her to task for speaking to them was beyond belief.

"It is true," Mrs. Bennington said fiercely, as though guessing my thoughts. "Ask Grady if you do not believe me. The last time he came to see me, he was in a horrible temper. He saw young Mr. Carew try to kiss my hand. Mr. Grenville threw his walking stick across the room and threatened to give the poor man a thrashing if he ever came near me again."

I blinked. "Forgive me, Mrs. Bennington, but I find this difficult to credit. Was this Carew behaving badly to you?"

She shook her head, golden curls dancing. "Indeed, no. Mr. Carew was quite the gentleman. But Mr. Grenville did not like it." She clasped her hands, pleading with me. "You must believe me, Captain. I am not lying. I do not know how to invent things. Mr. Bennington says it is because I have no imagination."

"Mr. Bennington should not be quite so rude to you."

She shrugged as though her husband's jibes slid from her easily. "Mr. Grenville said so, too. He also said that I should try to obtain a divorce from Mr. Bennington. Or an annulment. I have grounds, he says, because Mr. Bennington cannot father children."

She named Bennington's impotency without a blush, indicating that she did not share a bed with her husband.

"I did not marry him for children," she went on ingenuously. "I do not want children. I could not go on the stage if I were increasing. Mr. Bennington said he would allow me to continue acting, which is the only thing I like to do. I was very popular in Italy, but I had run into a bit of difficulty with debts, you see."

"And he offered to pay them if you married him?"

"Yes. He has ever so much money from a legacy, from the Scottish branch of his family, he says. He paid my notes as though they were nothing." She toyed with the frills on her bosom. "His name is not really Bennington, you know. I am not supposed to tell anyone that. But I felt I could trust you."

I wondered how many other people she'd babbled this secret to, and if Bennington knew she was the kind of woman who could not keep a secret.

"I do not know what his real name is, actually. 'I will be called Mr. Bennington,' he said to me. 'And you will be Mrs. Bennington. And none need to know any other.' " She did a fair imitation of Bennington's drawling voice, which might have amused me any other time.

I wondered. Perhaps the reason Bennington had lived in Italy most of his life was that he dared not return to England under his own name. Trouble with creditors? Or over a woman? Or was it some more sinister crime?

Perhaps those long-fingered hands had held a knife before, had thrust it with uncanny accuracy into a heart that had stopped beating.

Bennington, or whatever his true name had been, had promised to take care of Claire's debts and let her stay on the stage that she loved. So that he might return to England under a new name? His wife so eclipsed him that most people thought of him, when they bothered to, as "Mrs. Bennington's husband." A good hiding place. But hiding from what?

I also knew that a falsified name on a marriage license meant no marriage at all, unless he'd legally changed his name to Bennington first. Granted, he'd married in Italy, and I was not terribly familiar with the marriage laws there. I wondered what was going on.

This young woman seemed to find the arrangement perfectly acceptable, at any rate. She had what she wanted, freedom to remain on the stage and security from creditors.

And she provided a blind for a husband that she cared nothing about.

"I am beginning to agree with Grenville," I said, half to myself.

Her eyes widened. "Please do not say you will take his side. He has me very frightened. His jealousy will be the death of me, I think."

Her voice rose to a dramatic pitch. She clasped her hands and looked at me wildly.

"I will speak to him," I promised.

She sighed, putting every ounce of her stage presence into the throaty little moan. "Thank you, Captain Lacey. I knew you would not fail me."

She flung herself away from me, the skirts of her peignoir swirling. Then, rather anticlimactically, she stopped and rang for her maid.

"You attended the ball at the Gillises' the night Henry Turner died," I said, trying to bend to my true purpose for visiting her.

Her dramatic expression faded, and she made a face, much like a girl who has been given porridge when she expected sausages. "Yes, that was quite horrible."

"It was." I paused. "Did you know Henry Turner?"

She tilted her head. "No. I'd never heard of him until he got himself killed." She sounded sublimely uninterested.

I asked a few more questions about Turner and whether she'd seen him or Colonel Brandon enter the anteroom, but it soon became clear that she had noticed nothing. She had noticed only the people who noticed her.

The maid Grady entered the room in answer to her summons. She frowned darkly at me.

"Grady," Mrs. Bennington said. "Tell Captain Lacey how Mr. Grenville behaved the other night."

Grady looked me up and down, like a guard dog eyeing an intruder. "He did rail at her, that is a fact. I was afraid I'd have to call for the watch."

"And he threw his walking stick?" I asked, still surprised.

"Yes, sir. Look." She marched to the wall and put her hand on the cream silk. "Just there. It's left a mark."

Below her work-worn hand was a faint black mark and a tear in the fabric. "The footman couldn't quite get it to come clean. Have to do the whole wall over, like as not."

I straightened up, very much wondering. "I will speak to him," I repeated.

Grady gave me a severe look. So had my father's housekeeper looked at me when as a small boy I'd come home plastered from head to foot with mud. "See that you do," she said.

I would have smiled at the memory if the situation had not been so bizarre. I thanked Mrs. Bennington for her time, promised again that I would look into the matter of Grenville's strange tempers, and departed.

GRENVILLE and Marianne had gone from my rooms by the time Bartholomew and I returned to Grimpen Lane.

I felt I could hardly look up Grenville that night to make him explain what he meant by terrorizing the feeble-witted Mrs. Bennington, so I went to bed, conscious that not much later, I would be breakfasting with James Denis and my Frenchman.

In the morning, I dressed with cold fingers and rode across London in a gentle rain to number 45, Curzon Street. The facade of this house was unadorned, but the interior was elegant and understated, in a chill way. Mrs. Bennington's sitting room had reminded me somewhat of this house—cool and distant.

Denis's butler let me in and took me to the dining room. I'd seen this room before, but not for a meal. When I entered, two people sat at the table, Denis and the Frenchman. A third setting had been placed at one end of the table, for me, I assumed.

James Denis sat in an armchair at the head of the table, elegant in dress as usual, betraying no sign that he'd stayed up very late last night and had risen relatively early this morning. I reflected that I had never seen James Denis do anything so human as eat. I had always imagined that he must exist on water. However, he had a plate of real food before him, eggs and beef, a half-loaf of bread, and a crock of butter.

The other man at the table was the man who'd attacked me in my rooms. His close-cropped hair was a mix of gray and brown, and his eyes were dark. He wore a suit tailored to his lean body, a fact that spoke of expense. His emperor might have lost the war, but this colonel still had his fortune.

His plate held thick slices of ham, which he was shoveling into his mouth as I entered. Over his fork, he shot me a look of defiance.

"Captain Lacey," Denis said in his cool voice. "May I introduce Colonel Naveau."

Colonel Naveau nodded once, his eyes filled with dislike. I bowed to him before I took the seat that the butler indicated.

"Colonel Naveau is quite the pugilist," I remarked, as the footman slid a plate of steaming sausages in front of me. "Gentleman Jackson might be interested in some of his moves. Were you cavalry?"

Naveau watched me a moment, then inclined his head. "A hussar."

"Ah." I had guessed he was light cavalry because of his lean muscles, which spoke of hours in a saddle. French hussars had been known for their not-always-prudent courage. They'd been fond of throwing away their lives in some act of bravery that usually cost the English dearly. "They fought hard at Talavera," I said. "I was there. In the Thirty-Fifth Light Dragoons."

Naveau grunted. "The Thirty-Fifth Light did well at Waterloo." He barely moved his lips when he spoke.

"So I heard." I lifted my fork and cut a bite of sausage. "I had retired before then. I was injured."

"Captain Lacey's commander," Denis broke in, "was

Colonel Aloysius Brandon. The one who now awaits trial for the murder of Henry Turner."

"Yes, I have heard." Naveau's tone was clipped. "I read of Monsieur Turner's death in the London newspapers."

"You knew I had searched Turner's rooms," I said. "And you thought I had found the letter with which Turner had been blackmailing Colonel Brandon and Mrs. Harper. You followed me home and waylaid me in my own lodgings in an attempt to find it."

"I did." He seemed in no way ashamed.

"I have puzzled and puzzled why on earth you would want a love letter between Brandon and Mrs. Harper. Was Mrs. Harper your mistress? Or your wife, perhaps?"

Naveau's brows drew together. "I have no wife. And what is this love letter you speak of? I was not looking for a love letter; I was seeking a document. A very important document. Mr. Denis says you will know where to find it."

I looked from him to Denis. "What are you talking about?"

Denis broke in smoothly. "Mr. Turner stayed for a time in Paris, as a guest of Colonel Naveau. After Mr. Turner had departed for London, Colonel Naveau discovered that a document was missing from his house. He searched, but concluded that Turner had absconded with it. Naveau followed Turner to London, then learned of Turner's death after he arrived."

"So Henry Turner stole a document from Naveau. What has this to do with Colonel Brandon?"

"Because your colonel knows where it is," Denis said. "Or at least, where it last was."

The footman came forward to pour more hot coffee into my cup. "I am confused," I said. "Why should Colonel Brandon know anything about a French document?"

Naveau made a noise of exasperation. "Because Henry was blackmailing your colonel for the document. I know this."

"Turner was blackmailing Brandon over a letter to or from Imogene Harper," I said slowly. A letter that would make their affair embarrassingly public. Adultery was against the law, after all.

"No, no, Captain. Not a love letter. A letter he and Mrs. Harper wrote while we were all in Spain. A letter to me."

I blinked. "To you?"

"Yes." Naveau seemed annoyed at my disbelief.

"What is this document?"

"Nothing of concern to you," Naveau snapped back. "It is in French."

"I read French."

"Still you would not understand it."

"And Colonel Brandon would?" I asked.

"Mrs. Harper would."

"Why Mrs. Harper?"

For answer, Naveau gazed at Denis. "You told me he would help, without question."

"No," Denis replied. "I said that he would find the document, but Captain Lacey must always ask questions. It is his nature."

"It is an inconvenient nature."

I ignored him. "Why did you promise him that I would find it?" I asked Denis.

Denis laid his knife and three-tined fork carefully across his plate. "The matter is simple. Colonel Naveau needs this document. He has entered a bargain with me to restore it to him. You are close to your colonel and can persuade him to tell you where it is. If it has not turned up among Turner's things, that means he either destroyed it or passed it to someone, most likely, to Colonel Brandon."

"He has paid you," I said, my eyes narrowing.

"Yes," Denis said.

"In that case, you should have told him that one of your own men would find the document."

Denis looked at me a long time. Nothing existed behind his cold expression but more coldness. "I did."

I understood the implication. From the first, James Denis had told me that he wanted me to work for him. I had refused, because the man was a criminal, no matter how

well he lived or what good deeds he might have helped me
do. Any help he'd given me had been to suit his own pur-
poses.

He had done me favors in order to make me beholden to
him. I would pay him back, he said, in his own coin.

Now, he was calling in a favor. He knew that I'd want to
find the document in any case, in order to clear Colonel
Brandon. He was holding my feet to the fire.

"I do not work for you," I tried.

"No," he agreed. "But you need this paper. Colonel
Naveau will remain here as my guest, and you will bring it
to him."

I felt my quick temper stir. "I want the paper only to help
prove Brandon's innocence."

Denis lifted his slim shoulders. "If you wish, but you
will bring it to me and not give it to the magistrates."

His gaze, if anything, grew colder. I remembered what
had happened to a young coachman who had once disobeyed Denis. Denis had never told me of the matter, but I
knew that Denis had had one of his lackeys murder the
man.

"I searched Turner's rooms thoroughly," I said. "I also
paid a visit to his father in Surrey, and looked over his
rooms there. I found nothing. No documents, no letters of
any sort." I looked at Denis. "What makes you believe I can
find this for him?"

"Because you have an uncanny knack for turning up
things that need to be found. You will do this."

I promised nothing. He watched me steadily, but
damned if I'd bow my head and obey him.

I pushed away my now cold sausages and rose to my
feet. The butler appeared in an instant, understanding that I
was going.

"I have no doubt that the man you have following me
will report my every action to you," I said.

"Yes." Denis's face was expressionless.

"Then I need make no vows to you that I will find and
return the paper. You will know what I do."

He inclined his head. He had no need to answer.

Colonel Naveau looked blustery, but I ignored him. I departed the room without taking leave or saying good-bye, and followed the butler down the stairs again to the street.

STILL seething, I walked the length of Curzon Street through Clarges Street to Piccadilly. As I walked, I again went over the extraordinary conversation I'd just had. A document, not a letter, written by Brandon and Mrs. Harper to Colonel Naveau, in French.

My temper began to cool as worry took over. James Denis had been strangely insistent that I pursue this. Why? So that he could claim that I worked for him? Or for some other reason?

And why the devil should Brandon care about the document? What was the fool trying so hard to keep from me? The only thing certain was that there was more to this than any party let on. Denis had not asked me to search for the paper to please Colonel Naveau, no matter how much the man promised to pay him. Denis did things for his own reasons, and not all of those reasons involved money.

I sighed, wiping rain from my face. I had searched Turner's rooms already and found nothing. But I might as well do so again. I might have overlooked *something*.

As I passed through Clarges Street, I wondered whether Grenville was in his house there, with Marianne. I deliberately turned my gaze away from the doors and windows, as though to give Grenville his privacy, even from the street.

Grenville was another person I was not happy with. Why had he gone to Mrs. Bennington and berated her so? I might be able to accuse Mrs. Bennington of exaggerating his behavior, overdramatizing it, but her plain and very sensible maid had said the same thing.

My friends, I reflected, were busily driving me mad.

I turned onto Piccadilly, making my slow way past Berkeley Street, Dover Street, Albermarle Street, and Old Bond Street. I passed Burlington House, a huge edifice that had dominated Piccadilly since the reign of Charles II. Owned now by Lord George Cavendish, the interior was lavish, I'd been told, with no expense spared on decoration. Grenville had pronounced it excessive.

Turner's landlord looked puzzled when I said I wanted to see his rooms again, but he took me upstairs, perhaps hoping I wanted to let them myself.

Turner's sitting room was a mess. Open crates stood about half-filled. The furniture had been lined up along one wall, apparently waiting for men to load it into a wagon and drive it to Epsom.

In the bedroom, I found similar disarray, along with Hazleton, Turner's valet. The man lay across Turner's bed, fully clothed, snoring loudly. Two empty bottles, which had probably held more of Turner's claret, stood on the night table.

I approached the bed and shook Hazleton's booted foot.

The man snorted. He fumbled his hand to his face and rubbed one eye. "Wha—? Devil take it, man."

"Hazleton," I said, shaking the foot more firmly.

Hazleton blinked some more, focusing on me at the foot of the bed. He sat up straight, then groaned and pressed his hand to his forehead.

"What a head I have," he mumbled.

"Emptying bottles of claret by yourself will do that." I dragged a chair from a corner and sat down. "While you are recovering, I want you to tell me everything you know about a Colonel Naveau, and Turner's last visit to Paris."

"Ah. You know about that, do you?"

"Not as much as I'd like. I have met Colonel Naveau. These bruises on my face are courtesy of him. You would have saved me much trouble if you'd told me about him from the start."

Hazleton gave me a belligerent look. "Well, you didn't ask, did you?"

"Did he come here the same day I did, looking for something?"

"That he did. Not two minutes after you departed."

"And you helpfully told him that I had already been here, and anything the colonel needed to find, I likely had?"

"Yes," Hazleton said defiantly. "I didn't know he would crack your face. I couldn't, could I?"

"What was he looking for?" I asked.

Hazleton looked surprised. "Well, now, you'd know about that."

"No. I looked, and I found nothing. Naveau has found nothing. I know the document is a paper written in French, but I do not know what it is."

He shrugged. "I don't know either. I can't read Frog-speak."

"Tell me why Turner went to Paris, what he did there, and why he came home."

"Persistent, aren't you, Captain?" He pressed his hand to his head again. "I'll need a bit of something to settle my head. So I can remember."

I conceded. Hazleton climbed down from the bed and opened the armoire. In the bottom stood four more bottles. He uncorked one and poured ruby red liquid into a glass. "Have some, Captain?" he offered.

I declined. I craved coffee, not wine, and I would reward myself with some after I finished with Hazleton.

Hazleton drank, then let out a long sigh. "That's good, that is. I'm knackered from straightening out my master's affairs. And then, once I'm finished, that is the end for old Bill Hazleton. Mr. Turner—senior, that is—said he'd look after me, but a man needs only one valet. So what is to become of old Bill?"

"Perhaps Colonel Naveau can avail himself of your services," I said, not entirely serious, but wanting him to get on with it.

Hazleton took another long gulp, then collapsed on the bed. "Oh, no, never him. That man frightens me, and not just because he's a Frenchie. And anyway, he was a spy. You did know that, didn't you? That he was an exploring officer during the war? For the Frogs?"

CHAPTER 13

No, I had not known that. Both Denis and Colonel Naveau had omitted that interesting detail.

Exploring officers had been those men sent off in the night to do covert missions for Wellington or for Bonaparte's generals. They crept across lands held by the enemy and spied out troop movements or intercepted papers or infiltrated the enemy camp itself. Men who could speak fluent French were prized by the English; likewise those fluent in English were prized by the French. So many Englishmen and Frenchmen had mixed blood, mothers from London and fathers from Paris, that it was difficult to decide sometimes who fought for whom.

Exploring officers had done a dangerous job, I recognized, but they had been more or less despised. Instead of standing and fighting in the open, they skulked about in darkness and lied and cheated their way into defeating the enemy. Commanders prized their exploring officers and found them distasteful at the same time.

Naveau had a fairly thick accent, so I doubted he'd ever

infiltrated English lines, but he might have been a receiver of information.

My heart grew cold. The fact that Brandon and Mrs. Harper had written to Naveau during the Peninsular War filled me with foreboding. Why the devil should they have written him? That Colonel Brandon, a high stickler for loyalty, would send a document to a French exploring officer for any reason seemed ludicrous.

Something was wrong here, very wrong.

"Tell me about your master's visit to Paris," I prompted Hazleton.

Hazleton rubbed his face and took a long gulp of port. "Well now, we went out to the continent there about a year ago. Mr. Turner likes to travel. Don't know why. The food is rotten, and I can't understand a word no one says, even excepting that some of the ladies in Milan and Paris are sweet as honey. Not as they wash as much as I'd like, but they're friendly. Mr. Turner met this fellow Naveau in Milan. After that, he tells me that we're packing up to go with Colonel Naveau to his home in Paris."

"What was the purpose of the visit to Naveau?" I asked. "Business?"

"He never told me why. I assume business. I know that the two of them didn't always agree. Shouted at each other something fierce, like me dad had come back to life, sometimes. I thought my master would want to stay in France forever, but one night, he wakes me up and says we're going back to England. 'Why?' I asks. 'Tired of the food, are you?' He boxed my ears for impertinence, but I got up and packed his duds, and we fled back to England."

He drained his glass and upended the bottle for more. His legs buckled suddenly, and he sat down on a chair. He looked up at me with a rueful grin. "A drop affects me more these days."

"What was Naveau like? Did you speak to him much?"

"Not I. Didn't have much to say to him, did I? But his own man, name of Jacot, had no complaints about him. Told me about his being an exploring officer and what they did in the war. Naveau was decorated for services to the French army, he said. Very intelligent man, I gather. Good at soldiering. A bit at a loss in civilian life."

I knew the truth in that in my own case. "Napoleon was deposed and the French king restored. Did Naveau remain a good republican?"

"Seems like he was glad all the fighting was over, no matter who was at the helm. I heard him say that war was bad for France and that so many men had died for so little. But Mr. Turner didn't like to hear about the war and the colonel's career. Every time Colonel Naveau started going on about life in the army, Mr. Turner would change the subject."

I thought of Turner, young and fresh-faced with his soft curls of brown hair. I imagined that listening to stories of an old war horse had wearied him.

"About this paper Naveau was looking for," I began.

Hazleton shrugged. "Don't know much about it. Naveau came bursting in here and started going on about Mr. Turner being a thief and ruining him. He demanded I return a paper what Mr. Turner stole. I said I didn't know nothing about it, but that you had been up here for a time by yourself, so maybe you'd taken it. Then he ran off after you." Hazleton glanced at my fading bruises again. "Didn't know he'd pummel you."

"I would like to know why that document was worth pummeling me for."

"No idea, Captain. No idea at all. At any rate, it's not here."

"It seems it is not. You never saw it?"

Hazleton burped. "If I did, I wouldn't have paid it much mind, if it were in Frenchie talk, 'cause I don't know it, as I said."

"Then how do you communicate with your ladies in Paris?"

Hazleton snorted. "Oh, I know enough for *that*. You don't need much language to tell a lady you fancy her, now do you?"

"No, I suppose you do not."

I asked him a few more questions, but it was clear that Hazleton did not know what the document was or where it could be found. I left him to finish imbibing the last of his master's claret.

Outside, I bought a bit of bread from one vendor and coffee from another. I chewed this repast, and thought about what to do.

The likeliest person to have that document, if it had not been destroyed, was Mrs. Harper. If Brandon had told me the truth, if he'd met with Turner at eleven o'clock, made the exchange—a bank draft for the document—and left the room again with Turner still alive, then he must have rid himself of the document between eleven o'clock and about one, when Pomeroy's patroller took him to Bow Street and made him turn out his pockets.

After meeting with Turner, Brandon had taken Imogene Harper aside in one of the alcoves in the ballroom. Had he passed her the paper and told her to hide or destroy it? Or had he strolled to a nearby fireplace and burned it himself?

It would have taken some time to push it into a fireplace and watch until it burned to ash. He would have had to ensure that the paper actually did burn and did not fall behind a log or into the ash grate. I could not fathom that no one would notice him doing this.

No, he must have passed it to Imogene Harper. But then, why had Mrs. Harper come to search Turner's rooms?

I ground my teeth in frustration. Nothing made sense.

Piccadilly ran before me, misty in the rain, skirting St. James's, the abode of clubs and hotels and homes, as well as gaming halls where a fortune could be lost on a single throw of dice. Not that well-heeled gentlemen did not lose fortunes and lands in the clubs—a man could wager his entire wealth in White's on whether the sun would come out the next day.

As I walked again in the direction of Green Park, I reflected on Mr. Turner's propensity for wagers and his keen luck. Leland had told me that he'd wager whether a cat would walk a certain direction or whether a maid would be sick or well, arbitrary events. I wondered if his machinations with the document were part of a wager—can Mr. Turner procure a document from a French colonel and blackmail an English colonel with it?

I found this far-fetched, but I wondered how Turner knew that the document would be important to Colonel Brandon and Imogene Harper.

It was only ten o'clock, and few of the *haut ton* were up and about. The streets were busy with servants and working people scurrying about to make ready for when their masters rose at two or three.

Not all Mayfair fodder slept late, however. I did see two or three gentlemen, one riding, two driving themselves in phaetons to whichever activity beckoned them. I strolled into Green Park, observing nannies with children who'd been brought to London with fathers and mothers for the Season.

I thought about my own daughter running about camp with little regard for danger, and her frantic mother railing at me to stop her. Carlotta had been raised by a nanny and a governess and had expected her daughter to be looked after in the same manner. I had hired a wet nurse, naturally, but after that, Carlotta was dismayed to find she'd have to take care of the baby herself.

I had not minded looking after Gabriella and had not understood my wife's distress. Louisa, too, had lavished attention on the child. But Carlotta had been miserable, and I had not been patient with her.

I wanted to see Gabriella again. I could taste the wanting in my mouth. I wanted to see Carlotta again, as well. I wanted to end things cleanly with divorce or annulment or whatever solicitors could cook up in their canny brains. I wanted to be free so that I could turn to the rest of my life.

Lady Breckenridge had told me that any victory she would have with me would be hollow. I did not want that to be true. I was an impetuous man and liked to rush into affairs of the heart, but this time, I wanted to ensure that what I had with Donata was real.

She had thought the reason for my hesitation was that my heart was engaged elsewhere. The truth was that I wanted to go to her a free man, so that if I offered her my heart, it would come with no impediments.

The surprising thing was that Lady Breckenridge seemed not to mind that I had nothing to offer her. She asked nothing from me but myself, and I knew better than to sneer at such a compliment.

I stood watching the nannies herd the children for a while longer, then turned my steps toward a hackney stand. I needed to consult Pomeroy to discover where Mrs. Harper lived, and then pay her a visit.

WHEN I left Bow Street later, a lad in the street tried to pick my pocket. My hand closed around a bone-thin wrist, and the small, dirty-faced boy attached to it cursed at me.

I released him and gave him a thump on the shoulder. "Clear off and go home."

He jumped and fled as fast as he could, no doubt thinking me a fool for not marching him off to the magistrate on the spot. He must have been desperate—or else highly confident—to try to rob me just outside the Bow Street office.

Mrs. Harper, I'd learned from Pomeroy's clerk, had lodgings in a small court north of Oxford Street, near Portman Square. I decided to take care of one other errand on the way, and took a hackney back to Mayfair and South Audley Street. At one o'clock, I was knocking on the door of Lady Breckenridge's townhouse. Barnstable opened the door to me.

"Has her ladyship arisen yet?" I asked.

"She has indeed, sir." He looked critically at my face. "Healing nicely, sir. Always swear by my herbal bath. If you'll come this way, sir."

He led me upstairs to Lady Breckenridge's sitting room and left me there while he ascended to her rooms to inform her I'd called. I steeled myself for her to send me away, but before long, I heard her light footsteps approach.

I turned as Lady Breckenridge entered the room. She looked awake and alert, but she did not smile at me. She wore a light green morning gown with a lace shawl around her shoulders and had pinned up her hair under a white lace cap.

"I apologize for visiting you at such an appalling hour," I said, bowing.

Her slim chin dipped. "I would have called it a beastly hour myself, but never mind. My cook informs me that she has prepared tea for me. I can offer that and cakes if you like."

"I am full of bread and coffee, thank you. I have been wandering about London eating from vendors' trays."

She gave a slight shrug as though she did not care whether I drank her tea or not. "I assume you had some reason for this call."

"I did." I hesitated. When I had decided to come here, it had seemed a good idea, but she did not seem happy to see me. After the manner in which we had parted the last time, I could hardly blame her. Her stance was most unwelcoming.

"I came to ask if you might give me an introduction to Lady Gillis," I said. "I would like to speak to her about the night Turner died, and I would like to look over the ballroom again."

Lady Breckenridge folded her arms over her gown, the lace shawl sliding down her shoulders. "I see." Her voice was cool.

"I have presumed," I said quickly. "I beg your pardon. I did not mean to take advantage of you."

"You do presume." She gave me a quiet look. "But I am happy that you did."

Something inside me relaxed. "The last thing I want is to take advantage of you."

"The last thing?" She gave me a half-smile. "I do not believe you, you know. There must be plenty of other things that you do not want more than that. But very well, I will take you to visit Lady Gillis, so that you may once more look at the scene of the crime. Give me a day or two to speak to her. From what I hear, she is most distraught, and has refused to leave her bed."

"I am sorry to hear that. I do not wish to distress her further, but I truly need to see the anteroom and the ballroom again."

"You will," she said, her tone confident. She trailed her long-fingered hands down her arms. "I will give you a bit of advice, however. If you wish to speak to ladies by the pillars at Covent Garden Theatre, you should not speak so loudly or so obviously."

Her face was very white, and I saw something flicker in her eyes. Hurt, I thought, and anger.

"Damn it all," I muttered.

I had hoped that my conversation with Marianne would go unnoticed, but I ought to have known better. My face warmed. "As I have observed before, you are a very well-informed lady."

"Good heavens, Gabriel, it is all over Mayfair. I could not stir a step last night without someone taking me aside and asking me whether I knew that my Captain Lacey had been pursuing a bit of muslin under the piazza."

"They should not have spoken to you of such a thing at all," I said indignantly.

"Yes, well, my acquaintances are a bit more blunt than necessary. They seemed to believe I would find this *on dit* interesting."

"They ought to have better things to talk about."

"I agree. I did tell them quite clearly to mind their own business." She was rigid, her eyes sparkling in anger.

"Gossip is misinformed, in this case," I said. "She was not a bit of muslin. She was Marianne Simmons."

Her brows arched. "And what, pray tell, is a Marianne Simmons?"

"Hmm," I said as I mused how to explain Marianne Simmons. "She is an actress. She occupied rooms above mine for a time, and made the habit of stealing my candles, my coal, my snuff, and my breakfast whenever she felt the need. I let her; she never had enough money. She is shrewish and irritating and smart and bad-tempered, and has fallen quite in love with Lucius Grenville, although I must swear you to silence on that."

She listened, interested. I told her of Marianne's habit of accosting me every time she perceived something wrong between herself and Grenville, which was often.

As I spoke, Lady Breckenridge relaxed, and by the end of my tale she looked slightly amused. "So you have become the peacemaker."

"Unfortunately. I do not know how effective a peacemaker I am. I generally want to shake the both of them. I hope that the storm has died down for now, but I know better."

She strolled to me. "Poor Gabriel. Besieged on all sides. Your colonel and his wife; Grenville and his lady-bird."

"True. They resent my intrusion, but they also expect me to have answers for them."

"That must be difficult for you." She spoke as though she believed it.

"It is difficult. And it is my own fault. If I minded my own affairs, I would not get myself in half the predicaments I do."

"No, you would sit at a club and play cards until numbers danced before your eyes. It is your nature to interfere, and you have done some good because of it." She laid her hand on my arm. "Besides, if you did not poke your nose into other people's business, you would not have journeyed down to Kent last summer."

She did not smile, but her eyes held a spark of amusement. Last summer, I had gone to Kent to investigate a crime and had met her there in a sunny billiards room, where she'd blown cigarillo smoke in my face and told me I was a fool.

I lifted her hand to my lips and kissed her fingers. Her eyes darkened.

"Here is where things grew complicated on your last visit," she said.

I kissed her fingers again. "I very much wish that everything was simple."

She grew quiet. Slowly, I slid my arm about her waist. The lace cap smelled clean with a slight overlay of cinnamon. She always smelled a little of spice, this lady.

I truly wished things were simple, that I could come here, as though I had a right to, and sit in her parlor and hold her hand. I wanted more than that, of course. I wanted to love her with my body and drowse with her in the comfortable dark.

I wanted things to be at ease between us, no secrets, no jealousies, no fear. I gently kissed her lips.

She smiled as we drew apart. "You must continue prying into other people's business until you put everything aright, Gabriel. It is your way."

"I wish I could put it aright. But this affair is a tangle."

"You will persist." She stepped from my clasp, but held my hand. "Who are you off to see this afternoon?"

"Mrs. Harper. I must discover what happened to that piece of paper she and Brandon were willing to pay Turner for."

"How exhausting for you. Go in my coach, no need to take a horrid hackney."

"I had decided to walk."

She gave me a deprecating smile. "Your stay in the country made you terribly hearty, did it? There is a dreadful damp. Take the carriage."

I gave her a mocking bow. "As you wish, my lady."

She lifted her brows, then she laughed. "Oh, do go away, Gabriel. I will send word when I have smoothed the way with Lady Gillis. And remember not to speak to your Miss Simmons under the piazza again, or tongues will continue to wag."

She mocked me as only she could, but as I departed, I thought only on how much I liked to hear her laugh.

•   •   •

LADY Breckenridge's coachman did drive me to Mrs. Harper's lodgings. Lady Breckenridge had apparently given orders to Barnstable to prepare the coach before she'd even spoken to me, and he had it waiting for me outside the front door.

I easily found the fashionable house near Portman Square in which Mrs. Harper resided, but the lady was not at home. "Your card, sir," said a flat-faced maid, holding out her hand. I put one of my cards into it, and she backed inside and closed the door. That, for now, was that.

I found myself at a standstill in my investigation, so I took care of more personal business, such as paying a few debts and purchasing a new pair of serviceable gloves. I stopped at a jeweler's and looked at a diamond bracelet. I envied Grenville, who could have swept in and picked up anything he liked. I would have to take up another secretarial position before long, if I wished to purchase trinkets for my lady.

I tried to call on Grenville, but he, too, was not at home. Matthias told me that Grenville had sent word that he would be staying at the Clarges Street house. He winked knowingly.

I hoped that the news meant a closing of the breach between himself and Marianne, though I was disappointed that I could not speak to him. If he cared for Marianne, his behavior toward Mrs. Bennington was most puzzling.

I went from there to Whitechapel and my appointment with Sir Montague Harris.

The room in the public office was a rather cold and austere place. The fire smoked and burned fitfully, and the wine Sir Montague offered me was nearly sour. I told him of all I'd discovered from Turner's funeral to my interview with Hazleton today.

"What you say about Bennington interests me," Sir Montague said. He shifted his bulk in his chair, which had grown to fit him. "If he is so clever, why does he tell his feather-headed wife to keep it secret that he's changed his name?"

"I cannot say. Either he is not as clever as he pretends to be, or he counted on Mrs. Bennington spreading around that secret. Although for what purpose, I cannot imagine."

"Why change his name at all?" Sir Montague mused.

"Running from creditors?" I suggested.

"Or the law. I will focus my eye on this Mr. Bennington. Dig into his past, find people who knew him in Italy, and so forth. I will enjoy it."

I had no doubt he would. Sir Montague was shrewd and intelligent and little got past him.

He turned that shrewd eye on me. "Anything else you wish to tell me, Captain?"

I had avoided talking about Colonel Naveau and the paper he wanted me to find. I was not yet certain what it meant for Brandon, and I somehow did not want Sir Montague examining the matter too closely.

"No," I answered.

His eyes twinkled, as usual. "This is where I, as a common magistrate, have the advantage over you, Captain Lacey."

I tried to look puzzled. "What do you mean?"

"I mean that when I investigate crime, I am purely outside it. I can look at the facts without worry, without knowing that a suspect is a dear friend."

I barked a laugh. "I hardly call Brandon a dear friend these days."

"But you are close to him. His life and yours are tied in many ways. You feel the need to protect him, for various and perhaps conflicting reasons." He spread his hands. "I, on the other hand, see only the facts."

I could not argue that he likely viewed things more clearly than I did where Brandon was concerned. "And what do the facts tell you?"

He gave me a serious look. "That Brandon was mixed up in something he should not have been. That the death of Turner was an aid to him. That Mrs. Harper knows more than she lets on. That you are afraid to trust yourself."

The last was certainly true. I had some ideas about Brandon's involvement that I did not like. I had admired Colonel Brandon once, and some part of that admiration still had not died. He'd disappointed me—as much as I'd disappointed him—but I still wanted that hero of old to exist.

"What do I do?" I asked, half to myself.

"Discover the truth. The entire truth, not just what you want to know. Does Saint John not say, 'The truth shall make you free'?"

I looked at him. "Will it?"

"It will." Sir Montague nodded wisely. "It always does."

I left Sir Montague more uncertain than ever, and returned home. I mused on all I had learned that day over the beef Bartholomew brought me, and then tried to distract myself with a book on Egypt that I'd borrowed from Grenville.

That evening, I put on a thoroughly brushed frock coat and traveled to Gentleman Jackson's boxing rooms in Bond Street to meet Basil Stokes.

When I entered the rooms at number 13, I saw the unmistakable form of Lucius Grenville. He detached himself from the gentlemen he'd been speaking to, came to me, seized my hand, and shook it warmly.

"Well met, Lacey," he said. "And thank you."

CHAPTER 14

BASIL Stokes came up behind Grenville and eyed him curiously. "You seem damned grateful, Grenville. Has the good captain given you a tip on the races?"

"More or less." Grenville released my hand and turned away, eyes sparkling.

"Perhaps I'll have more tips for you tonight," Stokes said jovially. "What shall you do, Captain? Box? Or just observe?"

"Observe, I think. The damp is making me long for a soft chair and a warm fire."

"Too much of that makes a man weak, Captain. You stride around well enough even with your lameness, but better take care." He laughed loudly.

I decided that Basil Stokes was the sort of man who said what he liked, then laughed afterward to soften the blow. He wore his white hair in a queue and dressed in breeches and shoes, not the newer fashion of trousers.

He was an old Whig, much like my father had been. He was probably cronies with Charles James Fox, the great Whig statesman, and vehemently opposed to the now con-

servative Prince Regent and his followers. I strongly suspected that my father had embraced Whigishness not because it was traditional for the Lacey family to do so, but
because most of the men to whom he owed money were To-
ries.

Stokes led us across the room and introduced me to several gentlemen of his acquaintance, bluff and hearty men
like himself. They already knew Grenville, of course. We
talked of the usual things: sport, politics, horses. Then Gentleman Jackson entered and attention turned to the lessons
he gave in the middle of the room.

"Gentleman" Jackson had been a prize pugilist until his
retirement, when he decided to open a school for gentlemen
who wanted to learn the art of boxing. These gentlemen, the
cream of the *ton,* would never fight a match in truth, but we
all enjoyed learning the moves that made pugilists famous.
Grenville made a decent boxer; he was wiry and strong and
could move quickly. I was more ham-handed in my moves,
but I could hold my own.

Tonight, I sat on a bench next to Stokes and watched
while two younger fellows stripped to shirt sleeves and took
up positions in the center of the room, fists raised.

"A quiet wager?" Stoke said into my ear. He might have
said "quiet," but I am certain everyone in the room heard
him. "Ten guineas on Mr. Knighton."

"Done," Grenville said before I could speak. Stokes
beamed at him and nodded.

"Captain?"

"I do not know these gentlemen," I answered. "Let me
study their form before I throw away my money."

Stokes chortled. "I like a careful man. I do not know
their form myself. That is why it is called gambling." He sat
back, laughing, but did not prod me to wager.

The gentlemen commenced fighting. They had apparently taken many lessons with Gentleman Jackson, and
boxed in tight form, keeping arms bent and close to their
bodies. After a time, Jackson moved in and gave them

pointers. The observing gentlemen watched or tried to imitate what he told them to do.

"Well, then, Captain, what did you want to ask me about the night poor Mr. Turner died?" Stokes startled me by saying.

I glanced about, but the others, except Grenville, were fixed on Gentleman Jackson and his instructions. "I want only a report from another witness," I said. "No one seems to have noticed much."

And did you happen to pick Brandon's pocket and steal his knife? I wanted to ask.

Stokes gave me a good-humored look. But I sensed, for all his bluff good nature, that he was a shrewd man.

"The truth on it, sir, was that no one saw much, because all the gentlemen were vying for the attention of the beautiful Mrs. Bennington. Many a man would be glad to escort her home for an evening."

Grenville shot him a stern glance, his smile dying.

I ignored him for now. "Is that what you did? Vied for Mrs. Bennington's attention?"

Stokes laughed out loud. "Not me. Oh, I'd love to give the woman a tumble, but at my age, a warm glass of port is more to my taste on a cold night than a lass who'd not look twice at me. That is what I was searching for at the fatal hour of midnight, drink. Gillis did not lay in near enough. I had to walk the house looking for more. Your colonel was doing the same."

"Was he?" I asked, interested. "You spoke to him?"

"Of course. He was growling about lack of servants. Where were they all? he wanted to know. I told him that the house had been built so that servants walked in passages behind the walls. That's why we couldn't find one when we needed one. Brandon said it was bloody inconvenient and walked away. He went toward the back stairs. I assume he was about to descend to the kitchens, but who knows, because I went back to the ballroom, still wanting drink. When I entered, Mrs. Harper began her screaming. She stabbed him, Lacey, mark my words. Women are easily excitable. Lord knows my wife was, God rest her."

"Would you be willing to say in court that you saw Brandon?" I asked. "If he was making for the back stairs at the time Turner's body was discovered, perhaps I can prove he did not have the time to kill him."

"Oh, he might have had the time," Stokes said cheerfully. "I did not see him until right before the screaming commenced. He might have done it before that." He chuckled at my expression. "But truth to tell, Captain, I do not believe he did. If Colonel Brandon wished to kill a man, he'd call him out and face him in a duel, not quietly shove a knife into him. A question of honor, don't you know."

Honor, yes. I agreed with him. But I thought of the missing document that Colonel Naveau wanted. Something dangerous was going on here that might make a man throw honor to the wind.

"Of course," Stokes went on. "I might have done it. Oh, good form," he shouted at Knighton below as the man began punching his opponent.

"You might have," I persisted. "But why would you?"

"Because I owed Mr. Turner a ruinous amount of money." Stokes watched the boxers for a moment. "Should have learned my lesson when I lost to him at the races, but I wagered on the outcome of a cock fight, and lost heavily. Not my fault, I could not have foreseen that the champion bird would expire of apoplexy so soon into the match. The lad had a nose for wagering. Saved my pocket when he died. But I didn't kill the chap. I'd have paid up, I always do."

The man was just ingenuous enough for me to believe him. He seemed a straightforward, no-nonsense sort of gentleman, one who might be persuaded to bet on a ridiculous outcome but turn over his money amiably when he lost.

Then again—Turner was dead.

"So," Stokes said. "If I didn't murder the chap, and Brandon didn't murder him, who did?"

"That is the question." I returned my attention to the

boxers. The gentleman called Knighton had just landed another good facer on his opponent. I felt relieved I had not bet against him. "And at this moment, I have no bloody idea who."

GRENVILLE invited me back to Grosvenor Street for brandy and hot coffee to chase away the chill of the evening after we left Gentleman Jackson's. I readily accepted.

The Knighton fellow had done well. I'd bet on him in a round against a tall, muscular boxer, and won a few guineas. I resisted the temptation to let it all go again and, flushed with success, accompanied Grenville home.

Now in his upstairs sitting room, the one that housed curios from his travels, Grenville reclined in a Turkish chair, clad in slippers and a suit meant for relaxing in his own house. He fingered a small golden beetle he called a scarab and let out a wistful sigh.

"Egypt is a magical place, Lacey," he said. "All of the wonders of a lost world buried in the sand, waiting to be discovered. The Turks don't care about it one way or another. I have read of that Italian fellow, Belzoni, out there looking for treasure. He used to do a strongman act at Tunbridge Wells. Would carry seven men on his back. Amazing fellow."

"And you wish to travel to Egypt to help him?"

"Not help, watch and learn. I doubt I would do much good chucking blocks of stone about. I long to return. It is a beautiful place."

"You speak of it much."

"I told you before, we could go together. I believe you'd enjoy it."

I had poured my brandy into my coffee and now sipped the spicy, warm mixture. "What would Marianne say?"

"I believe she would be furious with me. That is the trouble with falling under a woman's enchantment. A man becomes reluctant to leave her side."

"Are you reluctant to leave her side?" I asked curiously.

He gave me a rueful look. "I am, if you must know the truth. That young lady has gotten under my skin." He took a drink of brandy. "Well, you warned me. Perhaps I should flee to Egypt so I might come to my senses."

"She would never forgive you, I think."

Grenville made a face. "She might be happy to see the back of me. Especially if I left her with a great deal of money. Yes, I believe that is my solution."

"I believe you wrong her," I said.

He looked at me in surprise. "Do I?" he said, in a tone that conveyed disbelief.

"You stayed last night with her, did you not?"

He gave me a cynical smile. "A night with a lady does not mean a softening of that lady's heart. You are a romantic."

"Perhaps," I agreed. "What about Mrs. Bennington?"

His glass of brandy stopped halfway to his mouth. "Mrs. Bennington?"

"I visited her after her performance last night. Her husband introduced me. She asked me to speak to you."

His friendliness vanished. "Did she?"

"I found it rather incredible what she told me, that you shouted at her over a gentleman called Carew and threw your walking stick across the room. I was shown the mark you left in the wallpaper. I must wonder why you did so."

Grenville sat stiffly, his eyes glittering with anger and dislike. "Lacey, I often am amused by your curiosity, but this time, I am not. Please cease to ask me questions."

"You frightened her."

"Good. She ought not to let young fellows make up to her, nor should she have married that God-awful Bennington. The man is a mountebank."

"She told me his name was not Bennington. Who is he then?"

"The devil if I know."

"You seem extraordinarily angry," I remarked, sipping my coffee. "Do you know Mrs. Bennington well? I never heard you speak of her before she came to London."

"I told you, Lacey," Grenville said in a hard voice. "Cease asking me questions about Mrs. Bennington."

"I admit, her story seemed incredible. I thought it likely that you had a reasonable explanation for the entire matter, and that I would force it from you."

He stared at me, his face white, and then he suddenly began to laugh. "Good God, you have audacity."

"I know. That is why I anger so many people."

He laughed again. "I admire it, you know—even when it makes you a bloody nuisance."

I noted that his backhanded compliments let him nicely avoid the question. "Will you not tell me the explanation?"

He stopped laughing. "No. I will not. This event with Mrs. Bennington is none of your blasted business. That is all I will say on the matter."

I inclined my head. My curiosity was not satisfied, but I saw I would get no further with him tonight. "Very well, but I must ask you to cease frightening her. If she tells me again that you have thrown your walking stick or shouted in her face, I will definitely have words with you."

He gazed at me, his lips parting. "You truly do have audacity, Lacey."

"Yes."

I knew I jeopardized my friendship with him by being high-handed, but I could not sit by and condone his behavior. Mrs. Bennington had been truly frightened, and Grenville had not denied her accusations. He would not explain, not even to make peace between us.

He drank his brandy in silence for a moment, then said, tight-lipped, "I suppose we should turn the conversation to other things. What do you think of what Stokes told you?"

I shrugged. "I do not know. It is the first time I have been able to verify the truth of Brandon's story, but there are other things going on that I do not understand."

I told him of my meeting with Denis and Colonel Naveau, and the request to find the document that Turner had stolen from Naveau. Grenville listened, his animosity turning again to interest.

"I agree with you that Brandon most likely gave the paper to Imogene Harper," he said. "But if he did not? She must have been looking for it when you caught her at Turner's rooms. That tells me she does not have it."

"I plan to ask her when I visit her, and try to force her to tell me the truth. But if she does not have it . . ." I trailed off, taking a sip of coffee. "That means Brandon got rid of it somehow. I cannot imagine him passing it to any other person, except perhaps Louisa. But she has given no indication that she knew anything about a letter."

"Then what is your theory?"

I clicked my cup to its saucer. "That Brandon hid it. That he found a place to put it at the Gillises' house where even their servants would not find it. He hid the document before Pomeroy arrived, fearing that Pomeroy would find it. He probably meant to return to retrieve it or to send Mrs. Harper for it. But Pomeroy whisked him to Bow Street, and he did not get the chance to pass on the message. Mrs. Harper has not been to see him, nor has Louisa. And he does not want me to find the damned thing."

"Hmm," Grenville mused. "How could he be certain the servants would not find it?"

"I do not know. He must have thought the hiding place a good one." I studied the shelf beside me, which was filled with oriental ivory. "If a Gillis servant did find it, would they be able to read it? It was in French, and not all servants can read—even English. They might think it a stray bit of paper and destroy it."

"Or wrap fish in it or polish furniture with it," Grenville said. "My footmen use my old newspapers to polish the silver."

"Perhaps Bartholomew and Matthias can infiltrate the Gillises' servants' hall again and find out. I am not certain how I will explain to Lord Gillis that I want to search his house from top to bottom for a stray bit of paper, but I will try."

"I can speak to Gillis at my club."

"Lady Breckenridge has promised she will gain me entry through Lady Gillis."

His brows climbed. "Has she?"

I poured more coffee into my cup from the pot on the tray. I felt Grenville's keen gaze resting upon me, but I chose to ignore it. "Some things are none of my business," I said, keeping my voice light. "Some things are none of yours."

He looked pleased. "You will never have a moment's boredom with Donata Breckenridge. She is decidedly unconventional."

"She is intelligent," I said, defending her. "And does not waste time on frivolous conversation."

"Exactly."

He wore a faint, superior smile. I said, "Her marriage to Breckenridge I know was unhappy. She loathed him. I gather it was an arranged match?"

Grenville nodded, always ready to delve into the affairs of his fellow man, or woman. "Yes, it was a good match, or would have been if Breckenridge hadn't been such a boor. Her father was Earl Pembroke, and Breckenridge was the nephew of one of his friends. Both men had large and prosperous estates, and Pembroke wanted his daughter and grandchildren provided for." He turned his glass in his hands. "Funny thing, I met Lady Breckenridge at her come-out, when she was Lady Donata. She was quiet and well mannered and pretty, never spoke a word out of place. A regal young lady. Not until after she married Breckenridge did she blossom to what she is now."

I contrasted Grenville's picture of the unmarried Lady Breckenridge to the frank, acerbic lady with the cynical sense of humor I'd come to know.

I said, "Knowing Breckenridge, he must have infuriated her until she grew fed up. She must have dropped her polite veneer in self-defense."

Grenville shot me a look. "Breckenridge was horrible. You knew him only two days. Very few people could abide him. He paraded his mistresses about, in front of his wife;

I hear he even took a few of them home and forced her to share her dining room with them. I admire her for not running mad or shooting him outright. She must have the strength of ten to live through all that he did to her."

"She does have strength," I said softly. "She can stand up to me and tell me when I am a fool."

He chuckled. "So very few men would prize that in a woman."

And yet, I did. My wife, Carlotta, had been a fragile, tender creature. I'd needed a wife who could bash crockery over my head and tell me not to run roughshod over them. Carlotta had simply sat back and let me become more and more heavy-handed. I doubt I'd ever be able to be heavy-handed with Donata Breckenridge.

I decided to lighten the mood. "She is a very lovely woman."

Grenville grinned. "That does not hurt, either." He lifted his glass. "To comely ladies with sharp tongues. Bless them."

I lifted my cup and joined him in a toast.

THE next afternoon, I returned to the court near Portman Square to attempt another visit to Imogene Harper. This time, I found her at home.

She received me in a tidy parlor whose windows overlooked the foggy lane. This was a quiet court, rather like the one I lived in on the other side of the city. The house was respectable, the sort a well-to-do widow might hire.

Mrs. Harper looked the part of the respectable, well-to-do widow. Again, I was struck with what a pleasant-looking woman she was—not a beauty, but not displeasing, either. The disheveled look she'd had when I'd encountered her in Turner's rooms was gone. Her yellow-brown hair had been dressed neatly in a simple knot at the back of her head. She wore brown again, a high-waisted gown trimmed with black, tasteful and comely.

Once the requisite politeness had finished and we'd settled with the requisite tea brought by the maid, I told her, "I have met Colonel Naveau."

Her eyes widened, and she set her teacup down quickly. "Oh."

"He has commissioned me to find a letter stolen from him in Paris by Mr. Turner. I believe that same letter was sold to Colonel Brandon for five hundred guineas in the anteroom of Lord Gillis's Berkeley Square townhouse."

Mrs. Harper bowed her head, but a flush spread across her cheeks.

"Am I correct?" I asked.

"You believe so," she answered, her voice hard. "What does it matter what I think?"

"It matters a great deal, Mrs. Harper. I need to find that document. I want to find it. Will you tell me where it is?"

CHAPTER 15

❧

SHE lifted her head. "And if I tell you I have no idea where the bloody letter is, will you believe me?"

"I will, actually."

She looked surprised, then skeptical. "You will? Why?"

"Because I know Colonel Brandon better than you do."

She stared at me, then she collapsed limply into her chair. "Oh, what does it matter? No, Captain, I do not have the letter. I begged and begged Colonel Brandon to give it to me, but he would not."

"But you do have the draft for the five hundred guineas that Brandon gave Mr. Turner, do you not?"

"Yes, I found it in Mr. Turner's coat pocket. I took it and put it into my reticule."

"You searched his dead body for it. I admire your coolness."

"I was anything but cool! Believe me, Captain, when I screamed, I did so from the heart. When I searched Turner's pockets, his body was still warm, and it was ghastly. I was horrified. I saw his blood on my glove, and it sent me into hysterics. I do not know much of what happened after that."

"Grenville sat you down and gave you brandy. He also took your glove away."

"Yes, he did." She drew a long breath. "When I could no longer see the blood, I calmed somewhat. But even so, my maids had to take me home. It was horrible."

"You made the Bow Street magistrate feel sorry for you. He did not want to bring you there for questioning."

"No." Her lips thinned. "He came here."

"And what did you tell him?"

"Really, I do not remember precisely. I told him that I had danced and talked and done things one does at a ball. Yes, I stepped away with Colonel Brandon to speak to him privately, and why should I not? I went to the anteroom to snatch a quiet moment and found Mr. Turner."

"This is the story you told the magistrate?"

"Yes."

I took a sip of tea, which was weak and too sweet. I set it aside. "You and Colonel Brandon tell slightly different stories. He admitted he spent most of his time with you and that you were upset by Mr. Turner's insolence more than once. So much so that Brandon had to slip away to find you a glass of sherry at the moment when Turner was being murdered."

She flushed. "I never wanted to find Mr. Turner dead in the anteroom. My sole purpose in attending the ball was to obtain the letter and destroy it."

"So his death and Brandon's arrest inconvenience you greatly."

"Inconvenience?" She spat the word, then sprang to her feet. "It has been hell, Captain. I do not know where the letter is. Colonel Brandon might be hanged for murder. Now you tell me that Colonel Naveau has come from France to ruin us all."

"How can he ruin you? What is this letter?"

She stopped and looked at me, her eyes steady. "What do you believe it is?"

"I thought it a love letter between you and Brandon, but I only assumed that. You never corrected me, and neither did he. I have since learned that it is a document that Colonel Naveau very much wants returned. You and Brandon told me that the pair of you had an affair, but is that the truth?"

She nodded. "Yes. At Vitoria, just after my husband's death."

"You were grieving," I guessed, "and alone, and he was helpful."

"I was not simply grieving." She lifted her chin. "I was devastated. I loved my husband. He was a good man. I was angry that he'd been taken from me, and I was also in a good deal of trouble. Colonel Brandon was there. He was strong and helped me, and he was . . . I cannot explain what he was to me. I should not have; I felt the betrayal of my husband, but I could not help myself. I admired him, and I was so grateful."

She broke off. But I understood. Brandon was a leader when he chose to be. He needed followers and needed to be admired, but he had the confidence, the strength, to make men follow him. I had felt the same pull when I'd first met him, the need to do anything for him.

"Why were you in a great deal of trouble?" I asked.

"Because of my husband. He'd done a terrible thing. And I was afraid, so afraid that he'd be disgraced, even in death. He'd be stripped of his rank, and I, too, could be disgraced and worse because I'd helped him, albeit unwittingly. I did not understand the horror until I went through his things in preparation to return to England. I did not know where to turn. Brandon, unbelievably, said he'd help me."

"I am supposing that your husband had dealings with this Colonel Naveau?"

She hesitated. The look she sent me was filled with appeal. Though she was not a comely woman like Lady Breckenridge or Louisa, I was touched by the need in her eyes.

"Mrs. Harper," I said. "My purpose is to prove that Brandon did not murder Henry Turner. I am not here to condemn your husband for what he might have done, or you. The war is over. Many men died, but Napoleon was defeated at the last. What happened then no longer matters to me."

"It ought to matter," she said savagely. "What my husband did might have cost men lives, the lives of your men, perhaps your own, if you'd been unlucky."

"Naveau was an exploring officer," I said. "Did your husband give him information?"

She looked sad. "Yes. I discovered he did so when I went through his things. He had been taking money from Colonel Naveau in exchange for dispatches."

I fell silent. Spying could be a lucrative game, and a deadly one. If her husband had been found guilty of treason, he could have been shot at best, drawn and quartered at worst. He'd been fortunate to die in battle.

I did not tell the entire truth when I said I no longer cared what had happened on the Peninsula. Spies were the worst of men, men who dealt in secrets and underhanded exchanges. A dispatch sent to the enemy could ruin battle plans and slaughter thousands of soldiers who might otherwise have escaped death.

"What did you do?" I asked quietly.

"I destroyed all his papers." She quirked a brow at me. "What would you have me do, Captain, run at once to his colonel and confess that he'd been selling secrets to the French? My first loyalty was to my husband, who had been good to me. I destroyed every last scrap of evidence that he'd done anything wrong. But then, only a few days after my husband's death, Colonel Naveau sent a message. It was sheerest good luck that I found it before my husband's batman did. The message was odd, but I understood that Naveau was waiting for something. I did not know what to do. So I confessed to Colonel Brandon and swore him to secrecy."

"And he agreed?" I was baffled. Colonel Brandon was a stickler for proper behavior in a soldier, in an officer, in a gentleman.

"He agreed to say nothing. My husband was dead—he'd

died honorably, saving other men. And he did not want dishonor or punishment to fall on me. Aloysius suggested we send a message to Colonel Naveau explaining that Major Harper was dead and to leave me alone."

"That was foolish. Naveau was a professional exploring officer. If he received no more word from your husband, he would conclude that his source had dried up, and tried elsewhere. And likely he would have heard of your husband's death on his own."

"Naveau did not know when he wrote this message that my husband was dead. He was angry, and threatened to reveal to Wellington what my husband had been doing. Colonel Brandon wrote a letter to Naveau, in French, and somehow got it delivered to him; I have no idea how he managed it. As a peace offering, he included a dispatch that Naveau had been asking for."

"Good God."

"Yes, he risked much for me."

I had been angry at Aloysius Brandon in the past, but my rage rose to new heights today. "He did risk much. He risked ignominious death and disgrace. And for what? Your pretty eyes? Did he ask you to elope with him?"

She looked perplexed. "He asked me to marry him, yes. How did you know?"

"Because I was at the other end of the matter. Did you know that he planned to leave his wife for you? You must be a remarkable woman, to lure him from Louisa Brandon, who I assure you is quite remarkable herself."

Mrs. Harper flushed a dull red. "I refused him. He was very excited after we'd delivered the message, and begged me to marry him once he obtained the annulment of his marriage. But I could not. I'd loved my husband dearly. I did not want to rush to another man as though my husband had meant nothing to me. So I turned him away."

"Yet you admit you had an affair with him," I said.

"A very brief one. I was afraid and alone, and needed comfort. Then I told him to go."

Which he'd done. Brandon had returned to his wife to

discover that Louisa had run to me in her distress. He'd been furious and would not believe that we'd not had a liaison. But if he had been indulging himself in another woman's bed, small wonder he'd instantly believed I'd been indulging his wife in mine.

"And you returned to England?" I continued.

"Yes. Scotland, actually. My sister had married a man from Edinburgh, and they invited me to live in their house. She has two small children, and they welcomed me as part of the family. It was a peaceful existence."

"Until this spring?"

She nodded. She moved back to a chair and sank into it. "I received a letter from Henry Turner in February. He said he had the very letter that Colonel Brandon and I had written to Colonel Naveau. How he came by it and how he found me, I do not know. He told me I must come to London and to pay him the sum of five hundred guineas, or else he would take the letter to the Horse Guards and proclaim that my husband and I and Colonel Brandon had been traitors."

I understood Brandon's outrage at Turner. I felt it now myself.

"I hurried to London and wrote to Colonel Brandon. I was petrified. And he—" Her eyes sparked with anger. "At first Aloysius wanted nothing to do with me. He told me bluntly that the affair was long ago, and that he and his wife were happy, and that I should cease to bother him. I was very angry. He had as much to lose as I did."

"I read the letters you wrote to him," I said. "You told him that both your names would be revealed. I assumed then you meant that your love affair would be made public."

"Much worse than that. When Aloysius wrote again, he agreed to help, though he was not best pleased about it. Turner wanted to meet us at the Gillises' ball, knowing that Colonel Brandon and his wife had been invited. So we made the appointment and brought him the money."

"And then Brandon made a mare's nest of it." I sighed. "I do not know why anyone would suppose he could do anything covert. He got himself talked about, upset his wife, and was arrested for murder."

To my surprise, a smile hovered on Mrs. Harper's lips. "I do not think he anticipated being arrested for murder. And as for him being ham-handed, at least people only talked of us having an indiscreet affair; they did not guess the worst of it. Even you did not."

"No. I admit that I was sorely misdirected."

She studied her hands in her lap. "I regret hurting Mrs. Brandon. She does not deserve this."

"No, she does not." I resumed my seat. "Tell me now, exactly what happened at the ball. You may still believe that Colonel Brandon killed Turner to keep him quiet, but I do not. If you had the evidence back, there was no need to murder Turner. Unless he had something else?"

Mrs. Harper shook her head. "There was nothing else. Just that letter. And Aloysius told me he'd made the exchange."

"Tell me again what happened."

She pressed her fingers to her temples. "I want so much to forget what happened, and everyone wants me to remember." She laughed a little. "It is true that Aloysius called too much attention to us. But I feared Mr. Turner, and I did not want Aloysius to leave my side. He was angry at Mr. Turner, but also at me. Mr. Turner did offer to dance with me several times, but I knew that he simply wanted to talk alone with me. Aloysius chased him away."

Lady Aline's version of events confirmed this. "The meeting was to be at eleven o'clock?" I asked. "In the anteroom?"

"Yes. Aloysius told me that I was not to go, although I wanted to see the letter for myself. But he was adamant, and I obeyed. He and Turner went into the anteroom together. No one followed. Not five minutes later, Aloysius emerged, rather red in the face, and then Mr. Turner came out. Aloysius took me to an alcove and told me the deed was done."

"Colonel Brandon provided the payment as well?"

"He did. He insisted. I did not protest too much. While I am of comfortable means, I cannot part with five hundred guineas with impunity. Colonel Brandon spoke of the sum as almost trivial."

"Colonel Brandon has a large income. When he spoke to you in the alcove, did he show you the paper?"

"No. He refused. He told me he had it, and I was not to worry."

"If it was in his handwriting, he'd be anxious to keep it," I reflected. "But he did not have the letter when he was arrested. Do you have any idea what he did with it?"

"None. I was agitated, not surprisingly so. He said he would find me some sherry, and left me. I stayed in the alcove, trying to catch my breath. Then, when Aloysius was a long time coming, I decided to emerge. Others would wonder what I did there so long. I tried to behave normally and have a conversation with Lady Gillis, but I was too agitated. I decided to sit alone in the anteroom. But when I entered, I found Mr. Turner."

"Dead."

She shuddered. "Yes. I thought him merely foxed, and I was a bit angry at him, celebrating at our expense. But he sat too still, and I realized he was not breathing."

"And you decided to search him for the bank draft."

"Yes."

"Why? To save Brandon a bit of blunt?"

She flushed. "That was not all I thought. I did not think the draft should be found on a dead man. I did not want it to point to a connection between Mr. Turner and Aloysius."

"It was a good thought, but Brandon's foolish behavior did that for him. Well, I am back to not knowing what became of the paper. Brandon is most reticent to tell me."

"He is ashamed."

I snorted. "He is afraid I will use the knowledge against him. Unfortunately, Mrs. Harper, instead of clearing Brandon, I now have information that gives him still more of a motive. He killed Turner not to cover up an affair but to keep himself from being arrested for possible treason. Damn."

Mrs. Harper looked at me limply. "I know. I am sorry."

"Brandon is an idiot, which is not your fault," I said. "He never should have written that letter."

"I know."

"The only way I can save him is to discover who truly did murder Turner. Did you see anything that can help me?"

She shook her head. "I was in the alcove. By the time I made my way to the anteroom, he must have already been dead."

"You said his body was warm. He could not have been dead long. Are you certain you saw no one leave the room before you entered it?"

"I did not."

I imagined the small gilded room with its simple furnishing and scarlet and gold walls. I remembered the opulent staircase hall and Basil Stokes complaining that one never saw the servants because they walked through back passages behind the walls.

Anyone who knew how to get into those passages could have slipped into the anteroom (if indeed, another door led to the passages from the anteroom). They need not have been seen in the ballroom at all. Brandon had been observed striding to the back of the house, ostensibly in search of sherry.

Damn. Damn. And damn.

I rose to my feet. "Mrs. Harper, I thank you for being frank with me. I am going to find that blasted paper if I have to tear apart London to do it. And I will clear Brandon, too. Please, if you remember anything else, any small detail that might be helpful, send me word."

She promised to, but her face was white, her eyes tired.

I left her with my card and my direction penned on it. She said good-bye, her eyes quiet in defeat.

I knew that she believed I would betray her to save Brandon, if necessary. And, I thought as I left the house for the spring fog, she might not be wrong.

•   •   •   •

LADY Breckenridge had sent me a note via a servant that morning, telling me she'd procured an appointment for me with Lady Gillis. She instructed me to call at the South Audley Street house at three o'clock.

I had just enough time now to journey from Portman Square to South Audley Street, and arrived on Lady Breckenridge's doorstep at three o'clock precisely.

Lady Breckenridge greeted me in a swirl of silk and cashmere and pressed a cool kiss to my cheek. "You are amazingly punctual, Gabriel. Shall we go?"

I was pleased, first that she had done this favor for me, and second, that she felt comfortable enough with me for a kiss as greeting. I was pleased, too, to sit next to her in her carriage, resting my foot on a stool thoughtfully provided by Barnstable.

As we rolled toward Berkeley Square, her shoulder brushed my arm with the carriage's movement.

I remembered the things Grenville had told me the night before about her husband. I was for a moment sorry that Breckenridge was dead, because I would have liked to call him out. But then I recalled that I had, very satisfactorily, once bruised his face in an impromptu boxing match.

I reached down and took Lady Breckenridge's hand in mine. "You told me once that I resembled the late Lord Breckenridge."

Her brows arched under her flat bonnet. "You and he had a similar build. And hair the same color. But you are a completely different man, thank God."

"I share the sentiment. I promise you, Donata, that I will never subject you to the humiliations he did. Ever."

She gave me a half-smile. "I know. You have too much damned honor."

"Not only honor," I corrected her. "Affection."

She stared at me. I do not know who I startled more with the word, her or myself. She looked at me for a long while, then she laid her head on my shoulder and kept it there for the rest of our short journey.

The carriage stopped before the entrance to the Gillises'

home in Berkeley Square. The entrance was flanked with tall columns that led us into the rotunda of the front hall. Maids took our coats and hats and a stately butler led us to a drawing room somewhere in the vast interior.

There, I met Lady Gillis for the first time. When she entered, I was struck as to how much younger she was than Lord Gillis. Grenville had mentioned that she was younger, but to me, she seemed no more than a girl. When I bowed over her hand, I put her age at perhaps mid-twenties at most.

"Violet," Lady Breckenridge greeted her. "Captain Lacey wishes to poke about your house. Shall you allow him?"

CHAPTER 16

LADY Gillis did allow it, although she was flustered. "It is not a nice thing to have a murder in your home," she said, as though referring to finding a book of lewd poetry in her library. "We have been at sixes and sevens since the ball." She dabbed the corner of her eye with a handkerchief.

"I am sorry it had to happen," I said.

"It was dreadful. Absolutely dreadful. I have been abed for days."

"Did you know Mr. Turner?"

She started, then flushed. "No. Not well. He was an acquaintance of a friend, who suggested I invite him."

Lady Gillis suddenly said she felt unwell and declared she'd retire to her rooms. She would not stop me looking about the house, she said, but she made us promise not to disturb her servants. Lady Breckenridge offered to go upstairs with her, but Lady Gillis said quickly that she would be fine with her maid for company. I rather think that Lady Gillis wanted Lady Breckenridge to keep an eye on me.

The ballroom in daylight was a very different place than it had been in the middle of the night. The arched windows at the end of the room let in gray light, and the chandeliers hung empty, devoid of candles.

A footman obligingly lit sconces for us, then disappeared on noiseless feet.

"Lady Gillis's servants are well trained," I observed as the tall man glided out, leaving us alone. "They seem unperturbed even by a sordid murder in their midst."

"Lady Gillis is a duke's daughter," Lady Breckenridge said. "She brought many of her own servants with her after her marriage. They are an efficient lot, but rather cold."

I thought of Lady Breckenridge's butler, Barnstable, ready with a pleasant smile and a cheerful inquiry into my health. I, too, would prefer a human being to a silent, efficient automaton.

"I am surprised they allowed murder to occur," I remarked.

She shrugged. "Well, if their master will allow in the rabble . . ."

I smiled with her, then moved off to examine the room. Along the longest wall were arched openings, moldings matching that on the windows, that led in to small alcoves. Each alcove held a chair or two and a small table. Dark green velvet draperies were pulled back from the openings and held in place by silken ropes.

I loosened a tie-back and let the drape fall. Both drapes would easily cover the alcove, rendering the inside a private, if rather stuffy, compartment.

"To which did Colonel Brandon take Mrs. Harper?" I asked. "If you remember? After Colonel Brandon left the anteroom after eleven o'clock?"

Lady Breckenridge studied the alcoves a moment. "That one," she announced, pointing to the opening just to the left of me.

I entered it and seated myself on one of the chairs. Wainscoting covered the wall from the floor to a chair rail nailed about three feet above the baseboard.

I ran my hands around the chair rail molding, looking for openings into which a folded piece of paper could have been wedged. I did the same with the baseboard moldings, then turned over the little table and both chairs, examining the undersides and upholstery.

I found no rents or gouges into which a paper had been pressed. I examined the chair and table legs in case one was hollow—I did everything short of taking the furniture completely apart.

Lady Breckenridge watched me curiously. "They say that women ask too many questions, but I must know what you are doing."

"Looking for Colonel Brandon's letter."

I had not told her the story that Mrs. Harper had given me today. I could not. Brandon needed my silence. Let Lady Breckenridge continue to believe that the problem was a love letter and an affair.

I righted a chair and sat upon it, raking my hand through my hair. "He met Mrs. Harper here after he paid off Turner. Then he left her to search for sherry. Where would he likely have gone?"

Lady Breckenridge thought a moment then she beckoned me to follow her. She glided across the ballroom as silently as any of Lady Gillis's servants and led me out a double door and through a wide hall.

Several rooms opened off this hall, all dedicated to the comforts of guests and displaying more of the Gillis artwork. "He might have come into any of these chambers," Lady Breckenridge said. "There would be decanters and so forth for the guests."

"Brandon said he could not find any sherry." I stood in the middle of one small room and looked about at the gilded furniture and the paneled walls.

Lady Breckenridge shrugged. "Shall I ring for a footman and ask him in which room they'd put it that night?"

"Not just yet." I left that room, crossed the hall, and entered another little sitting chamber. This one had similar paneling, but everything was gilded in silver rather than gold. "Lord Gillis's servants do not seem the sort to leave guests thirsty. So was the search for sherry a sham? And why?"

I felt cold. Every bit of evidence I went over pointed more and more to Brandon having committed the crime. He was back here while Turner was being murdered, with none to see but Basil Stokes, who caught sight of him just before Mrs. Harper screamed.

Brandon had to have known, when Turner was found dead with Brandon's own knife in his chest, that he might be arrested for murder. In the confusion between the discovery of Turner's body and the arrival of Pomeroy, he'd strive to rid himself of the incriminating paper.

He might have handed it to Mrs. Harper, but she claimed he did not. He might have handed it to Louisa. Or he might have hidden it in a place he'd spotted when he'd been roaming these rooms truly looking for a servant to bring him a drink.

I turned in a circle, taking in the room. Lord Gillis's servants would be certain to clean these chambers thoroughly every day. They were correct and well trained and aloof, probably some of the most experienced in their class. Where could Brandon hide something where they would not find it?

Then again, this was Colonel Brandon. He had not made it through the ranks to colonel for nothing. He was a good and inspiring commander, and sometimes, uncannily perceptive. Only where his personal life was concerned was he a fool.

The place he would hide his letter was in plain sight.

My gaze went to the books in the glass-doored bookcase, and my heart beat faster.

I saw in my mind, clear as day, Colonel Brandon striding into one of these rooms, snatching a book from one of the shelves, sliding the letter between the pages, jamming the book back among its fellows, then striding out again before anyone in the ballroom wondered where he'd gone. By the time Pomeroy arrived to begin his questioning, the letter was well hidden.

I crossed the room, pulled open a bookcase door, and examined the books. The leather spines were uncreased and unbroken. The pages on the few I pulled out likewise were uncut. When a man bought a book, the pages were still folded; one used a paper knife to cut the pages open so that the book could be read. Some men purchased libraries for the look of them rather than for intellectual pursuit; often pages of entire collections remained uncut.

In one of these books, unread by the inhabitants of the house, must lay the secret Brandon was willing to go to the gallows to protect.

"Help me," I urged. I began pulling out books, running my thumb over the pages.

Lady Breckenridge's cinnamon and spice perfume filled my nostrils as she came to help me. I was close—so close. Her slender hands touched mine as she pulled out books and copied my movements.

The books in the silver room yielded no secrets. Anxiously, I shoved the last book back to the shelf and hobbled back to the gold leaf room. Only about ten books decorated a bookcase here—I thumbed through those and found nothing.

There were four more rooms along the corridor. Lady Breckenridge and I looked through every book in them. By the time I slit open the last book, I'd found nothing. My leg was hurting and I wondered if my supposition was wrong. But it felt right—it seemed right. My vision of Brandon's actions had been so clear.

I sank down on one of the chairs, in too much pain now to stand.

Lady Breckenridge stopped before me and smoothed a strand of my always unruly hair from my face. "Are you all right?"

"Disgusted, mostly," I said. "The bloody thing must be here. I know Brandon. He would have hidden it. He would not have risked Pomeroy finding it and handing it over to Sir Nathaniel."

Lady Breckenridge's cool fingers felt good. She rested herself on my lap and continued to stroke my hair.

I did not want to push her away. My head ached from speculating, and her presence, her touch, soothed me. I closed my eyes.

"I am not a man of complex thought," I said slowly. "In the army I solved problems as they came to me. I did not sit in a chair and contemplate them."

"You were a soldier," she said, her voice low. "Not a general."

I snorted. "And what the generals decided after sitting back and contemplating was often foolish. They could not solve problems that were right in front of them." I sighed and opened my eyes. "Neither can I, it seems."

"You are working your way through lies."

"I know. The only person who has not lied to me is you."

She smiled a little, her pale mouth curving. "Are you certain?"

"You never hide your opinions."

"True. I was brought up to be demure, which I was until I married my foul husband. Then I realized that timidity would bring me nothing. But I did lie to you, Gabriel."

"About what?"

Her cheeks colored. "About why I helped Louisa Brandon that night. I told you I did it for your sake, because she was your friend. That was not entirely true."

She had my full attention now. "Tell me what you mean."

"I helped her because I wanted to observe her," she said. "To know what sort of woman had won your adoration."

I studied her in silence. Her eyes held a defiant light, but behind that lay—worry?

"It is not adoration," I said quietly.

"Is it not?"

She challenged me. She wanted truth. I was not certain what truths I could give her, because I was confused about truth these days myself.

One thing I knew was that she was warm, and her touch delighted me in ways I had not known in a long time.

"No," I answered. "It is not. Admiration, certainly. And friendship."

"And love," she supplied.

"Love." I touched her face. "But not love that is covetous. I would see her happy, but I do not need to possess her."

She looked unconvinced. "Gentlemen often express admiration, when in truth they mean desire."

"Your husband might have," I countered. "My desire lies along another path." I drew my finger across her lips.

Her eyes still held caution. "I can never be this paragon you admire. No matter how I try."

I smiled. "I do not want you to be. I want you to be witty and acerbic and blow smoke in my face when I am stupid and soothe me when I am hurting. You have proved excellent at all these things."

She dropped her gaze. "From the beginning I have made a complete cake of myself for you. That you do not despise me amazes me."

I stared in surprise. Lady Breckenridge had always seemed a woman who did exactly as she pleased for reasons of her own.

"You make me long to be tender," I said.

She looked up at me. In that moment, when her eyes met mine, I knew that I'd never in my life met a woman like her.

"We do not have time to be tender," she reminded me. "We must find your colonel's letter so you may save him from the noose."

Thus, Colonel Brandon, even imprisoned, reached out to make my life difficult.

"Yes," I conceded. "But damned if I know how I will do it."

Lady Breckenridge slid from my lap and pressed a kiss to the top of my head. "You will find a way."

I gave her an ironic look. "I am pleased at your faith in me."

She took my hand and helped me to my feet. "If Colonel Brandon did not leave the letter in a book, then we must look elsewhere."

"He did," I said. "I know he did."

I thought glumly that perhaps a servant had found it in truth, had not cared what it was, and had destroyed it.

I moved across the room to investigate what I'd been too tired to investigate a few moments before. Near a corner of the room, the paneling did not fit quite right, and closer scrutiny showed that it was a door that opened right from the wall, giving onto the servants' passage behind the walls.

No attempt had been made to completely hide the door, but the paneling had been fashioned to make it unobtrusive. No one would pay attention to it until the servant came through to carry in tea or lay the fire or whatever his particular duty might be.

I ran my fingers down the edges until I found a piece of gilded molding that moved. The designer had cleverly used the molding to conceal the door's latch. I pressed the latch, and the door swung smoothly toward me.

I looked inside and saw a narrow passage, roughly finished and lit with sconces. A footman, hurrying through on some errand or other, saw me and started, his eyes wide.

"I beg your pardon," I said.

The footman rapidly regained his composure, changing from human being to well-trained servant in an instant. "Sir?" he said coolly. "May I assist you?"

"Yes." I motioned with my stick. "Where does this passage lead?"

His brows lifted the slightest bit. "To the ballroom. And in the other direction, to the stairs to the kitchens."

"Do all the rooms have access to this passage?"

"Yes, sir." I heard the "Of course they do, why would they not?" in his voice.

"May I look?"

The eyebrows climbed. "It is no place for a gentleman, sir. Or a lady."

"Even so. Please show us."

He gave me the same look a put-upon colonel had when wives new to the regiment requested a tour of the army camp. Lady Breckenridge and I did not belong there. This passage was the servants' territory, and ladies and gentlemen were not welcome. The levels of the house were separated as much for the privacy of the servants as the privacy of the masters.

The passage was dark and close and stuffy, but I could see that it would be handy for moving about the rooms quickly, not to mention unseen.

The walls were plastered, but not painted, and the doors were rough wood, distinct and not hidden.

The doors also looked all alike. "How do you know which door leads where?" I asked. "For instance, which would lead to the anteroom in which Mr. Turner was killed?"

The footman led us along to the door second from the end on the left. "This one, sir."

"But how do you know?"

He gave me his look of faint disdain. "We know."

Lady Breckenridge peered around me. "You are thinking the murderer came this way. How would he have known which door it was?"

"Either he knew someone in the house who told him," I answered, "or he scouted beforehand." I turned to the footman, who'd puffed up, affronted that I'd implied that any of the Gillis servants would ever dream of assisting a murderer. "Did you or any of the other servants observe anyone back here who should not have been the night of Mr. Turner's murder? Or anything unusual at all?"

"I did not, sir. But I will ask Mr. Hawes. He is our butler."

His air of offense was beginning to amuse me. "One more question. Did you or any maid or footman remove a paper from any of the books in these rooms? Say the day after the murder? While they were cleaning? Perhaps they found something sticking from a book and pulled it out?"

"I clean these rooms myself, sir. And I did not find anything unusual among the books. But I will ask Mr. Hawes, sir."

Mr. Hawes seemed to be the font of all wisdom. "Please do," I said. "We will wait in the anteroom."

The footman opened the door to the anteroom, and I ushered Lady Breckenridge through. I examined the door carefully, but could find nothing to differentiate it from the other doors. Inside, it fitted well into the scarlet and gold wall, though the line was visible. The door was not a secret.

The footman disappeared, obviously relieved that we'd gone back to our side of the wall. I studied the gilded molding and scarlet silk above the wainscoting. The scheme was bright and a bit overwhelming. "Overdone," Grenville had said.

"The murderer entered through the servants' door," I mused. "I am certain of it."

"Which is why no one noticed him enter from the ballroom," Lady Breckenridge said. "Guests roamed in and out of the ballroom and all over the downstairs rooms all night. I do not think anyone would notice who was not in the ballroom at a given time."

"No," I agreed. "Turner might have used the servants' passage as well. He had made an appointment with Colonel Brandon in here, why not with someone else? It seemed a convenient place."

"The murder must have been very quick," Lady Breckenridge remarked.

"It likely was." I paced the room as I thought, laying my walking stick across the writing table. "The murderer has made up his mind to kill Turner. He makes the appointment, leaves the ballroom, enters the servants' passage through one of the other rooms. He comes here, meets Turner. He has Colonel Brandon's knife, which Brandon must have left about somewhere, though the devil if I know where." I turned to Lady Breckenridge. "He approached Turner. Turner knew him and did not fear him. There was plenty of noise in the ballroom, the orchestra, the dancing, the conversation. Before Turner knows what is happening, the killer steps to him, possibly covers Turner's mouth so he won't cry out, and drives the blade home."

I saw it in my mind. Without realizing what I was doing, I covered Lady Breckenridge's mouth with my hand and pressed my fist against her chest, right where the killer would have plunged the knife.

It would have been fast and silent. Turner probably had grunted if he'd made any noise at all, then fallen, limp. The killer had caught him, easily lowered him into the chair, and arranged him to look as though he were drunk or asleep. The murderer then left the way he'd come.

Lady Breckenridge's eyes glittered above my hand. "Very exact," she said, stepping away.

I came back to the present. "I beg your pardon."

She smiled in her intelligent way. "Not at all. It was an apt demonstration. You do know, do you not, that you are only succeeding in making the case against Colonel Brandon tighter? He was in a room with a door to the passage; he admitted it. Basil Stokes saw him."

"And likewise, he saw Basil Stokes. Stokes said they exchanged a few words, then Brandon made for the back of the house. Stokes claims he went back to the ballroom and then heard Mrs. Harper scream, but we have only his word on it."

"But why should Basil Stokes kill Henry Turner? Mr. Stokes is rather irritating, but he hardly seems the sort to kill in such a clandestine fashion. He'd challenge Turner to a fight if he truly wanted to harm him. Loudly."

"I agree with you, in part," I said. "But Stokes, by his own admission, owed Turner a huge debt. And he expressed relief that Turner was dead and that he no longer had to pay it."

Lady Breckenridge shivered. "It is all so horrible."

"Murder is horrible. Death while fighting is one thing; a deliberate and underhanded murder is another."

"It is good of you to help your colonel," she said softly. "No matter what I think of your motives."

"I need to," I answered. "Not simply because of Louisa.

Brandon aided me when I needed it most. He took me, a callow young man with no future, and made me into something. No matter what else is between us, he gave me that."

She did not answer. She did not need to. She slid her arms about my waist and rested her head on my chest.

At this inauspicious moment, the butler, the all-knowing Hawes, entered the room.

Lady Breckenridge stepped away from me, looking in no wise embarrassed.

Hawes, like a good butler, pretended not to notice. "Sir," he said, bowing. "My lady. With what may I help you?"

Lady Breckenridge answered. "The captain wished to ask you a question or two about the night of the murder."

"Yes, my lady." He turned to me, his butler hauteur in place. "John told me that you wish to know if anything unusual was seen in the passage or any person not meant to be there."

I nodded. "That would be helpful."

"I am afraid none of the staff saw any person untoward. Most of the footmen were circulating champagne in the ballroom or cleaning up the supper rooms. The passages would be empty for a time, so someone might slip through without us noticing. However, one of the maids did mention that she noticed a scrap of lace caught near one of the doors."

I came alert. "A scrap of lace?"

"Yes, sir. As might come from a lady's gown."

"Near which door?"

"The door to this room, sir. I will show you."

He glided across the room in an elegant walk and unlatched the panel that led to the servants' corridor. He pointed to a small nail that stuck out a little from the wooden doorframe. "Just there, sir, I believe. The silly girl left it there, and when she reported it to me, I ordered her to return and take it away. But she claimed that when she returned, the lace was gone. Possibly another footman saw it and took it away."

Or possibly, I thought, excitement rising, the killer had

taken it from the door and put it into Turner's pocket, where Mrs. Harper found it when she examined the dead man's coat.

"Will there be anything else, sir?" Hawes asked, his stance stiff.

I distinctly felt his wish for us to leave. We were intruding on his and his staff's routine.

"That will be all, thank you. You have been quite helpful."

Hawes bowed again. "Her ladyship has retired to bed. She asked me to bid you good afternoon when you take your leave."

I inclined my head. "Tell her ladyship that we wish her good health."

Hawes saw us upstairs and the footmen brought our wraps. He handed me a folded piece of paper, written over in fine printing. The writing was English and seemed to be about cakes, so I dismissed the idea that Hawes was handing me the document that Colonel Naveau and I sought.

"Begging your pardon, sir," Hawes said. "The cook asked leave to give you this receipt for cakes that Mrs. Brandon admired."

"Mrs. Brandon?"

"Yes, sir. She expressed a liking for the cook's lemon cakes when she visited, and asked for the directions, so that her own cook might prepare them for her."

"I see." I took the paper. "I am certain that Mrs. Brandon will thank you."

"Not at all, sir." He saw us out the door, and then Lady Breckenridge's footmen took us in hand. I tucked the paper into my coat and climbed into the carriage, trying to stem my excitement.

Lady Breckenridge saw through me. She quirked a brow at me as the carriage started. "What is it, Gabriel? You look positively triumphant."

I settled back and stretched my leg toward the box of hot coals while she watched me. "I know what became of the letter."

Her eyes widened. "Do you? Shall you retrieve it at once, then? What direction shall I give my coachman?"

"It will keep. First, I would like to return to Bow Street and look at the scrap of lace that Pomeroy took from the dead man's pocket."

Without waiting for explanation, she told her coachman to drive to Bow Street, then sat back and looked at me. "You are very interested in this lace. Do you think a woman did this murder?"

"Not necessarily," I answered.

"But the lace was caught outside the door. Do you not believe that a woman slipped through the passage and tore her gown on the protruding nail?"

"No. If I am correct, then the lace was not torn, but cut. It was used to mark the door to the anteroom, so the killer would not be confused when he hastened down the rather dark servants' passage."

"I see." She mused. "You seem suddenly sanguine about the whereabouts of the love letter of Colonel Brandon."

"If it is not where I think it is, then it has been destroyed."

"You believe that Louisa Brandon has it," she said, with sharp perception. "You believe that she came to retrieve it on her husband's orders. Perhaps she raved over the cakes and demanded the recipe in order to have time to slip down to the ballroom and retrieve the paper."

"I imagine she truly liked the cakes. She is fond of lemon."

She gave me a steady gaze. "Mrs. Brandon must love her husband very much."

"She does."

She laid her hand on my arm and did not speak.

We rattled through the streets of London against a breeze that held the promising warmth of spring. Still it was chilly enough that I was grateful for the warm interior of the coach. When we reached Bow Street, I told Lady Breckenridge to stay inside the carriage. The rooms of the magistrate's house were no place for a lady.

Pomeroy, luckily, was in. I asked him what he had done with the things he took from Turner's coat. For a moment, as he paused in thought, I feared he had rid himself of them, perhaps sending them to Turner's father.

"I still have 'em," he said, to my relief. "Upstairs. Was saving them for the trial, in case they could tell us anything about how Mr. Turner got himself stuck."

He took me to a small room on the second floor and removed a wooden box from a cupboard. He emptied the contents onto the table and separated what he said were Henry Turner's belongings. They consisted of a snuffbox, a few silver coins, and the scrap of lace that Mrs. Harper had mentioned.

I picked up the lace. As I'd suspected, the ends were blunt, not raveled. It had been cut. The lace was stiff, because, I saw when I examined it, strands of real gold had been woven through the silk thread.

I closed my hand around it. I knew which lady at the ball had worn this lace, because I had seen her in the gown after the ball. "May I take this?" I asked Pomeroy.

"It ain't much use to me," he said. "Mr. Turner didn't pull it off the coat or dress of his killer. It was tucked, nice and safe, in his pocket. Can't imagine what for."

"Thank you."

"The trial is day after tomorrow, Captain," Pomeroy said. His usually jovial face was grim.

"I know. But Brandon did not murder Mr. Turner. He is only guilty of misplaced honor."

"Best you come up with a way to prove it, sir, or the colonel will swing."

"I am proving it now, Sergeant. Good afternoon."

I descended through the house and back outside to the carriage. "Did you find it?" Lady Breckenridge asked, her eyes animated with interest.

I climbed in next to her, and she gave the order for her coachman to drive on. "I did." I took her gloved hand and laid the scrap of lace into it.

She stared at it. "Good lord." Her face lost color. "You

said this was found in Mr. Turner's pocket? How on earth did it get there?"

"I hoped that you would tell me," I said. "This lace is from the ball gown you wore to the Gillises' last week, is it not? I remember seeing you wearing it when I arrived at Mrs. Brandon's."

CHAPTER 17

L ADY Breckenridge looked up at me, bewildered. "Yes, this is from my gown. But I never gave this lace to Henry Turner. I confess to be amazed."

"I would be less surprised were it torn from your gown. Anyone might have found a bit of lace torn off while you danced. But it was deliberately cut—"

"I know that," she broke in impatiently. "I cut it myself. For Mrs. Bennington."

I blinked. "Mrs. Bennington?"

"Yes. We were in a withdrawing room—my maid was lacing me into my dancing slippers. Mrs. Bennington began admiring the lace on my gown. She asked me for a snippet so she might have her dressmaker find some like it. So I cut a little bit off where it would not show and gave it to her."

I took the lace back from her and laid it on my glove. The innocent scrap glittered with wires of gold against my glove's cheap leather. It was feminine and pretty, and yet strong.

"This killer is of ruthless and nasty mind," I said. "This person does not mind using another man's dagger to do the deed, nor stealing from an innocent woman to assist him. Every clue left will point to a different person, each one completely removed from the crime. The killer planned this with deftness and care, then sat back and laughed."

She watched me with intelligent eyes. "What will you do?"

I thrust the lace into my pocket. "Speak to Mrs. Bennington. I wish to ask her, fairly bluntly, why she wanted a piece of your lace and what she did with it."

"She is performing tonight," Lady Breckenridge said thoughtfully.

"I will try to make an appointment to see her after the play. She invited me once before; she might be persuaded to invite me again."

"She will."

"You seem confident," I said.

She smiled. "My dear Gabriel, you are handsome and polite and unattached. She will see you."

"But penniless," I reminded her.

"Some ladies do not mind this. Sit in my box tonight, and we will visit her afterward. We are in Russel Street now. Shall I have my coachman set you down here?"

I agreed, and she told her coachman to stop.

"Until this evening, then," she said as I descended. "And tell your Miss Simmons not to accost you under the piazza." She chuckled, then the footman closed the door, and the carriage pulled away.

I smiled to myself as I hobbled down Grimpen Lane to my rooms. Bartholomew greeted me with hot coffee, and I reflected, as I often did, what luxury it was to have a valet in training.

I found a letter from Sir Montague Harris waiting for me. As I read it, I mused that I envied his network of sources. He'd managed to find, through inquiries, a man who'd known Mr. Bennington on the continent.

Said gentleman, a solicitor by trade, had moved from Italy back to London shortly after Bennington had. Bennington, the man had told Sir Montague, had come to Italy from the north of England. That interested me, because Bennington certainly did not have a north country accent.

The next statement interested me further. This man who'd known Bennington said that Bennington had been known as Mr. Worth, but shortly before his marriage had changed his name to Bennington. Why he'd changed his name, the man did not know, but then, Bennington—or Worth—had always been whimsical.

Armed with this knowledge, Sir Montague had found the man of business of this Bennington-Worth and visited him.

Yes, Mr. Worth had spent time in Italy, said the man of business, and arranged to have his name changed before he returned to England. Mr. Worth did have a legacy; he'd inherited a fortune about five years ago when a Scottish gentleman, Mr. Worth's fourth cousin, had died. Mr. Worth drew a large sum—how much, the man of business refused to specify—every quarter, a substantial living.

The man of business had not asked Mr. Worth why he wanted to change his name, and speculated that it might be scandal over a woman. No, Mr. Worth was not heavily in debt. He paid his bills regularly, and so was not hiding from creditors or money-lenders.

Mr. Worth seemed to have a stellar reputation. And yet, the drawling, sardonic man had decided to drop *Worth* and become *Bennington*.

"Make of that what you will," Sir Montague finished the letter. "I am certain you will come to some interesting conclusion."

For some reason, I imagined that Sir Montague had already formed his own conclusion and was waiting for me to catch up. I could see him smiling as he wrote.

I read the letter again, shook my head, then sat down to pen a note to Mrs. Bennington, asking to see her again that night.

• • •

LATER, I sat in Lady Breckenridge's box with Lady Aline and a few other ladies and gentlemen of the *ton* with whom I'd become nodding acquaintances.

As usual, the audience talked to each other while the play dragged on and paid attention to the stage only when Mrs. Bennington stepped upon it. She was particularly brilliant tonight, her voice clear and ringing, the character coming to life through her. I even forgot for a moment that she'd possibly been involved in Turner's death.

Grenville's box remained dark and unused. I heard people speculate on where Grenville was hiding himself this evening. I ventured, when my opinion was asked, that Grenville had chosen to have a quiet night at home, but none believed me. They wanted to hear something more interesting than Grenville staying tamely indoors.

After the performance, Lady Breckenridge offered to take me to Cavendish Square in her carriage. I accepted. I knew she was as curious as I, and I believed she deserved to hear the explanation of how her lace got into the pocket of Mr. Turner.

I wanted also to bring Grenville along. Lady Breckenridge acquiesced and told her coachman to drive first to Grosvenor Street. Something was in the wind between him and Mrs. Bennington, and I did not want to chance that it had nothing to do with Turner's murder. He would not thank me, but in the choice between saving Colonel Brandon and not offending Grenville, I had to choose Colonel Brandon's life.

Grenville, however, was not at home. Matthias, who answered the door, informed me with a conspiratorial look that Grenville was spending the evening in his house on Clarges Street.

I spent a few moments wondering whether I should intrude upon Grenville's privacy, then I decided to intrude. I told Lady Breckenridge's coachman to drive us to Clarges Street, and we stopped before the house.

"I will have to ask you to remain here while I go inside," I said to Lady Breckenridge. "There are reasons."

She laughed. "My dear Lacey, it would hardly do for a lady of the *ton* to enter the house in which a gentleman keeps his mistress."

I let out my breath. "You know far too many things for comfort, Donata."

She gave me a knowing smile. "Gossip is the most popular entertainment in London. There is little I do *not* know."

The thought unnerved me a bit. I descended from the carriage into the rain, and plied the doorknocker. A haughty maid opened the door and looked me up and down.

Lucius Grenville employed the best-trained servants in London; even more so than Lady Gillis's elegant horde. The maid who confronted me stolidly refused to admit me. I had to talk long and hard to convince her that the matter was of utmost urgency.

She at last let me in, but forbade me to move farther than the front hall. She sent the footman upstairs with a message for Grenville, then she hovered nearby, as though not trusting me not to dash up the stairs the instant her back was turned.

After an appallingly long wait, a door opened above, and I heard Grenville's footsteps on the stairs.

In the year or so that I'd known Grenville, I had never seen him in dishabille. Even now he was in only relative dishabille. He wore pantaloons and a lawn shirt and a frock coat, all covered with a silk dressing gown. His hair was only a bit mussed. His expression was wary and not a little annoyed.

"Lacey," he said, in his cool man-about-town voice. "I respect and admire you, but this is hardly the best time for a visit."

"I realize that," I answered. "But I was on my way to the Benningtons, and I hoped you would come with me."

His brows rose. "The Benningtons? Why?" He stopped on the last stair, which put his height about level with mine.

"Because I believe they are the key to this murder. I thought you might want to be present."

He came alert, all thoughts of privacy forgotten. "Yes. Yes I do. I must dress. Wait here."

"Be quick, please. I do not want Mrs. Bennington's dragon of a maid to refuse to admit me because I am late for the appointment."

Without answering, he turned and dashed back up the stairs. The sound of a door banging followed.

I waited impatiently while the clock ticked steadily in the corner. I wished that Grenville was a man who could simply snatch up a greatcoat and dash out the door. But he would refuse to do so. He'd once told me that if he was seen on the streets of London without waistcoat and cravat and the proper footwear, the newspapers would be filled with stories that he'd run mad. Not even for murder would Grenville take chances with his reputation.

When the door banged again, I looked up in anticipation, but the voice that sailed down to me was not Grenville's.

"Lacey, what the devil do you think you're doing?"

Marianne Simmons, in true dishabille, raced down the stairs to me in nothing but a loose peignoir, her hair floating free.

"Trying to discover a murderer, Marianne."

"You come here and snatch him away to visit *Mrs. Bennington*, of all people! Why, I'd like to know? Let me come with you. I will claw her eyes out."

"No," I said firmly.

"Dear God, Lacey, why must you torment me?"

"I want to question Mrs. Bennington about the murder. I want Grenville there as well."

"And I suppose you will not tell me why?"

"No."

She looked as though she might fly at me, claws raised, but she stopped, her face taking on a canny expression. "Did Mrs. Bennington do the murder? That would suit me."

I looked past her at Grenville, who was at last descending the stairs. He had heard her. "Mrs. Bennington had nothing to do with Turner's death," he said. "I am accompanying Lacey to prove it."

Marianne sent him a look of fury, but I saw the hurt in her eyes. She dropped her gaze and turned away before Grenville could spot it. "Mary," she called to the prim maid. "Come upstairs and dress me. I am going out."

Grenville's face set. Saying nothing, he strode past her and out of the house.

So great was his anger that he'd climbed into the carriage before he realized that the coach belonged to Lady Breckenridge, and that she was waiting inside.

He flushed. "My lady."

"Mr. Grenville," Lady Breckenridge returned, her eyes glinting with humor.

Grenville sent me an accusing glance. He was angry, and he was embarrassed, but I could not wait upon the nicety of his feelings. As the carriage wound through the streets to Cavendish Square, I showed him the scrap of lace and explained about the servants' passage at the Gillis house and my speculations. As I talked, Grenville's expression became grim.

"If this is true, Lacey," he began. He broke off, as though unable to complete the thought. "I never believed—"

He broke off again, closed his mouth, and looked away in uncomfortable silence.

The Benningtons' house in Cavendish Square was quiet. We were admitted by a maid, who curtseyed to us and led us to a reception room to wait. Grenville paced, moody and quiet, while Lady Breckenridge looked about her with interested dark eyes.

Mrs. Bennington's maid, Grady, entered the room not long later. She sent the three of us a look of disapproval.

"My lady has decided that she is not receiving tonight," she said.

I had feared as much. "I do not wish to disturb her for long." I took the scrap of lace from my pocket and handed it to Grady. "Please give her this, and tell her Captain Lacey wishes to ask her about it."

Grady frowned at me, then when she saw what I held out, paled. "She will know nothing about it."

"Take it to her, please."

Grady pressed her mouth closed. She snatched the lace from my hand and marched swiftly from the room.

Grenville shot me a dark look. "You cannot mean that Claire Bennington committed this crime, can you? I simply will not believe it."

"I do not know whether she committed it. That is why I want to ask her questions."

He paced again, his distress evident. "She could not have killed Turner. She is not strong enough. She's only a girl."

He seemed inordinately upset, more so than a gentleman with simple concern for a young woman. Before I could speculate further, Grady returned. She did not look best pleased, but she said that we could all go up to Mrs. Bennington's private room.

Grady led us upstairs to the sitting room in which Mrs. Bennington had received me before. Again, the room struck me with its elegant anonymity, except this time, the salmon-striped sofa and chairs were strewn with gowns and bonnets and shawls. I was reminded of Turner's rooms when the valet, Hazleton, had emptied the cupboards in preparation for sending away all of Turner's things.

Grenville looked at the jumble in surprise. "You are leaving London?"

Mrs. Bennington flinched and avoided his gaze. "Grady, why did you let him come here? I wanted Captain Lacey."

"I came to help you," Grenville said, anger in his tone.

"We don't want your help," Grady retorted. She put her hands on her hips.

Mrs. Bennington sank to a chair and put her hand to her forehead. "I have such a headache. I do not want these people. I feel unwell."

"You see?" Grady said to Grenville. "You have upset her again."

"I have done nothing of the sort," Grenville returned. "Lacey has come to question you about the murder of Henry Turner, Mrs. Bennington. I know you had nothing to do with it, and if you answer honestly, I believe I can make him take his questioning elsewhere."

I looked at him in amazement. His face was red, his gaze uncomfortable.

Mrs. Bennington's eyes swam with tears. "My head. Grady, I need my draught."

Grady rushed to the cupboard and pulled out a glass bottle full of dark liquid.

Lady Breckenridge, who had lifted a silk shawl to admire it, suddenly burst into a peal of laughter. "Good heavens, how dramatic we are." She folded the shawl and replaced it on the chair. "We are not on the stage, Mrs. Bennington. Captain Lacey only wishes to know to whom you gave that bit of lace that you asked of me."

"Oh." Mrs. Bennington sat up, looking relieved. "I see. I gave it to my husband."

"Your husband?" I asked. "What on earth for?"

She blinked. "Because he asked me."

"It did not occur to you to wonder why? Did he wish to buy you a gown?"

"I do not know."

"You do know," I answered. "I believe that you know more than any of us about this matter."

Her eyes filled. "How could I?"

"You play the fool well," I said gently. "But I believe you are not a fool."

She looked at me in stunned disbelief. Then the blank look left her eyes, and she bit her lip.

"Leave her be, Lacey," Grenville said suddenly.

I shook my head. "She is key to this. I want Colonel Brandon released, and I will do what I must to bring it about."

"Including browbeating a young woman?"

I stared at him. Grady had accused him of shouting at Mrs. Bennington and going so far as to throw his walking stick, and now he bristled at me like a dog guarding its master.

"Mrs. Bennington," I said, softening my voice. "Why

did your husband ask you to obtain a piece of lace from Lady Breckenridge?"

She shook her head. "I do not remember. It was a game of some sort."

Grenville and the maid Grady both looked thunderous, Lady Breckenridge, interested.

"A wager?" I supplied.

Her brow cleared. "Yes, that was it. He wagered that I could not obtain a piece of lace from a high-born lady. Because I am so low-born, you see."

"He said that?" Grenville asked, incredulous. "What the devil made you marry that man? Do not tell me you could not have the pick of gentlemen on the continent."

Mrs. Bennington looked confused again. "He was good to me. I had debts—he paid them. He must be kind to do that."

Or he wanted something, I thought. But Claire Bennington, absorbed in herself and her life on stage, did not realize that.

"Is he kind?" I asked.

"I suppose he is." She pressed delicate fingers to her temples. "Really, Captain, my head does ache."

Grady, her face set, poured a thick liquid into a small glass and pushed it at Mrs. Bennington.

Lady Breckenridge, looking more amused than angry that she'd been the butt of a wager, sat down amid a pile of velvets. "So you handed over the scrap of lace to your husband. When was that?"

"Oh, good heavens, I hardly remember." Mrs. Bennington took the draught from Grady and drank it down. She sighed happily when she handed the glass back, as though her headache was fading already. "Before supper, certainly. My husband escorted Lady Aline to the supper room. He had wanted me to get a scrap of lace from *her*, but I only had the opportunity to speak to Lady Breckenridge. He was annoyed, I remember, that I had not approached Lady Aline."

Who was large and strong and could have driven a knife into Turner's heart if she was cruel enough to do it.

"Do you love your husband, Mrs. Bennington?" I asked abruptly.

Her eyes widened. "Why ask that?"

"Because he is a murderer," I said. "And I wondered if you would help me or be loyal to him."

CHAPTER 18

LADY Breckenridge looked at me in complete astonishment. "Mr. Bennington?" She blinked, then grew thoughtful. "Yes, I see."

Mrs. Bennington lowered her gaze. "I should be loyal. He is my husband."

Grady broke in fiercely, "She had nothing to do with it. I'll not see her in the dock for this."

"Nor will I," I said.

I tried to sound reassuring, but Grady moved between me and her mistress. "She is an innocent. She cannot help what that fiend of a husband does."

"I know," I said, "I imagine that Mr. Bennington used her from the moment he met her. He knew that as her husband, he would be eclipsed by her, and he was correct."

Grenville did not look terribly surprised by my assessment, but he was not happy.

Lady Breckenridge's eyes sparkled with interest. She was possibly the only person in the room not charged with emotion.

"I can work out how he must have done it," she said. "He

challenged Mrs. Bennington to obtain a bit of lace from a lady, which she did—from me. Mr. Bennington goes into the anteroom at some time, possibly before supper, opens the door to the servants' passage, and affixes the lace to the nail to mark the door he needed. He does not want to use something of his own or his wife's in case it is found.

"He makes an appointment to meet Turner in the anteroom at midnight. Just before midnight, he slips out of the ballroom and into one of the sitting rooms along the hall. He waits until the servants' passage is empty, enters it, finds the door he marked, and enters the anteroom, taking the bit of lace with him. He stabs Mr. Turner, lowers him into the chair, and places the lace in the pocket. He leaves Colonel Brandon's knife in the wound, to implicate him, and exits through the servants' hall just before Mrs. Harper enters."

She stopped and drew a breath. "I believe that explains everything neatly."

"True," I said. "Though not how he obtained Brandon's knife."

"Nor why Mr. Bennington should want to murder Mr. Turner at all," she added.

"I've made some guesses about that. Both men were on the continent and have only recently returned to London. Perhaps Turner knew things that Bennington did not want others to know. Things that led him to change his name." I fixed my gaze on Grady. "Do you know?"

Grady glanced at her mistress, who kept her gaze fixed on her lap. She wet her thin lips and said, "Bennington is a bad sort. But my lady, she was deep in debt—she will wager recklessly, she will. That was not the first time she'd been in deep."

Mrs. Bennington flushed, but did not raise her head. Grenville looked unhappy. "You should be careful," he said.

"Aye, that's what I tell her. One of her creditors, he was threatening her with arrest. And us being in Italy, what would happen if she was taken by foreign police? Then Mr. Bennington, he comes backstage one night and says he'll pay the debts, all of them, free and clear, if only she'll marry him."

"That must have seemed an answer from heaven," I observed.

Mrs. Bennington raised her head. "I was so relieved, I could not refuse him. I saw no reason *to* refuse him. He said I could do what I pleased, and he would keep me out of trouble with the creditors. Why should I not marry him?"

"Because he is a blackguard," Grenville said. "Did you not sense that?"

Mrs. Bennington looked puzzled. "No. He offered to help me. I wanted to go to London to perform, and he enabled me to do so. He has heaps of money. He was left a grand inheritance."

"He was," I said. "From a relative in Scotland."

"Oh," she asked. "Is he Scottish?"

"No," I answered. "I have not been able to place his accent, in fact; it seems very neutral, but perhaps that is because he lived so long in Italy. His true name is Mr. Worth. Does that mean anything to you?"

Mrs. Bennington shook her head. "He never told me."

"Did your husband know Mr. Turner on the continent?"

She looked blank. "Who is Mr. Turner?"

I wondered whether she was acting or if she'd truly felt no need to pay attention to the explanation that Lady Breckenridge had just put forth.

"Young man what was killed," Grady said, her face grim. "Aye, Mr. Bennington knew him."

I swung on her. I started to ask why the devil she hadn't mentioned this when I'd visited before, but I remembered that she had not been in the room when I mentioned Mr. Turner to Mrs. Bennington.

"You saw him? In Italy?"

"Yes," Grady said. "Not long after my lady married. Young Mr. Turner came to visit Mr. Bennington. Talked to him like he wasn't a stranger, like they'd met before, but Mr. Bennington wasn't best pleased to see him. I heard Mr. Turner call him Mr. Worth—and then, funny thing, said he was not even Mr. Worth. Mr. Bennington got jittery. Then Mr. Turner went away."

"A magistrate would be interested in knowing this," I said. "Why did you say nothing before?"

"I didn't want my lady bothered by Bow Street," she said indignantly. "That Runner, the one who came to the ball, was a great bully. And my lady had nothing to do with it."

"But you said nothing?" Grenville asked angrily. "Even about overhearing what Turner said? If you believed Bennington was hiding something, why did you say nothing to your mistress?"

"Because he paid the debts. She needs his money. She deserves it. Why should she not have it?"

"If Bennington is a murderer, she will lose all of it," I pointed out.

Grady looked stricken. Mrs. Bennington seemed more resigned. "I have my money from the stage. And I have been poor before."

"You will not be again," Grenville said. "I will see to it."

Both Lady Breckenridge and I looked at him in surprise. His face was flushed with anger. "I will take care of you, Claire," he went on. "I offered to before, remember?"

She turned to him, her hazel eyes wide. "You frightened me. You said I must divorce him. I did not know what to think."

Neither did I. Grenville and Mrs. Bennington looked at each other, and the pair of them seemed to forget that the rest of us were in the room.

"When you are free of Bennington, I will take care of you," Grenville said, his voice softening. "I told you this, and I promise it. I should have done so long ago."

I exchanged a glance with Lady Breckenridge. I shrugged slightly, to indicate that I did not know what to make of the conversation.

"Turner is dead now," Lady Breckenridge broke in. "So who can know what he wanted with Bennington? To blackmail him, presumably, over the fact that Bennington was not Bennington. Did he want to leave Italy because of Turner, or because others had got wind of his deception?"

"I plan to ask him," I said. "Where is Mr. Bennington at present?"

Mrs. Bennington looked blank. "I never notice where he goes."

"He likes to sit in a hotel in Piccadilly," Grady supplied. "I've heard him say so. He doesn't have a club like a proper gentleman."

I took up my walking stick, my usual impatience getting the better of me. "If I can get a confession out of Bennington and have him arrested, that will solve many problems."

Lady Breckenridge looked alarmed. "He is a murderer, Gabriel. He killed one man who knew his secrets; why would he not kill you?"

"Because I have one thing that Turner did not—a very large and loud former sergeant who is now a Bow Street Runner."

"I would like to come with you," Grenville said. "If Bennington is guilty, I want to put my hands on him." He looked restless and dangerous.

"Shall we adjourn to Piccadilly?" Lady Breckenridge asked. "In my carriage. I will accompany you, gentlemen."

"No, you will not," I said immediately. "We will return you home and go from there."

She gave me a scornful look. "I am not a wilting flower, Gabriel. I do not intend to enter a gentlemen's hotel, but I certainly will not sit home and wait for you to remember to call on me and tell me what happened."

Grenville seemed uninterested in our disagreement. "Let us away, Lacey. I am ready to arrest a murderer."

"I want Pomeroy," I said.

"Very well. We'll fetch him." He swept out of the room without taking leave of Mrs. Bennington. I bowed to her, but she gazed after Grenville with a mixed expression of hope and fear.

Lady Breckenridge and I descended the stairs together.

Grenville paced in the foyer, waiting for us. I held him back as Lady Breckenridge hurried out the door to the carriage.

"Do you love her?" I asked in a low voice. "Mrs. Bennington, I mean."

"What? Of course I love her." His scowl suddenly softened, then he sighed. "I ought to have told you. But it caught me a resounding blow when I found out, and I have not yet recovered." He lowered his voice and said, with a little smile, "Claire is my sister."

WE found Mr. Bennington in the sitting room of the Majestic Hotel in Piccadilly. The hotel itself was not far from the house where Henry Turner had kept his rooms.

Mr. Bennington sat in an armchair reading the *Times*, his immaculate suit attesting to the exactness of his valet. He had crossed his legs and held the newspaper carefully in manicured hands.

He glanced up when I walked into the room alone, but betrayed no surprise. "I will be with you in a moment, Captain," he said. "I am reading a fascinating story about a gentleman's journey through the wilds of Prussia. I must ask, if he complains of not having the comforts of London in the middle of Germany, why did he leave home in the first place?"

"I could not say," I answered.

He hummed a little tune in his throat as he read on, then he finally laid the paper aside. "Sit down, Captain. We might as well be civilized. You have found me out, have you? I wondered how long it would take you. People talk about your cleverness, but I believe you are not as clever as your reputation paints you."

I did take a seat, but one far out of his reach. We were the only ones in the sitting room, and late afternoon sunshine slanted through the windows. The room was quiet and genteel, with a gilded clock ticking on the mantelpiece and decanters of wine and brandy resting on tables for the guests' convenience.

Grenville and Pomeroy waited without for me to call them in. I wished I could have had time to speak to Grenville a bit more after he made his astounding statement about Mrs. Bennington, but we had no moments of privacy. His revelation, however, explained some of his odd behavior—he was a worried brother, not a jealous lover.

"In this instance, I was distracted by Colonel Brandon," I said to Bennington. "The knife pointed too much to him, and he did not help by being stubbornly vague with both me and the magistrate."

"He is a stubborn gentleman," Bennington said with a smile. "I was pleased, quite pleased, actually, to discover that I was not the only person that horrible young man tried to blackmail. I did Colonel Brandon a favor."

"By landing him in Newgate?" I asked, my temper rising.

"That is unfortunate," Bennington agreed. "But I saved him from whatever Turner was threatening him with."

"You did not know what it is?"

"No, nor did I care. My dear Lacey, I cared only that Turner knew I should not have enjoyed my glorious inheritance."

"You stole the inheritance," I said, everything coming together. "You pretended to be the heir, when you were not."

"Excellent, Captain," Bennington said. He applauded me softly. "A man can steal an inheritance, you know, if he is very lucky. And I was. The male line of the family was in an obscure branch, and I convinced the solicitors that I was that obscure heir—made easier because I knew that my friend Mr. Worth was dead—fell down a mountain in Bavaria, poor fellow. He was all alone, with no one to know but me."

"So you convinced them," I said. "Then you went to Italy to live far from people who'd known the true Mr. Worth—and yourself, for that matter. But then, Turner discovered your secret."

He watched me with an amused expression, as though he'd been indulging in a wager and now realized he had finally lost it. "Five years I'd enjoyed the income. I was able to live in a manner I'd never dreamed possible. Why the devil should I lose it?"

"How did Turner know that you were not the true Mr. Worth?" I asked.

"My bad luck. Mr. Turner apparently met someone who'd known Worth, and they'd mentioned that either Worth had changed mightily, or I wasn't the same man. I suppose Turner, bored, decided to dig around and find out. He was a careful gambler—was good at doing his research so he'd more likely win. He took me aside and explained this to me one day while I was strolling about for my health, smiling in a rather nasty way. He liked money, so it was quite easy to press a bank draft into his hand and make him go away."

"But he returned?"

"Oh, yes. I made a mistake believing that giving him money would see the end of it. I'd never dealt with a blackmailer before, you see. I thought I had been so careful to cover my tracks."

"But he persisted."

"Yes, he was quite obnoxious. He told me he planned to settle on the continent—I'd heard rumor that he had a paramour in Paris—so I decided to return to England. I changed my name so that it would be more difficult for Turner to find me again. I married Claire, who'd gotten far over her pretty head in debt to some nasty creditors. I had to tell the solicitor about the change in name so that he'd know where to continue sending the money. I pay him marvelously high fees, and he agreed without argument. He thought me an eccentric in any case, for preferring the rain and gloom of England to living in the sunshine of Italy. Mr. Bennington I became, and Claire and I returned to London. Claire enjoyed the adulation of the crowd, and I became 'Mr. Bennington what married that famous actress.'"

"But Turner came to London."

He grimaced. "Yes, worse luck. He quarreled with his mistress and returned to England. There he was, smiling and demanding more money. I knew that if he told the solicitor my secret, I was finished."

"So you killed Turner."

"I had no choice. I feared to call him out, because if I did, he'd likely spread the tale of why I did, and second . . ." He smiled. "Henry Turner was reputed to be a dead shot. He'd have potted me good."

"You would have died with honor," I said.

He blinked. "Dear me, I have no honor. Honor is for cavalry captains. If I had honor, I'd not have pushed my friend Mr. Worth down the mountain five years ago after I learned he'd come into a large inheritance. His face was completely smashed, poor fellow, and there we were, in a foreign country, no one there knowing which of us was which. So I stole his identity. The old me was buried, and a new George Worth wrote to the solicitors saying he was moving on to Italy and to send the funds there. Then I met Claire." His look turned sardonic.

"Why did you marry her?" I asked curiously.

He gave me a pitying look. "For the most basic reason of all, Captain. I fell in love with her. How could I not? She bewitched me. She had hordes of young men dancing attendance on her, but I had one thing she could not resist. Money. I promised to pay her debts if she'd do me the honor of becoming my wife. I fondly thought that once I'd paid her creditors and charmed her with my wit, she would fall in love with me. Alas, no." He smiled at himself. "She is too fond of pretty young men, and adores their attentions. And unfortunately, I have a sad affliction and cannot bother her in the carnal way, which I assure you she does not mind. She never pretended that she'd married me for anything but convenience. And so, you see, if Turner took my legacy away from me, I would have nothing left to keep Claire at my side. Therefore . . ." He made a dismissing gesture, as though brushing Turner away.

I watched him for a moment. "You are correct about one thing. You have no honor."

"Oh, come, come, Captain. Where would that legacy

have gone? George Worth told me he had no heir that he knew of, unless his man of business could find some fellow living in the wilds of America or some such place. Why should all that money go to waste? I put it to excellent use."

"Money is no replacement for friendship and esteem," I pointed out.

"Spoken like a true gentleman. I suppose that in the army you threw yourself in front of bullets to save others?"

"Not quite," I said, "but I did pull others out of the way of bullets."

"All for pittance. You are a poor man, Captain. You always have been. What can you understand of a man's need for wealth and comfort?"

"Grenville is the wealthiest man I've ever met," I said quietly. "He loves his comfort, and yet he has honor and generosity and charity."

"Ah, well. Blame it on my birth. My father was a poor man who blew his brains out when he lost his little all on a horse. He left a son buried in a school with no one to care for him. Pity me, Captain."

"I pity your wife. And even Turner, although, by all accounts, he was not a pleasant young man."

"He was not. I did the world a favor, my dear fellow."

I stood up, my patience at an end. "Had you killed him in a duel, or even murdered him in a straightforward way, I might understand. But you deliberately endangered Colonel Brandon and Mrs. Harper, both of whom were innocent. You tried to implicate Lady Breckenridge, although that, to her good luck, came to nothing."

"Well, I could hardly continue to enjoy my legacy if I owned up to murdering the chap, could I? And besides, Colonel Brandon and Mrs. Harper were not innocent. They were carrying on a frightfully sordid affair. I found it amusing that Turner was blackmailing them as well."

"Colonel Brandon is in prison for murder. I intend to get him out of that prison one way or another, even if I have to drag you by the neck to Bow Street myself."

To my satisfaction, Bennington looked slightly alarmed.
"You are a man of determination."

"I owe Colonel Brandon much. I will not see him die for
something he did not do. And you, if you have spoken the
truth today, are long overdue for paying."

He continued to watch me. "Think of my wife, Captain.
Claire Bennington cannot be left alone for a moment. I love
her, but she is one of the stupidest women alive, even if she
is brilliant behind the footlights. What will become of her?"

I thought of Grenville. "She will be cared for. Quite
well, in fact. She no longer needs you."

He paled. "Never tell me some gentleman is waiting in
the wings to sweep her off." He gave me a faint smile. "I
just made a pun, did I not? Waiting in the wings?"

"Very amusing. I am fortunate to have friends, Mr. Bennington. One of them is a Bow Street Runner."

As if on cue, Pomeroy entered the room.

At the sight of tall, jovial Pomeroy, anticipating a reward
for the conviction of Henry Turner's murderer, Bennington
lost his sangfroid. "Oh, God."

"A most illuminating conversation, Captain," Pomeroy
boomed. "Criminals, especially the clever ones, do like to
talk. Mr. Bennington—or Mr. Worth—or whatever you
would like to be called, I arrest you in the king's name for
the murder of Henry Turner. Shall you come with me and
speak to the magistrate? Since you like to talk, you'll be
able to tell your story all over again. I am looking forward
to it."

CHAPTER 19

I wanted the matter to conclude simply, by letting Brandon
out of his prison room and putting Bennington into it.

But of course, that could not be done. Pomeroy took
Bennington to Bow Street, where he would wait until the
next morning for Sir Nathaniel to examine him. I had very
little evidence to give Pomeroy, save for the conversation
that he had overheard and my explanation of how Bennington had managed to kill Turner with no one seeing him.

Lady Breckenridge, who'd been delighted to observe us
emerging from the hotel with Bennington and see Pomeroy
drive off in a hackney with him, kindly had her coachman
take us to Grenville's house in Grosvenor Street.

Grenville descended first. As I prepared to follow, Lady
Breckenridge stopped me with a hand on my arm.

"I thank you for not shunting me aside, Gabriel. That
was most fascinating," she said, her eyes alight.

"You ought to curb your fascination at such a sordid
business," I said, but I returned the smile. A fainting flower
she was not. Past experience had shown that I had not the
patience for a fainting flower.

"Nonsense," she said briskly. "It was just the thing. Life in Mayfair is deadly dull, you know. The same people at the same soirees and balls and garden parties, talking of the same things, day after day. You and your investigations are refreshing."

"I am pleased to entertain you."

"Do not tease me; you like my interest. When you have finished all you need to finish, Gabriel, pay a call on me. I would be happy to receive you."

Her tone was light, but I sensed wariness behind it. She was still not certain where we stood, and somewhere inside her existed the young woman who'd been bruised by her unhappy marriage.

I bowed. "I would be most happy to call."

She gave me a faint smile as though she did not care one way or the other, and lifted her hand from me. But her eyes as she turned away told me she was pleased.

I left the carriage and followed Grenville into his warm and splendid house.

Grenville invited me to supper. I declined. "I have many things to do this night," I said. "I must go to Louisa and tell her what has happened."

"You are right. What I have to say can wait."

"You should say it to Marianne," I suggested. "Tell her the truth. She deserves to know."

"Claire does not know, yet," Grenville said, his eyes quiet. "Her mother wrote me a letter a few weeks ago. She told me that she was very ill, and that Claire was a by-blow of my father's. My father certainly indulged himself; the woman I always thought of as my cousin turned out to be his by-blow as well. He fathered Claire twenty years ago, and apparently provided for her mother adequately, if not lavishly."

"Not to throw cold water," I said, "but you are very rich, and this woman could simply claim that your father sired her daughter."

"I know." He gave me a rueful smile. "When one has a great deal of money, there are those who feel it is natural that you should give it to them. But Claire is his, I am certain of it."

"You wish to be certain of it."

"True. I am foolishly pleased to find another sibling. We shall gather for Christmas and exchange New Year's gifts. Claire is beautiful and talented, and I am proud to help her. I knew the moment I saw her she belonged to my family." He grinned. "She has the Grenville nose."

LADY Aline was not with Louisa when I arrived at the house in Brook Street. Louisa explained, when she received me, that she had sent Lady Aline home.

"She is so kind to me," Louisa said. Her face was wan, her fingers, too thin. "But I wanted to be alone. It is difficult to keep up my spirits to please her."

"You will not have to do so much longer," I said.

We were in her yellow sitting room, a fire on the hearth chasing away the gloom of the evening. I told her about Bennington and his arrest and said that in the morning I would ask Sir Nathaniel to dismiss the murder charge against Brandon and let him go.

Louisa sagged as I finished my tale, her lips bloodless.

"You did this," she whispered. "You did this for me."

"Yes," I answered.

"Why are you so impossibly good to me, Gabriel?"

"There have been times in my life when you were strong for me. I wanted to be strong for you, this once."

Tears spilled down her face. "I have not been strong at all. You say he is truly innocent of this?"

"He did not kill Turner. I knew from the beginning that the crime was all wrong for him. Nor is Imogene Harper his mistress."

She lifted her head. "She was. On the Peninsula. However briefly."

"I know. I am not certain I can forgive him that."

"I will." When I looked surprised, she sighed. "He is my

husband, Gabriel. We have weathered much together. We will weather this, too."

"You love the idiot."

"Yes. I always have." She touched my cheek. "And I love you, too."

"A fact which warms my heart." I kissed her forehead lightly, then let her go. "I hope that our friendship may weather all this, as well."

"It will. I will not be so ungrateful as to shun you simply because I am embarrassed."

"Good." I paused. The cheerful room had grown still more cheerful, and in a few moments, I would not be able to bear it. "What did you do with the paper, Louisa?"

She stopped. "Paper?"

"The one Brandon told you to fetch from the Gillises'."

Her cheeks darkened. "Must you know everything?"

"It is a dangerous thing to have."

"I know that. But the greatest danger he fears is from you."

I held on to my temper. "Does he truly believe I would betray him? Please give it to me, Louisa. Unless you have already destroyed it."

"I have not." She walked away from me. "How did you know I had it?"

"Because there is no one else in the world he would have trusted it to. I had toyed with the idea that he gave it to Mrs. Harper, but she did not have it. He probably meant to hide it and fetch it the next day. I do not think he dreamed he'd be bound over for trial. He did not murder Turner, he knew, and expected everyone else to believe him. You read French," I finished gently. "You must have known what the document was."

She lowered her gaze. "Yes."

"You went to see Brandon after I'd admonished you to?"

She looked at me. "I did. And he told me an extraordinary tale. He bared his soul to me. He must have been quite desperate to do that. He does hate to appear weak, especially to a woman, most especially to his wife."

"He craves your respect."

"Yes, well, he does have that. He told me where the paper was and begged me, for God's sake, not to give it to you."

"I already know his secrets." I gave her a look of appeal. "Will you trust me and let me have the document? No one in the world but you and I and he will know what becomes of it."

"What about Mrs. Harper?" Louisa asked.

"Mrs. Harper should bless her luck that Brandon decided to help her at all—and that Bennington stabbed Turner. I will send word to her that it is all over, and that she should return to Scotland."

"Good," Louisa said. She was still pale, but her eyes began to sparkle with their usual fervor. "I might forgive Aloysius all he's done, because he can be so easily led into mischief. But Mrs. Harper is another matter. She had no business pinching my husband."

I laughed. "I am pleased to see that you will not simply be walked on."

"Indeed no. I expect Aloysius to be quite kind to me for a very long time." She placed her hand on my arm and gave me a warm smile. "Now, drink some coffee while I fetch the paper. Mary made it special for you, and she will be distressed if you do not have at least a cup."

AN hour later found me at Newgate prison with the incriminating letter tucked into my pocket. The turnkey was reluctant to let me in at this late hour, but he was easily bribed. Besides, Colonel Brandon was a posh guest, and he received privileges that the lower masses did not.

I found Brandon still dressed, sitting on his bed with his head in his hands. He looked up when I was ushered in, then sprang to his feet. "What are you doing here?"

I waited until the turnkey shut the door, then waited again until I heard his footsteps retreat before I spoke.

"I came to tell you that you will soon be free. I found the man who truly committed the crime."

Brandon stared at me in shock. "But—"

"Had you convinced yourself that I never would? Mr. Bennington was arrested this evening. I hoped you could be released at once, but magistrates take their own time."

In a few short sentences I described how Bennington had done the murder and how I'd found him out. Brandon gaped at me through the story, then when I finished, he began to splutter.

"The blackguard. Using my knife, sitting by quietly as you please while I waited here for trial. Good lord." He raked his hands through his hair until it stuck out.

"Would it help to know that he is terrified?" I asked.

"What? No, of course not. I long to call the fellow out, but that would not be the thing, would it?"

He paced the cell, animation flowing back into his body. Brandon dejected was a sad sight. Now his eyes flashed, and his back was straight and strong.

I said, "If you had told me the truth from the beginning, sir, you might not have had to come here at all."

He swung to me. "Oh, yes I would have. When I admitted the knife was mine, Pomeroy blamed me at once, damn the man."

"Which he would not have if you'd stayed in the ballroom within sight the entire night with your wife." I glared at him. "I know about Naveau, and the document, and Mrs. Harper. What were you thinking?"

His stopped. "You know what the document is?"

"Why the devil didn't you come to me when Mrs. Harper first wrote you about Turner? I could have retrieved the paper from him without all your machinations at the ball. I know people, like Grenville, who could have made him hand it over, and if we were more desperate still, I know Denis. I could have gotten it back for you. Why did you not trust me?"

He looked at me with infuriating stubbornness. "Because I know how much you hate me. Would you not use the opportunity to bring about my downfall? I could see you doing that, with glee."

"Then you read me entirely wrong. I have been loyal to you since the day I swore allegiance to you, twenty years ago. That has not changed."

"I hurt you." He shot a guilty look at my walking stick.

"I know. And I haven't forgiven you for it, believe me. But you were angry—you thought I'd taken Louisa, whom you love more than life. You feared that she'd leave you for me, even after you retracted your plan to divorce her. You would have deserved it if she had, but she loves you. The pair of you are so romantic, you make me weep. I never bedded your wife, Brandon. Never. She would not have done that."

"But you would have," he said sullenly.

"Of course I would have. Louisa has always been special to me. If she had wanted to give herself to me in that way, I would have done it and felt privileged to do so. But it never happened, and it never will."

He glared at me with his old fire. "That does not make me feel disposed to trust you."

"You might be a complete fool concerning your wife, but it is also true that I owe you my life. All of it." I gave him a firm look. "And so I will do my damndest to keep you safe."

I took the document from my pocket and held it up for him to see. I'd read it in Louisa's sitting room and had nearly groaned in dismay. In Brandon's handwriting, in French, the letter told Colonel Naveau of Mrs. Harper's husband's death and that there would be no more information from that source. The letter also included a copy of a dispatch that Major Harper had set aside for Naveau.

"This is what everything has been about. Good God, sir. What possessed you? Mrs. Harper's eyes? The fact that you might coerce her to marry you and bear you children? Was that truly your reason to betray us to the French? Other men have done so, but I never in a thousand years dreamed *you* would."

Brandon ignored my tirade. "Where did you get that?"

"Louisa gave it to me after she'd found where you'd hidden it."

"I told Louisa expressly not to show it to you."

"What did you fear I'd do? Sell it back to Naveau? I am, in fact, supposed to do that very thing, for James Denis."

Brandon whitened. "I will never let you. I will kill you first."

"Your faith in me is overwhelming."

I turned on my heel and stalked to the fireplace. There I knelt down and thrust the paper into the flames.

"What are you doing?" he bleated.

"Burning the thing. Or would you like to go on trial for treason?"

He approached me, his footsteps slow. I took up the poker and held the paper right into the heart of the fire. I watched while the entire document burned. When any scrap fell, I lifted it with tongs and shoved it back into the flames.

I waited until the paper had burned completely to ashes, then rose.

"There. Let that be an end to it."

Brandon was staring at me like he could not believe what I'd just done. "James Denis told you to take it to Naveau?"

"Yes," I said tersely.

"What will you tell him?"

He looked a bit worried. I wondered if he worried on my behalf, or feared that Denis would retaliate against him for not stopping me.

"I will think of something." I leaned on my walking stick. "Why did you not have Louisa destroy it?"

"I hadn't time to examine it closely at the ball. I wanted to be certain it was the right letter. Turner had closed it into another paper, and I barely had time to break the seal and see that the handwriting was mine before I fled the room. I fancied I'd heard someone coming. Then when he was dead, I panicked."

I stared at him, seeing the last turn of the labyrinth

straighten before me. "That is how you left the knife in the anteroom, is it not? You pulled it from your pocket to break the seal and left it on the table in your haste."

He looked blank. "Yes, I suppose I must have done. At the time I was not worried about the damned knife."

"Careless of you, but even if your knife had not been found, your behavior made you suspicious enough that night." I let myself grow angry. "How could you have written such a letter in the first place? How many men did we lose because you sent Naveau that dispatch?"

Brandon gave me a look of contempt. "The information was false."

I stopped. "I beg your pardon?"

"I changed the dispatch when I copied it. The information Naveau received was false. I imagine that a French troop scoured the hills looking for the English for many hours. Meanwhile we were far away." He peered at me. "Do you think I would pass on information to the French, Gabriel? What do you take me for?"

I let out my breath. "Do you know, sir, sometimes I could cheerfully strangle you."

"We are already in prison. You would not have to go far."

Brandon rarely tried for levity, so I could not know whether he was attempting a joke.

"If the information was false, why the devil were you so anxious to get the document back?"

He gave me a pitying look. "Well, I could not prove the information was false, could I? I would have to find the original dispatch, or Wellington would have to come forward and claim he remembered the original battle plans. I knew it was false, and Naveau does probably by this time. A tribunal, on the other hand, especially one influenced by any enemies I made during the war—I hardly liked to risk it."

I stepped close to him. "If anything of this nature happens again—though I will likely strangle you if it does—*tell me*."

He faced me, eye to eye. "When I require your help, I will ask for it."

We regarded at each other in silence for a moment.

Then I turned away. "Be happy that I am both fond of your wife and bad at obeying orders," I said. "You will be released tomorrow. Good night."

The turnkey let me out. I left Brandon in the middle of the room, staring at me with an unreadable expression.

CHAPTER 20

THE next morning, Sir Nathaniel listened, in his quiet way, to the story I told him about Mr. Bennington. He listened to Pomeroy's assertion that he'd heard Mr. Bennington's confession. Grenville added that he'd heard it as well.

Bennington sat before Sir Nathaniel wearing his usual air of faint scorn, and smoothly said that yes, indeed, he was a murderer twice over. Love of money, he said, was the root of all evil. That was in the Bible. In Paul's letters to Timothy, if one wanted to be precise.

Sir Nathaniel, looking neither shocked nor amused, committed Mr. Bennington to trial for the murder of Henry Turner. The other murder, occurring in another country with no witnesses, would not be tried here, although he would keep Bennington's confession to it in mind.

Mr. Bennington, however, never did come to trial. He was found the morning his trial was to begin hanging in his room in Newgate by his bedsheets, quite dead. I assumed that fastidious Mr. Bennington could not bring himself, in the end, to face the public hangman.

Brandon was released when Sir Nathaniel sent Mr. Bennington to Newgate. I do not know what Louisa did when Brandon arrived home, because I was not there to witness it. I left the two of them alone to rejoice, to scold, to decide what they would do from there, together. They did not need me.

That afternoon, as I rested in my rooms, I received the inevitable summons to Denis's Curzon Street house.

I met with Denis and Colonel Naveau in Denis's study, the room in which Denis usually received me. Denis sat behind a desk that was habitually clean—I did not know if he ever used it for anything other than intimidating his visitors.

Colonel Naveau, tense and irritated, rose as I entered the room. "Have you got it?"

"No," I answered. "I burned it."

"What?" The colonel trailed off in French, his language becoming colorful. Denis said nothing.

I laid my walking stick on a table beside me. "I burned it because its existence was a threat to Colonel Brandon. I could not risk that you would not try to extort money from him, or from Mrs. Harper."

"Brandon sent it to me," Naveau spat. "He took the risk. He will have to live with that."

"Not any longer. Why did you keep the paper, by the bye? To prove that you were a good republican and an excellent spy? Louis Bourbon is not a strong king. Perhaps the Republic will rise again, and you will need to prove your loyalty to it."

"Please do not tell my motives to me," Naveau said stiffly. "I kept it for my own reasons." He glanced at Denis, who had not moved nor spoken during our exchange. "He promised he would obtain it. I paid money. Much money."

"I will return your fee," Denis said, his voice dry. "Captain Lacey, like you, does things for his own reasons."

Naveau gave him a hard look. "And you do nothing?"

Denis cleared his throat. The two pugilists who stood near the windows came alert. "Please pack your things and return to France, Colonel," he said.

Naveau looked at me for a moment longer, stark anger

in his eyes. But he was not foolish enough to argue with Denis. He bowed coolly, then strode past me and out of the room.

A lackey in the hall closed the door. Silence fell. The pugilists returned to their relaxed stances by the windows. Denis said nothing. He folded his hands on the top of his desk and regarded me with quiet eyes.

"You must have known that I could not give that paper back to him," I began.

Denis inclined his head. "I suspected so."

"Then why did you ask me to find it?" I frowned. "Not to placate Naveau, surely."

"It was a test, of sorts."

"I see. And I failed."

"No," he said. "You passed."

I lifted my brows.

"I wished to see where your loyalties lie," he said. "And what you would do for them. You are a man of great loyalty, even when it conflicts with your heart."

"I am pleased I could provide you with entertainment," I said, not a little annoyed.

"No, you are not." He regarded me a moment longer. "Was there something else?"

I hesitated, my fingers brushing my engraved name on my walking stick. "My wife." A familiar lump rose in my throat. I suppressed it with difficulty. "Did she ever marry her French officer?"

He shook his head. "Never officially. I believe they found it easier to let others simply assume them man and wife. She has had four other children with him, as a matter of fact."

"Good lord." So, Carlotta had found family and happiness at last. I continued, my lips tight, "If I dissolve the marriage with her, they will no doubt be pleased."

"You will likewise be free," he pointed out.

I knew that Denis could help me, that he waited for me to ask him to help. He could no doubt reach out and scoop up my wife, pay the money to get me a divorce or have the marriage annulled, and land her in France again to marry her Frenchman.

He could, and he would. But I was not yet certain I was ready.

"Very well," Denis said, as if knowing my thoughts. "Good afternoon, Captain. My carriage will return you home."

I left him, still tempted and uncertain. I knew that one day soon, I would return to him, hat in hand, and ask for his help. He knew it, too.

I told him good-bye, and his butler led me out.

I did not return home, but asked Denis's coachman to leave me in South Audley Street. Lady Breckenridge's drawing room was full this afternoon, of high-born ladies, wits and dandies, and a poet and an artist.

They'd heard that Mr. Bennington had been arrested for murder, and wasn't that dashed odd? Poor Claire Bennington, they said, but he'd always been a queer chap. Best she put him behind her as quickly as possible.

Lady Breckenridge smiled at me from across the room. She lounged in a silk gown that bared her shoulders, and smoke from her cigarillo wreathed her face. A decadent lady, she liked her sensual pleasures, but she had heart.

When I at last was able to speak to her, she leaned to me and whispered, "Stay behind."

I obeyed. As the callers drifted away, I lingered, shaking hands with the wits and dandies who were trying to become closer to the great Grenville.

Finally, the last lady bustled away, and Lady Breckenridge and I were alone.

"Let us adjourn upstairs," she said. "This room reeks of perfume. Lady Hartley does like exotic scent, and there's nothing for it that we all must be drenched in it by the time she leaves."

So saying, she ascended to the next floor and to her private boudoir. Barnstable, after his inquiries about the state of my bad leg and rejoicing how quickly my bruises had gone away, brought us coffee and brandy then left us alone.

I told Lady Breckenridge about Bennington's examination, and the fact that Brandon had gone home.

"Thank heavens," she said, pouring a large dollop of brandy into my coffee. "The poor woman. How awful for her. It will not be easy for her to forgive him."

"No. But she loves him enough to do it."

Her brows arched. "Love and loyalty in marriage. What an odd idea."

I smiled over my coffee cup. "Rather old-fashioned."

Lady Breckenridge drank in silence for a moment. "This summer I will spend time at my father's estate," she said presently. "It is a beautiful place, and the gardens are quite grand. People pay a shilling on Thursdays to look at them."

"Do they?" I asked.

"I am going to be so bold as to ask you to visit. For a fortnight, perhaps. My mother would approve of you."

I smiled. "Of a penniless captain who cannot even be a captain any longer?"

"My mother is a true blue blood. She cares nothing for money. Or at least, she does not now that her only daughter is provided for. She can retreat into lofty ideals. She does it very well." She smiled, the affection in her eyes outweighing her acerbic words.

"I would be honored to accept such an invitation."

"Good," she said.

I set down my cup and rose to my feet. She looked surprised. "Goodness, are you going?"

"No." I reached down, took her cup from her, and put it on the table beside her. Then I took her hands and raised her to face me.

"Donata," I said. "I want never to be less than honest with you. You once guessed that I had been married and thought I was a widower. The truth is that I am still married."

Her eyes widened. I went on quickly. "Fifteen years ago, Mrs. Lacey deserted me. I have not seen her since then. I re-

cently discovered where she lives in France with her lover."
I tightened my grip on Lady Breckenridge's hands. "I want
to find her and dissolve the marriage if I can. And after I
have done what I need to set her free, I would like to ask
leave to court you."

Lady Breckenridge said nothing. Any other woman
might have been overwhelmed with what I'd just told her,
or grown furious or burst into tears. But I knew she would
forgive honesty far more than she'd forgive pleasing lies.
She was resilient, this lady.

"I have no idea how to make pretty lover's speeches," I
said when the silence stretched. "Not like your poets."

"Poetry can be tedious. Too many words to say a simple
thing." She studied me a moment longer, the pressure of her
fingers warm on mine. "Very well, Captain. I give you
leave."

Something stirred in my heart. I leaned down and
brushed her lips with mine.

When I made to pull away, to take my leave, she held on
to my hands. "Stay," she said.

We studied each other a moment longer.

"Very well," I replied, and did so.